WALK ME HOME

SEBASTIAN FITZEK is one of Europe's most
successful authors of psychological thrillers.
His books have sold twelve million copies, been
translated into more than thirty-six languages
and are the basis for international cinema
and theatre adaptations. Sebastian Fitzek was
the first German author to be awarded the
European Prize for Criminal Literature.
He lives with his family in Berlin.

www.sebastianfitzek.com

SEBASTIAN FITZEK

WALK ME HOME

translated from the German by
Jamie Bulloch

An Aries Book

First published in Germany as *Der Heimweg* in 2020 by Droemer Knaur

First published in the UK in 2022 by Head of Zeus Ltd,
part of Bloomsbury Publishing Plc

Der Heimweg copyright © 2020 Verlagsgruppe Droemer Knaur
GmbH & Co. KG, Munich, Germany
Translation © 2022 Jamie Bulloch

The book has been negotiated through AVA international
GmbH, Germany (www.ava-international.de)

The moral right of Sebastian Fitzek to be identified
as the author and Jamie Bulloch to be identified as the translator
of this work has been asserted in accordance with the Copyright,
Designs and Patents Act of 1988.

9 7 5 3 1 2 4 6 8

A catalogue record for this book is available from the British Library.

ISBN (HB): 9781804542286
ISBN (XTPB): 9781804542293
ISBN (E): 9781804542279

Typeset by Divaddict Publishing Solutions Ltd

Printed and bound in Great Britain by
CPI Group (UK) Ltd, Croydon CR0 4YY

Head of Zeus Ltd
5–8 Hardwick Street
London EC1R 4RG

WWW.HEADOFZEUS.COM

Dedicated to all those to whom fear is a constant companion.

One woman in four has experienced physical or sexual violence by a partner at least once in her life. Women of all social classes are affected.

Report by the Federal Ministry for Family Affairs, Senior Citizens, Women and Youth, 2 February 2020

A study compiled by the Federal Ministry for Family Affairs has highlighted that women who grow up with domestic violence in the family home are more than twice as likely to be victims of domestic violence themselves. Women who are physically abused by their parents are three times more likely to experience violence by a partner.

Astrid-Maria Bock, BILD-Zeitung, 27 June 2017

Do you see the moon in the sky?
Only half of it can we spy,
And yet it is beautifully round.
Much in life is like the moon,
Which we laugh at all too soon,
Because it is invisible to the eye.

Matthias Claudius (1740–1815), (trans. Jamie Bulloch)

AUTHOR'S NOTE

All the events in this thriller are obviously (and fortunately) the product of my imagination. But the telephone service to support people who feel anxious on their way home at night does actually exist. The idea originated in Stockholm where the service is run by the police force. In Germany, apparently, there is no money available and the job has to be done by volunteers. Regrettably, therefore, this important service often finds itself struggling to survive. More information can be found at www.heimwegtelefon.net.

A similar UK-based helpline is run by Strut Safe, a voluntary service that provides support for callers across the UK. For more information visit www.strutsafe.org.

TRIGGER WARNING

This story deals with domestic violence, an all-too-common criminal offence that is not talked about enough in our society. For people who have been, or are, victims of domestic violence, the depictions in this book may cause extreme emotional reactions.

PROLOGUE

After all the injuries her bruise-covered body had sustained in the most sensitive places; after the blows to her face, back, kidneys and stomach, which turned her urine the colour of beetroot for several days; after all the pain inflicted on her with the garden hose and iron, she'd never have imagined she'd ever be able to feel something like *that* again.

The sex was awesome! she thought as she lay on the bed in the dim light. The man she'd fallen hopelessly in love with had got up to go to the bathroom.

Not that she had much to compare him with. Prior to her husband she'd only had two lovers, but all that seemed an age ago. The negative experiences of the present had long buried the positive ones in her past.

For years now, she'd associated what happened in the bedroom with nothing but pain and humiliation.

And now I'm lying here. Breathing in the scent of a new man in my life and wishing our night of passion could begin all over again.

She was astonished at how quickly she'd put her trust in this guy and told him about the violence she suffered in her marriage. But she'd felt drawn to him from the very first moment she heard his deep voice and gazed into those dark, warm eyes that looked at her in a way her husband never had: openly, honestly and affectionately.

She'd almost told him about the video. About the evening her husband had forced her to undergo. With those men.

Lots of men, who'd abused and humiliated her.

It's hard to believe that I've willingly surrendered to a member of the 'stronger' sex again, she thought as she listened to the whoosh of the water coming from the bathroom, where her dream man was taking a shower.

Usually it was she who spent hours trying to scrub the disgust from her body after being 'used' by her 'husband', but now she was savouring the tangy scent of a lover on her skin and wanted to preserve it for ever.

The sound of the water stopped.

'Fancy doing something now?' she heard him ask cheerfully from the bathroom after he'd got out of the shower.

'Love to,' she replied, although she had no idea how to explain to her husband that she was going to stay out longer.

And it was already…

She looked at her watch, but it was too dark to make out the face. Apart from the narrow opening in the bathroom door, the only other light came from a faintly lit work of art. A slightly curved samurai dagger with a mother-of-pearl hilt hung on the bedroom wall, its green shimmer picked out by two dimmed LED spots which were as muted as nightlights.

As she reached for her mobile she noticed a strip of light switches embedded in the bedside table.

'How about we go for a cocktail?'

She pressed the outer button on the strip and couldn't help giggling when she saw what it did. The sheet had slipped, giving her a view of the mattress, which was now illuminated in a halogen-blue colour that made it look as if she were on a lilo in a swimming pool.

She sat up cross-legged on the mattress, in which the water shone brightly and as luminescent as a glow stick. It also changed colour. From azure to phosphorous yellow to dazzling white *to…*

'What's that?' she asked.

Softly. More to herself, for at first glance she was taken aback. She leaned forwards and found herself peering through the diamond formed by her legs and crotch.

Oh, Jesus Christ…

She slapped a hand over her mouth in shock and stared at the mattress on which she'd been making love with a man just a few minutes earlier.

I'm hallucinating. That can't be…

'You found it, then,' an unfamiliar voice said, before the stranger appeared in the bathroom doorway. As if he were holding a remote control to operate the terror, the bed beneath her glowed blood red, and what she could now see was so horrific that she wanted to tear her eyes out.

Yes, she had found *it*, but *it* made no sense. Her mind refused to accept the sheer horror for the simple fact that what she was looking at defied all logic.

'Where is he? What have you done with him?' she screamed at the stranger, louder than ever before, as the monster in human form came over to the bed with a syringe and said, grinning smugly, 'Please forget your lover for the moment. I think it's time you got to know *me*.'

1

JULES

Jules sat at the desk, thinking how the hissing in his ear went perfectly with the blood on the wall.

Even though, if asked, he couldn't have said where this morbid association came from. Perhaps because the sound he was hearing in the receiver reminded him of a liquid straining its way through a narrow gap.

Like blood spurting from a dying person's artery.

Blood you could daub bedroom walls with to leave a message for the world.

Jules averted his eyes from the television set, which in close-up was showing the grotesquely large digits, smeared in red above the bed on the wall of the victim's room. The handwriting of the Calendar Killer. A greeting stating: 'I was here and you should thank your lucky stars we didn't meet'.

Otherwise you'd be lying on this bed too. Your face a picture of surprise and your neck gashed.

He spun through ninety degrees on the swivel chair and the television disappeared from view, which helped him to concentrate on the telephone call.

'Hello? Is anyone there?' he asked for the third time, but whoever was on the hissing line still wasn't saying a word.

Instead, Jules heard a man's voice at his back. It sounded familiar even though he'd never met the guy before.

'*So far three women have been found murdered in their homes,*' said the stranger he knew by sight and who ensured that people were served up Germany's most horrific crimes within their own four walls and at regular intervals.

Case XY... Unsolved. Germany's oldest true crime show.

Jules was annoyed he couldn't find the remote control to switch off the TV, which was probably still showing the Calendar Killer's latest crime scene.

It was a re-run of the 20:15 programme, supplemented by the latest information from viewers since the primetime broadcast.

The study in this period apartment in Charlottenburg was a through room connecting the living and dining area, and like the rest of the flat it had impressively high stucco ceilings, from which the first residents would no doubt have hung heavy chandeliers. Jules preferred indirect light; even the glare from the television set was too harsh for him.

The wireless headset, with its small headphones connected by a wire frame at the back of the neck and the microphone on an arm in front of his mouth, allowed him to search for the remote control on the desk cluttered with magazines and documents.

He remembered having it in his hand not long ago; it must be buried somewhere beneath all this paper.

'*And at the scene of every crime, the same gruesome image. The date of the murder on the wall, written in the victim's blood.*'

30/11
8/3
1/7

'The modus operandi to which the Calendar Killer owes his name.'

The first killing, its anniversary just a few hours away, had been all over the media last November.

Interrupting his search for the remote, Jules looked out of the large, slightly convex panelled window, which was holding firm against a heavy snowstorm, and down at the street. Once again he was surprised by his lack of recall for weather. He was able to recollect the strangest things he'd heard only once, like the fact that Hitchcock didn't have a belly button, or that ketchup was sold as a medicine in the 1830s. But he couldn't remember last winter.

Had it snowed in the first week of advent last year, as it was doing in large parts of Germany at the moment? The record-breaking summer with tropical temperatures nudging forty degrees had been followed by filthy weather with what felt like nothing in between. Although it wasn't especially cold, at least not in comparison to Greenland or Moscow, the sudden switch to snow and rain, stirred up by a strong easterly wind, drove people straight home after work. Or to the ear, nose and throat specialists. There was, however, something comforting about the view outside, and not only because it afforded a contrast to the Calendar Killer's murals.

Through the tall windows it looked as if a film crew had emptied a confetti cannon in front of the street lamps of Charlottenburg to give the residents of these desirable nineteenth-century apartments around Lietzensee an early Christmas show. Countless snowflakes danced like a swarm of fireflies in the cone of warm light and from there were propelled across the icy surface of the lake towards the television tower.

'Is anybody preventing you from talking to me?' Jules asked the hypothetical person on the line. 'If so, then please cough now.'

He couldn't be sure, but Jules fancied he'd heard a faint panting, like a runner choking on their own breath.

Was that a cough?

He turned up the volume on the laptop which was streaming their conversation using the telephone companion software, but he could still hear the XY presenter droning in his ears. If Jules didn't find the remote control he'd have no option but to pull the plug out of the wall.

'We have agonised over the question of whether to show you images from the original crime scene in such detail. But to date these recordings are the only clues the investigation team has on the so-called Calendar Killer.

'As you can see...'

From the corner of his eye Jules saw the camera perspective change, zooming in on the bloody writing on the wall. So close that the coarse plasterwork looked like a moonscape the serial killer had used inappropriately as a canvas.

'... there's a squiggle at the top of the number 1. With a little imagination the figure which the killer wrote on the wall at the scene of the first murder looks a bit like a seahorse. Our question to you, therefore, is: Do you recognise this handwriting? Have you ever come across it in any context before? Any relevant leads...'

Jules gave a start. He'd definitely heard something on the line.

A clearing of the throat. Breathing. All of a sudden the hissing stopped dead.

The ambience he picked up in the headphones had changed, as if the caller had moved from a wind tunnel into a sheltered area.

'I haven't been able to understand what you're saying, which is why I'm assuming you're being threatened,' Jules said, and at that moment he found the remote control on the desk, hidden beneath a prospectus for a rehab clinic.

Berger Hof – Be Healthy in Harmony with Nature

'Whatever happens, stay on the line. Don't hang up under any circumstances!'

He switched off the television and looked at himself in the sudden black of the flatscreen, now a dark mirror. Jules shook his head, unsatisfied with his reflection, even though he had to admit that he looked much better than he felt. More like twenty-five than thirty-five. More healthy than ill.

Though that had always been a curse. Even when he was lovesick and suffering from gastroenteritis, Jules was the very picture of health to all those around him. Over the course of their relationship, Dajana was the only person who'd learned to 'read' him. She'd spent a long time working as a freelance journalist and her strong sense of empathy had allowed her to coax a hitherto well-hidden secret from many an interviewee. And what worked with strangers obviously worked even better with those closest to her.

She spotted the signs that he was on the verge of collapse

from exhaustion when his brown eyes shone a shade darker after a double shift at the emergency control room, or when his prominent lips were a touch drier than usual because he hadn't succeeded in instructing a mother how to resuscitate her child down the phone. Without saying a word, Dajana would take him in her arms and massage his tense shoulders. When they lay on the sofa and she buried her face in his thick, untamed hair, she could practically smell his stomach aches and fatigue, and the deep melancholy he often felt. Maybe she'd studied him in his sleep too, his nervous twitching, his murmuring, and perhaps she'd comforted him with a gentle hand on his forearm when he screamed. *Perhaps.* He'd neglected to ask her and he would never have the opportunity to again.

There!

This time he was absolutely certain. The caller had groaned. He couldn't tell if it was a man or a woman, only that the person was clearly in pain and trying to suppress it.

'Who... who is that?'

Finally. The first complete sentence. And it didn't sound as if the caller – a woman – had a gun pointing at her head, but you could never be sure.

'My name is Jules Tannberg,' he replied, then he focused, and began the most intense and momentous conversation in his life with the words: 'You're connected to the telephone companion service. How can I help you?'

Her answer almost ripped his eardrum.

It was a single, terrifying scream of despair.

2

'Hello? Who is that? Please tell me how I can help you?'

The scream died away.

Jules instinctively reached for a biro and a pad of paper to note down the time of the call: 22:09.

'Are you still there?'

'What?... er, no, I...'

Heavy breathing, the sound of someone in a rush. Desperate.

'I'm really sorry, I...'

Clearly a woman's voice.

Male callers were rare. The telephone companion service was mainly used by women on their way home at night who had to walk through multistorey car parks, empty streets or even woods. They might have been working late, escaping an awful date or just leaving a party where their friends had stayed on.

All of a sudden alone, at a time of the night when they were reluctant to call and wake a relative, they would feel very scared in the dark as they entered poorly lit underpasses or took carelessly chosen shortcuts through deserted areas. In such a situation they wanted a companion to escort them safely through the night. A companion who, if the worst came to the worst, knew their precise location and could instantly call for help, although this had happened only seldom in the history of the service.

'I have... to hang up...' she said. Worried that she felt intimidated by his deep voice, Jules realised he had to act quickly if he wasn't going to lose her.

'Would you prefer to talk to a female companion?' he asked, speaking as clearly as he could; he suspected that the caller (probably early thirties, he noted) had difficulty concentrating. 'I understand if you're uncomfortable talking to a man in your situation.'

Like most fears, the anxiety felt by the person seeking help from the service was usually unfounded. But in most cases, either for a perfectly explicable reason (such as a drunkard on the underground platform making unwelcome advances) or because of a trick of the imagination, it was connected to a man. And so Jules found it totally normal that a woman might be hesitant to talk to a member of the sex which had been the cause of the fear in the first place, no matter how irrational it was.

'Would you like me to transfer you to a woman?' he asked again, and finally got an answer, albeit a confusing one.

'No, no, it's not that. It's... it's just that I didn't realise.'

She sounded scared but not panicked. Like a woman who had felt much worse fear before.

'What didn't you realise?'

'That I called you. It must've happened while I was climbing.'

Climbing?

The hissing on the line – wind, surely – had started up again, although not as intensely as before, thank goodness.

Jules's pad filled with questions:

Why does a frightened woman go climbing at night? In the driving snow?

'What's your name?' he asked.

'Klara,' she said.

She sounded dismayed at herself, as if the name had slipped out unintentionally.

'Okay, Klara. Are you telling me that you called us by mistake?'

He said *us* because the idea of having a team in the background gave the caller confidence, and in truth there were a number of volunteers working for the service. Right now, for example, a Saturday at hotline prime time, four volunteers in Berlin were sitting by their laptops, waiting to take calls between 10 p.m. and 4 a.m. via the national number. They were not, however, in an open-plan office like where Jules used to work for the emergency control room.

Thanks to the software that directed every incoming call to an available assistant, the volunteers could look after the frightened, lonely and sometimes confused callers from the comfort of their own homes. Ever since information about this new service, which was financed by donations, had spread virally across the social networks, the number of calls had risen steadily, but the phone didn't ring all the time.

While they waited, the volunteers could do things like watch Netflix, listen to music or read. And the wireless headset allowed them to move around at home even if they took a call. Many of them would lie in bed, some would even be in the bath. Only a few, probably, sat at a desk like Jules, but this was a habit developed in his former career. Although he liked to wander around in mid-conversation, when making contact at the beginning he needed some structure.

Ideally he'd have typed all the information the caller was giving him into a computer, but here it made little sense. Unlike when he was handling a call for the fire brigade, he didn't have to ensure an engine had the necessary equipment for the particular emergency. Nor was he looking at the approximate location of the caller on a digital map. Nonetheless Jules felt better organised behind a desk; it gave him a sense of security when he was talking to the caller.

'Yes. I must have deactivated the lock screen by accident,' Klara said. 'My mobile did it by itself. I'm really sorry for disturbing you, I had no intention of calling.'

A saved number, Jules noted. This wasn't the first time Klara had been frightened. Nor the second or even the third time. She must have been scared so often that she'd saved the telephone companion number among her favourites.

'I'm terribly sorry, I dialled the wrong number. Anyway, now I'll...'

Klara evidently wanted to end the call. And Jules couldn't let that happen.

He got up from the desk. The old parquet floor, scarred by countless pairs of shoes, rearranged furniture and dropped objects, creaked wearily beneath his sneakers.

'Please don't take this the wrong way, but you sound as if you need help.'

'No,' Klara replied, a touch too rapidly. 'It's too late for that.'

'What do you mean?'

The whimpering he heard down the line was so clear that for a moment he thought it was coming from the hallway.

'What's it too late for?'

'I've already got a companion. I don't need another one.'

'Are you saying you're not alone at the moment?'

The wind at Klara's end of the line had picked up again, but her voice was more than a match for it.

'I haven't been alone for a second these past few weeks.'

'Who's with you?'

Klara breathed heavily, then said, 'You don't know him. At most you know the feeling he triggers.' Her voice cracked. 'He frightens you to death.'

Is she crying?

'Oh, God, I'm truly sorry,' she said, trying to compose herself. Before Jules could ask what she meant by that, she quickly added, 'We have to finish this conversation. He won't believe it was just an accident. That I dialled the wrong number. Christ, if he finds out I've called you he'll come to see you as well.'

'And do what?'

'Kill you too,' Klara said. Her morbid prophecy gave Jules a sense of déjà vu.

3

'If you cock it up you're dead,' Caesar joked. His laughter dissipated when he saw how crestfallen Jules looked, and he realised his flippant comment had gone too far.

'Sorry, that was bad taste.'

Magnus Kaiser, known affectionately as Caesar to his friends, looked guiltily at his best friend of many years. Jules, who was standing beside him at the desk, shook his head and made a dismissive gesture with his hand.

'How often have I told you not to treat me like a baby? Being so careful with every word doesn't make me feel any better.'

'All the same, maybe I shouldn't utter words like "death", "dying" and "murder" so snappily in your presence.' Caesar sighed and pointed to the laptop with the telephone companion software he'd brought over to Jules. 'Listen, maybe this is a really lousy idea. Maybe it's better if you don't spend all night with mentally fragile people.'

'You've just got a bad conscience because you didn't agree this with anyone. But don't worry, nobody's going to find out. I'll man the companion service for you, don't fret about it.'

Caesar didn't look convinced. It was a bit awkward that

Jules was stepping in for him like this, because the laptop and software were the property of the organisation and should only be used by a fixed list of people. Roping in a friend without approving it first wasn't quite kosher.

'I can get someone else to cover my shift...' he began, but Jules stifled the protest by ruffling his friend's long blond hair that he still wore surfer-style. Even though it was ages since Caesar had seen the sea. And he wouldn't ever ride the waves on his beloved boards again.

'How many more times do we have to go through this? Tonight is your how-many-eth date over the past God knows how many months?'

Caesar gave him the finger, which he'd had tattooed with a paragraph symbol during the first semester of his law degree. He regretted it now, because the tattoo had been the reason for his rejection by the big law firms, and he was dependent on occasional business, working for a bog-standard outfit.

'Precisely, your first date,' Jules clarified. 'And on a scale from one to ten, how hot is this dragon?'

'Her name is Ksenia. And she's definitely a twelve. I'm not the only person in our self-help group who fancies her.'

Caesar looked nervously at his watch, a Rolex Submariner he'd never been diving with and probably never would. The time when Caesar matched up to his nickname as an outstanding competitor in every sport had come to an abrupt end over a year ago. These days even having a shave seemed to pose a challenge. Caesar's beard clearly hadn't seen a blade in a week and made him look substantially older than thirty-six.

'So, what are you waiting for?' Jules prodded him. 'Get yourself out of my flat and score with your dream woman!'

Jules stood and took the handles of the wheelchair, but

Caesar applied the brake, preventing his friend from pushing him away from the desk.

'I've got a really bad feeling about this,' he said softly, raising his head and staring with his blue eyes right through Jules as if he weren't in the room. People who didn't know Caesar found this daydream gaze slightly unsettling, but he did it several times a day, often for no apparent reason. Although he looked completely absent, Jules knew that his friend had his most lucid thoughts in these moments. For example, Caesar would be struck once more by the realisation that he'd never walk again because the alcoholic who'd knocked him down at the McDonald's drive-in couldn't jump into a time machine and undo his drunken outing.

'Calm down, mate. For years I dealt with the weirdest calls to 112. I'm sure I'll be able to reassure a few scaredy-cats.'

'That's not what I'm talking about.'

'What are you talking about, then?'

'You, Jules. After everything you've been through. You of all people should keep away from people in crisis.'

'From people like you, you mean?' Jules kneeled in front of the wheelchair to look his friend directly in the eye.

'What are you saying?'

'Have you really got a date?'

Shocked by the turn the conversation had taken, tears sprung to Caesar's eyes. 'Are you my best friend?' he said, taking Jules's hand.

'I have been ever since primary school.'

There had been one short phase during which their relationship cooled, and that was in the eleventh class, when both of them fell in love with the same girl. But they overcame this, and in the end Caesar and Dajana developed a very close friendship even though the school beauty had given Jules the nod.

'If I were gay I'd marry you,' Jules joked.

'Stop the interrogation now then, okay?'

Jules got to his feet and raised his hands as if to show that he was unarmed. 'You won't do anything silly, will you?' he asked Caesar, who was steering his wheelchair to the hallway.

'He'll get to the stage when he can't cope with it anymore,' Dajana had predicted to Jules. *'Caesar didn't have the willpower to stop smoking when he was playing basketball, so how's he going to get over being a paraplegic?'*

'Tell me what you've really got on this evening,' he called out as Caesar was leaving.

By way of an answer his best friend gave him the Tom Cruise quotation from *Top Gun*, which had been an in-joke between the two of them since their schooldays:

'I could tell you, Jules. But then I'd have to kill you.'

4

Kill me? Jules now thought, four hours later, repeating in his head the last words Klara had said to him: '*We have to finish this conversation. He won't believe that it was just an accident. That I dialled the wrong number. Christ, if he finds out I've called you he'll come to see you as well.*'

To kill me?

Even though he didn't seriously imagine he was in danger, Jules felt an unsettling, alarming anxiety. A bit like that nightmare when time and again he found himself in front of a group of teachers doing an oral exam he hadn't prepared for.

'What do you mean?' he asked Klara, straightening his headset. 'Why should someone come over to my place and want to kill me?'

And who are we talking about, anyway?

'I'm sorry to have said that, but it's the truth. As soon as he finds out we've been in contact, he'll come looking for you and get rid of you too.'

He?

Jules had to move. Without realising it, he wandered through the study and living room.

'In ringing the telephone companion service you've done

20

exactly the right thing,' he said to build up Klara's trust and reassure her. As was usual in these nineteenth-century apartments around Lietzensee, the hallway was a narrow tunnel connecting the kitchen at one end with the living room at the other. For the stretch in between, which went past the children's, parents' and guest bedrooms, as well as the dining room and utility room, the corridor was so long you could have done with a bike or at least a skateboard.

Jules knew that to keep the conversation going with this woman he needed to consider carefully his choice of words and avoid saying anything negative. On the other hand he was no longer sure that this was such a smart strategy. After all, Klara had just told him his own life was in danger. Which was absurd, of course, even though – and this worried him – it wasn't totally crazy.

Less-experienced assistants would probably think Klara had a screw loose; a patient suffering from hallucinations who'd managed to call from a secure unit, which wasn't all that uncommon.

But her voice betrayed no signs of being affected by drugs, nor did her wording or intonation sound as if they'd been shaped by dozens of therapy sessions.

Jules sensed that there was a rational basis to Klara's fear, and this was what he wanted to figure out.

'Where are you at the moment?' he asked after a brief pause for thought.

The most important question of all, the one he'd always asked first to the thousands of callers in the past, when he still worked in the emergency control room in Spandau. Twenty-four workstations, each equipped with five monitors; four thousand calls per day, half of which resulted in a deployment.

A major fire in Marzahn, a stroke in Mitte, premature labour in Lichtenrade. Nobody could be helped if they didn't say where the emergency vehicle had to go to. Although a call made from a mobile could locate the caller to an area around the nearest radio mast, in the outer districts of the city this could encompass several kilometres.

'Why do you want to know where I am?'

'So I can help you.'

'Didn't you hear what I said? I'm lost. Hang up now and at least save your own skin.'

He screwed up his eyes, an involuntary habit when he concentrated. 'So you're being threatened. A man, I take it. Is he close by right now?'

Klara gave a sad laugh. 'He's always with me. Even when I can't see him.'

There was silence in Jules's apartment. The only sound was the humming of the old fridge, but it was muted by the distance it had to travel down the corridor, which meant Jules was able to form a clear acoustic image of Klara's surroundings. Her shoes were crunching on gravel and he heard the rustling of leaves: she must be on a path surrounded by trees. A solitary car accelerated in the background. The area was secluded but not deserted.

'I've got to hang up.'

'Please tell me how I can be of help.'

'You weren't listening. Nobody can help me anymore. You've got to think of yourself.'

There was a firmness to Klara's voice now; she sounded a bit like a teacher.

'Is this meant to be a joke?' Jules asked. 'Are you trying to put the wind up me?'

'For God's sake, no. That's the last thing I'd do.'

'Tell me what's wrong, then.'

Silence.

A silence so extreme that Jules could hear the faint tinnitus in his right ear. A buzzing that was ever present, but which he sometimes forgot for weeks on end until something irritated or worked him up. It was as if the high-pitched, mosquito-like sound was triggered and intensified by negative emotions.

'Have you ever been so frightened that each cell in your body was filled with pain?' she asked him.

The mosquito buzzing in Jules's ear canal receded again as he racked his brain for an answer.

He closed his eyes, now blocking out the dim glow of the nightlight in the hallway, but the darkness beneath his lids almost immediately gave way to an image in his head that was far too bright and colourful.

It was the summer and thirty-two degrees outside. In the air hung the scent of the storm approaching the city. Jules swallowed, loath to think about this yet again, but it was already an hour since he last had done, which was unusual for him. Normally he spent every spare moment dwelling on the moment when he'd lost everything.

'Do you mean, have I ever been so frightened that I wanted to rip my skin from my body because I felt as if I were burning inside?'

'Yes,' Klara said.

Right then Jules knew she wouldn't hang up. Not while he was telling her about the worst experience of his life. The one experience that still made him wish he were no longer alive.

5

They said that once you'd spent an hour in this place you'd never look at Berlin in the same way again when you drove through its streets. The city's face would have changed for ever, into a countenance that was sick, ugly or pitiful, depending on how you viewed it. And yet in the middle of where it was all happening it appeared rather calm: a room the size of a warehouse that looked like the control centre of a missile base, equipped with two dozen computer desks, sitting at which were call handlers who, like Jules, were usually staring at a map of Berlin on their monitor while at the same time working through the form that had to be completed for each emergency.

Right now, however, Jules didn't have the time to run through a checklist with the panicky caller. Instinctively he went over all the points he'd learned in training for this situation.

One of the most appalling you could be confronted with while on shift at the control room.

Patient: male
Age: 4 to 7
Condition: critical

'Are you still talking to the boy?'

'No, he's not saying a word. How much longer now?' The caller, who'd identified himself as Michael Damelow, sounded like he was racing up a steep staircase. And yet according to his description he was standing in the hallway of a new-build flat in Brandenburgische Strasse, staring at a locked bedroom door.

'Number 17, fourth floor, left. It's on fire. You've got to hurry!'

'The emergency services are on their way,' Jules told the man, who sounded frightened to death.

His eyes wandered to the large screen that took up almost the entire wall at one end of the hall. Current hotspots in Berlin were marked on the digital map. Apart from the usual rush-hour madness of a Friday afternoon, there were no incidents of particular note.

Apart from an accident on the ring road.

Jules glanced at the monitor to the left. According to the GPS signal, it might take the fire brigade at least another three minutes to get there.

'Okay, I'm getting out of here.'

'No, wait,' Jules begged the postman. The poor chap had just gone to deliver a parcel (*The Haubachs, Brandenburgische Strasse 17, 4th Floor*) and was surprised by the stench of smoke coming from the flat, then by the woman's bare foot he'd seen in the hallway when he peered through the front door that was curiously open. And finally by the blood.

'Listen, mate, I'm shit scared. Everything's about to go up in flames here.'

'Is smoke still coming out from under the door?'

'Yes, of course.'

Jules drummed the keyboard with his fingers. According to the regulations he should be in agreement with Damelow; indeed he *must* order him to leave immediately. No third party ought to risk their own life by opening the door to a bedroom on fire.

But Jules couldn't ignore the locked-in boy either.

'Christ, he's scratching at the door!' the postman groaned. He sounded nasal and muffled because he'd covered his nose and mouth with a wet cloth, as Jules had advised. It had been a mistake to direct him into the flat. The floor tiles must have looked as if a slaughtered animal had climbed out of a blood-filled bath. In all probability the woman had tried to take her own life and dragged herself into the hallway with slit wrists.

'What did you just say?'

'The boy's scratching. At the door. From the inside.'

Jules closed his eyes and saw a dying boy digging his fingernails into the wood of the locked door in a hopeless attempt to get free.

'Are you certain it won't open?'

'Oh, of course, I'm not quite right in the head,' Damelow said, his voice cracking. 'Maybe the door's wide open. Maybe the dead woman I stepped over in the hallway here isn't real but just a doll. And maybe—'

'That's enough. Calm down!'

The postman coughed and shouted at the same time: 'You can bloody talk! You're not standing in a pool of blood outside a child's bedroom with smoke pouring out of it.'

'Look at the other doors. Can you see any keys?'

'What?'

'Keys in the locks. Often in flats they work on all the doors.'

'Wait a sec. No, I can't... hold on, yes!'

Jules heard footsteps. Squeaky shoes on lino or laminate. 'What do you mean, yes?'

'I've got one.'

'Try it.'

'Okay, hold on.'

More coughing, this time louder.

If the postman was having difficulty breathing in the hallway it must be like a chimney inside the child's bedroom.

'I can't hear scratching anymore,' Damelow said.

'Doesn't matter, does the key work?'

'What? Yes. But I don't dare. Won't opening the door just feed the fire with oxygen?'

'No,' Jules lied.

'I, I don't know. I don't want to risk it. I'd rather...'

Jules's gaze darted left, back to the monitor showing him the location of the fire engine. 'Stay on the line,' he told the postman, then called the leader of the squad.

Who answered immediately. 'Hello?'

'Where are you?'

'We've arrived,' the officer in charge said. 'But there's nothing here.'

The mosquito in Jules's tinnitus-plagued ear piped up at full blast. 'What do you mean?'

'I mean there's no emergency here. The Haubachs are fine, apart from the fright we've given them.'

Out of the corner of his eye he could see his team leader talking to the deputy below the wall with the huge screen. He bet they'd tuned into his conversation a while back and were listening in.

'Have you spoken to the family?' Jules asked the officer in charge.

'Father, mother, daughter. All fine.'

Daughter?

'Hang on a sec...'

Has the bastard been pulling my leg?

An angry Jules switched back to his conversation with the alleged postman. It wouldn't have surprised him if the man had hung up by now, but Michael Damelow was still on the line.

'Where are you?' Jules asked.

'I already told you. In Brandenburgische Strasse.'

'No, you're not.' Jules relayed what his colleague had just told him.

'But that... Oh, God... I'm r–really sorry,' Damelow stuttered.

'What?'

'In all the commotion, I...'

'Stay calm. Take a deep breath. What's going on there?'

Jules rolled his eyes.

A dead woman. A bedroom on fire. A child scratching at the door, crying for help. And now a panicky witness too...

'... I gave you the last one.'

'The address of your previous delivery?'

'Yes. I'm somewhere else now.'

'Where. Exactly. Are. You?'

It took all of Jules's self-control to avoid screaming down the phone, and it took the man a while to finally give him the correct answer.

'Prinzregentenstrasse 24, third floor, 10715 Berlin.'

Jules made him say the address three times.

The first time he stopped breathing, the second time his heart stopped beating. And the third time he was dead.

Dead inside, a zombie who could still move and speak, who leaped up from his seat, tore off the headset and gaped like crazy at the faces of his staring colleagues.

But he was no longer alive.

No longer like the people around him.

'Jules,' he heard his team leader call out as he hurried over, but there was no stopping him. He shook off his colleagues, shoved his boss to one side, and ran out the door and down the steps. Blind with panic, deaf with fear, he jumped into his car parked outside and raced off.

To Prinzregentenstrasse 24.

Third Floor.

10715 Berlin.

Home.

6

KLARA

'Have you ever been so frightened that each cell in your body was filled with pain?'

'Do you mean, have I ever been so frightened that I wanted to rip my skin from my body because I felt as if I were burning inside?'

'Yes.'

After this exchange her telephone companion had gone quiet for an unsettlingly long while and for a moment Klara couldn't be sure if Jules had hung up or not.

But then he said, 'Excuse me, I've just been reminded of a particularly traumatic episode in my life. It's still relatively recent.'

Klara stopped and bent over, a hand braced on her left side to ease the stitch around her spleen. Not that she'd been walking particularly quickly.

Even though she was carrying a few extra kilos, something Martin never tired of pointing out ('At least your doe eyes haven't got fat – they're about the only part of you that's still pretty'), it wasn't the physical exertion that was troubling

30

her, but the near-death experience just before her pocket call
to the telephone companion service. Her conversation with
the caring, amiable-sounding stranger was draining her of
the little energy she still had and which she needed for much
more important things. Indeed, she had no idea why she was
still talking to him.

'I'm very well acquainted with the situation you're
describing,' Jules said after another pause, during which
she felt almost viscerally that something was troubling him.
Something weighing so heavily on his mind that he'd never
be able to shuffle it off for as long as he lived. Jules's words
struck a chord on her heart strings, which she believed had
fallen silent for ever, and maybe even snapped.

Jules – if this was his real name (he pronounced it 'Chools')
– sounded so *sincere*. She couldn't find a better word to
describe him, although she didn't know if her senses were
playing tricks on her out here in the dark. Perhaps he was
merely an actor sporting his reassuring voice like a mask,
employing it in such a way that you were ready to believe
anything he said, however improbable it sounded. 'Nobody
understands me.' Klara stood up straight again and loosened
the hairband with which she'd tied her thick brown locks
into a ponytail, well aware that the pressure in her head had
nothing to do with her hair being tied too tightly.

Klara breathed in the fresh, damp air of the woods. The
branches of densely growing pines formed a natural canopy
protecting her from the snow. Because the wind had died
down briefly, it felt a little warmer, but she couldn't stop
shivering. The waterproof she'd hastily put on over her
Norwegian sweater before going out and the jeans that were
now ripped and wet weren't much use against the cold. The

clothes she'd chosen wouldn't even have been appropriate for an autumn stroll.

A *stroll*, she thought, with a hint of melancholy she hated herself for. *Something I haven't done often enough in the thirty-four years of my life. I always thought setting off without a fixed destination, without something concrete to do, was a waste of time. And now I'm standing here, bleeding, with less hope than someone being strapped to the electric chair, and I'm missing all those walks in the woods that I never wanted to do.*

'My fear doesn't fall into any category. So please don't insult my intelligence claiming you understand me even though you know absolutely nothing about me.'

She felt her brow, happy that the blood had dried, but her skull was droning like a church bell that had been struck by a hammer. The punishment for climbing a rock in the middle of the night, a rock that very few Berliners knew even existed. A secret tip without an address: eight-, nine- and ten-metre artificial towers of sprayed concrete. In truth, only the members of the German Alpine Association were allowed to manoeuvre themselves across the protrusions, ledges and recesses up to the cross at the summit.

But who's checking GAA passes in a snowstorm at night?

'I don't know how you're feeling, but I know how you're behaving, and that's more like a truculent child than a grown woman.' Once again Jules gave the right answer. *Fuck it.* Had she by chance come across the best-trained volunteer at the service, or were all of them trained these days? When she last called she'd got a very nice, but far-too-young, girl on the phone, who kept beginning her sentences with the platitude, '*Like I said…*', even though she hadn't actually said anything.

She bet that all the volunteers had to go on regular courses and attend seminars with creative titles such as *'Crisis intervention – you bring them home on your own'*, during which they analysed snippets of telephone conversations like the one she was having now.

Klara came out from beneath the pines, which had sheltered her from the wind and snow, and trudged down the narrow path that wound its way through the woods from the Teufelsberg to Teufelsseechaussee. She was on the very edge of the city, and the light pollution it gave off was strong enough to provide a twilight between the clouds of snow confetti that were whirling around.

She was dragging her leg behind her; hopefully she hadn't broken her ankle, but in truth it didn't matter now. Essentially the pain was good for her. It was so acute that tears welled in her eyes, and this kept her awake for the last few metres.

'What led you astray?' Jules asked.

Klara closed her eyes briefly. The darkness that then enveloped her matched the cosmos-like cold here outside.

Christ, why don't I just hang up?

If he'd simply asked, *'What happened?'* or *'Tell me!'*, she would have ended the call. But his question showed that he'd judged her correctly. That she'd once been a woman with a goal. She'd embarked on a long journey hoping for satisfaction and even love, maybe, but then was forced to discover that its paths were paved with landmines you could only avoid with a great deal of luck. And luck, well, that was the first friend who'd parted company from her, who'd torn up the ticket for the ride – my God, that felt like a long time ago now.

'Do you know Le Zen on Tauentzienstrasse?' she asked.

'The luxury hotel?'

'Exactly.'

'On my salary I couldn't even afford a coffee there, but yes, I have heard of it.'

'How about the speakeasy lift?'

'Speak what?'

'That's a no, then.'

Klara pushed aside a branch that was in her way. 'You have a good view of the lifts from the lobby, especially if you sit on the narrow futon sofa right beside the vases with the purple orchids. At first glance you'll just see three chrome-plated lift doors, beautifully decorated with Chinese lettering, matching the oriental design of everything in that place.'

'But?'

'But if, at exactly 11:23 p.m. on the last Saturday of each month, you sit on that futon sofa, peer through the orchids and focus on a narrow door beside the lifts, you'll realise that this door covered in tissue paper is not an entrance or exit to a utility room or anything like that.'

'It's another lift.'

She could have smiled. In normal circumstances she'd have loved to chat to Jules about everyday things. Politics, art, travel or his views on bringing up children, if he had any. He sounded like a father who was able to be both loving and firm. How often did you meet men who followed what you were saying and even finished your sentences correctly because they'd drawn the right conclusions from what you'd said?

'Precisely. It's a fourth lift.'

'Why "speakeasy"?' he asked.

'During Prohibition you could only get alcohol in the back rooms of bars. And the secret doors to these rooms would open if you whispered a password to the barman. Hence "speak easy": whisper.'

'What's the password that opens this lift?'

Good. He was delaying the real question: *Where does the lift take you?*

She would clam up if he got to the heart of the matter too quickly – she sensed he knew that. She'd feel cheap and used, like a girl allowing her date's hands to wander too quickly while kissing.

'Nowadays "speakeasy" has become established on the scene as a term for any secret establishment.'

'What scene are we talking about?'

She heard a rustling nearby, a fox perhaps or a wild boar searching for food in the snow.

'One in which pain is worshipped.'

'Did you get into the lift?'

Jules continued edging forwards with his questions, while Klara, with a sharp pain in her side and ankle, kept teetering down the path, now just a few metres away from the Teufelsseechaussee, which luckily was free of cars. In this weather and given her appearance, only an antisocial arsehole wouldn't have stopped. And what would she have said? *'Everything's okay, I'm fine. I like walking in snowstorms with an injured ankle and covered in blood.'*

'Yes, I did,' she replied to Jules's last question.

I got in.

'At 11:23 p.m., just as Martin had told me, the door opened. Silently.'

'Who's Martin?'

'Wait. You'll meet him very soon,' Klara said, and started telling Jules the story that didn't begin everything. Which perhaps didn't even herald the beginning of its end. But which certainly marked a turning point from which there was no way back. At the point when she crossed the threshold of evil, entering the dark lift that catapulted her into a world far worse than she'd imagined in her most terrible nightmares.

7

KLARA

A FEW MONTHS EARLIER

'Put on something businesslike,' Martin had told Klara. 'Your dark-blue suit with the pencil skirt and the white blouse beneath your blazer. The Prada pumps, no peep-toes, no high heels. It's got to look like you've come straight from a meeting at the office.'

She knew he was ashamed that his wife was a 'mere' medical–technical assistant at a psychiatric clinic rather than a management consultant or lawyer.

'And tasteful jewellery: the Chopard watch I bought you in Istanbul, a pearl necklace and the matching ear studs.'

She'd listened to Martin, as ever. Over the seven years of their relationship, three of which had been formalised with a marriage certificate, she'd learned not to ask too many questions. And dressing in 'businesslike' clothes was harmless compared to many of his other requests – even rather agreeable, in fact. Last time she'd been forced to wear thigh-high boots and a latex skirt to meet him at a porn cinema on Adenauerplatz. Compared to that dump, a luxury hotel like Le Zen was paradise on earth.

Or so Klara thought, even though she was fully aware that the gateway to hell could be held open by a liveried pageboy with a charming smile, who showed you the way through the lobby to the lifts across the Chinese marble floor. Where she entered one of the cabins. The fourth – evidently secret – speakeasy lift, its lighting so dimmed that it took a while to get used to the gloom.

Old, Klara thought, as the contours of her face became sharper in the lift mirror.

Wrinkly and shapeless.

Martin made her aware of it daily. Ever since Amelie was born he'd never tired of pointing out the effects of the pregnancy on her body and cursing how feeble she was because she'd done nothing to remedy this.

The door to the nineteenth floor opened.

Her knees unsteady, Klara stepped into the hotel corridor that smelled of patchouli room spray and looked nothing like a hotel corridor. The lift seemed to have taken her straight to the stairwell of a multistorey luxury penthouse. An absurdly wide staircase made of precious wood curved its way up to a gallery in front of the larger-than-life oil painting of a white-haired, toothless Chinese man. On either side of the bottom step, the staircase was flanked by head-height vases containing the largest sunflowers Klara had ever seen.

And in between, as if she'd just descended the stairs of a stage set, stood a smiling fairy, or at least that's what the creature dressed totally in black looked like to Klara.

'Hello, and welcome to VP. My name is Lousanne.' She laughed.

She pronounced the letters the English way; it sounded slightly like VIP.

'How lovely to see you. Have you been here before?'

Klara shook her head, intimidated by the woman's beauty. Very young, with large, dark Disney eyes that would unleash the protective instinct in any man and convince any woman that she would be powerless if Lousanne set out to seduce her husband.

Klara felt a twinge because she was reminded of her own life, of her time studying at vocational college, when she worked afternoons on reception at the law firm on Kurfürstendamm. When she used to greet every client with a similar smile, offer them coffee and request they take a seat in the waiting room if the lawyer or notary was still tied up. This was how she'd met Martin. At the time she'd felt as assured and free as Lousanne, whose posture radiated pride, but understatement too, with which she let every guest know that her time here meeting and greeting was just an intermezzo and that she was destined for higher things.

The higher you climb, the further you fall, Klara thought, and then was surprised by Lousanne's request: 'If you're honouring us with your presence for the first time then I'd kindly ask you to fill out our member questionnaire.'

Lousanne turned around and Klara was taken aback by how deep the back neckline of her dress was. 'If you'd like to follow me.'

She led Klara to a chest-high marble column beside one of the vases of sunflowers. On it sat a leather case that she opened smartly. She took out a padded envelope that she handed to Klara along with a white porcelain Montblanc fountain pen.

'Have you already chosen a level?'

Level?

She shrugged.

'Not to worry, you can change colour anytime.'

Colour?

Klara was trembling in her attempt to open the envelope, when it was snatched from her hand.

'That's not necessary, darling. I've already sorted out the formalities for you.'

She spun around in fright. Martin had slipped into the room through a secret door and was suddenly standing beside her. The envelope *(with a membership application? For what? Was this a club?)* was now in his hand and he was smiling mischievously. Shaven, showered and his curly grey hair tamed with wax, he smelled as good as he had when they first bumped into each other at the law firm.

'Can I have a quick word?' Klara asked, essaying a smile which failed miserably and pointing to the door through which Martin had presumably entered. The way to the lavatories seemed to be beside the lift; they might well be able to talk in private in the corridor down there.

Martin shook his head. 'Afterwards. There'll be much more to talk about then anyway.' He grasped her hand, slightly more firmly than necessary.

He nodded to Lousanne and led Klara upstairs.

'What's going on here?' Klara whispered in a choked voice.

Martin nodded as if she'd asked an intelligent question, but left it unanswered as he pressed a hand on her shoulder blade and guided her upstairs with a gentle thrust.

'I'm being serious, Martin. What are you planning this time?'

'Don't be such a spoilsport,' she heard him say with a smile, one step behind her.

At the top of the stairs the gallery led into a corridor with a grey carpet, at the far end of which stood a large, black double door. A pi symbol was painted on it in red.

Martin opened the door with an electronic key card.

'Please...' Klara begged, thinking of her six-year-old daughter Amelie, who hopefully was sleeping peacefully and innocently in her little bed, under the watchful eye of the babysitter. She followed Martin into the hotel room even though all her senses urged her not to.

Her eyes were lowered because she was afraid of what awaited her.

'I need the loo,' she croaked.

'That can wait,' Martin declared. Then something moved inside the room and Klara could no longer look away.

She'd been expecting a suite, a bed, and maybe a sofa and chair by floor-to-ceiling windows with a view of the Gedächtniskirche and Zoo Palast. All that was there too, but the bed was circular and set in the middle of the room which must be three times the size of the bedroom in Prenzlauer Berg where she'd lived before moving in with Martin.

'What's going on here?' she said, slightly unintelligibly because she'd unwittingly slapped her hand over her mouth.

Klara was staring at half a dozen identical faces. All the men were wearing the same mask. A tears of joy emoji.

She felt like howling herself.

'What are you going to do to her?' she asked weakly, paralysed by terror. Klara wished that the young girl on the bed, around whom the faceless men in dinner jackets were now standing, was the work of a make-up artist too.

But the blood dripping from her mouth and down her naked breasts was real.

8

The torture victim was cowering on all fours on the mattress like a dog. Supporting herself with one hand only, as the left arm hung like a broken wing from her scrawny body.

Please, she implored silently when her eyes met Klara's. She was missing two front teeth at least.

'Say "hello" to Shaniqua,' Martin laughed. 'Of course that's just her stage name, but doesn't she look like an American Indian beauty?'

More like someone dying at the stake, Klara thought. The dark-haired and dark-skinned girl – she couldn't be older than eighteen – had a slight build. With each fitful breath her ribs dug through her skin like an old man's fingers. Her chest was covered in bruises and open wounds.

The dog collar around the girl's neck was so tight she could barely take in any air. The leash was held by a strong-looking man in a crumpled dinner jacket. In his other hand was a soldering iron which he must have already used to inflict injury to her back and buttocks.

I'm in hell.

Klara wanted to rush to help the girl, but Martin held her tightly from behind, pulled her back towards him and embraced her as if they were a loving couple enjoying a gorgeous view on a balcony.

'VP's just a game, darling,' he whispered in her ear. He was wearing a smiley mask now too, which scratched Klara's cheek. She felt sick when he explained the abbreviation: 'Violence Play'. Two English words so horribly contradictory that they should never be brought together in any circumstances.

Violence? Play?

Good God.

Klara had hoped that when Martin became a father things might get better with his 'ideas' and 'role plays'. But the opposite had been the case, for the child gave him a bargaining chip.

'If you don't play along, everyone will find out what Mummy's been up to. They'll see photos and videos of it on the internet and they'll have to listen to how messed up this poor mother is, because that's exactly what people will be whispering about in the playground and at parents' evening. Then I'll take the child away from you and all you'll have left is a view of a rear courtyard in Marzahn that you can eye up from the window of your prefab block.'

'Let her go right now, you bastards!' Klara shouted. When Martin loosened his grip she made use of the opportunity and took a step towards the girl, who recoiled in horror. Losing her balance, she tried to support herself with her broken arm and howled in pain.

'Shut it!' barked the man holding the leash, as he jerked it.

Klara was next to him in a trice and screamed, 'Let the girl go, you fucking pervert!' She looked around the suite for a telephone she could use to call for help. On Martin's instructions she'd left her mobile in the car.

'You heard her,' Martin now told the assembled company. 'My wife isn't wearing a mask or an armband. Which means she's the queen this evening.'

All those present nodded. Klara felt as if she were witnessing the voting procedure of a secret lodge whose laws she didn't understand.

'Queen?'

'Yes, my darling,' Martin said. 'Tonight you get to decide the final measure.'

The man with the leash raised his hand holding the soldering iron. The lead was plugged into an extension and the tool was glowing.

'What final measure?' Klara asked, although she didn't want to know the answer. All she wanted was to run away. Away from here. Out of the room, the hotel, her life.

'We bought our toy (Martin actually said *toy*!) from her owner with no restrictions. Which means we can do what we like with her.'

Klara was sure he was grinning diabolically beneath the mask.

'And by "what we like" I mean anything and everything.'

'As our final measure tonight we're either going to blind her or penetrate her.'

'You're not doing anything else to her you sick fuck—'

'Exactly,' Martin interrupted her. 'Not us. *You*. The choice is *yours*. Do you want to grace her eyes or her vulva with the soldering iron?'

The words alone were like a kick in the stomach. Klara felt like doubling up with pain. She'd always suspected that there were women who had to put up with much worse than what she did. Girls from poor countries forced into prostitution, sold when young by their families to pimps, who then offered them to psychotically sadistic clients abroad – 'without restrictions'. She'd hoped she'd never actually have to encounter such horror, to which even she, a victim of domestic violence, closed her eyes in the hope it would go away.

'You say I'm the queen?' she asked Martin, an idea forming in her head.

'Yes, you are.'

'And I get to decide?'

'Exactly.'

She took a deep breath. 'Then I demand that all of you let her go. Right now.'

Klara held her breath in expectation of a slap to the face.

'Okay.'

To her amazement, her husband raised no objection. Instead he clapped his hands three times. A sliding door covered in tissue paper opened.

'Ah, Doctor, if you wouldn't mind. The queen has decided that the VP session is over for our toy.'

Another man, also wearing a mask but in a doctor's coat, said nothing as he pushed in a patient trolley from the neighbouring room.

Two men in dinner jackets lifted the semi-conscious Shaniqua – or whatever the seriously injured girl was called – from the mattress like a sack of potatoes and carried her to the alleged doctor.

Klara made to follow them but Martin gripped her arm firmly.

'Where do you think you're going, my love?' He pulled her towards him as a dancer might his partner in a pirouette.

'To call the police.'

Martin shook his masked head furiously. 'Oh, I ought to have explained, darling. Our VP session isn't over yet. Not by a long way.'

Without relaxing his grip around Klara's wrist, her husband watched the doctor and the girl as they left the suite.

'Let go of me!'

'I'm afraid I can't. Our rules state that if the queen sets the toy free, she herself becomes the toy. And as you're not wearing a colourful armband...'

The door closed behind the 'doctor' and the girl.

Martin grabbed Klara by her hair and yanked her head so violently that her eyes filled with tears.

'... it means we can do what we like with you. No taboos.'

He gave a sign to the man who'd been holding the leash and who now stepped over to Klara and gave her the first of many punches to the stomach she'd suffer tonight.

9

JULES

TODAY

'They could do with me whatever they wanted. Stub out their cigarettes on my body, urinate on me, kick, bite and hit me. A ruptured spleen wasn't the worst of my worries.'

'Christ. And did they—'

'Blind or penetrate me? No, my husband didn't let them poke out one of my eyes or rape me with a red-hot soldering iron.'

'But did they...?'

'... rape me otherwise?' Once again Klara finished his sentence. 'Literally, yes, without a doubt. In a sexual sense? No. That's not what the sadists' club is about.'

It took Jules some time to digest Klara's account. Then a while longer to find the right words. Eventually he said, 'Most women who call me are scared of walking home on their own. Is it possible that you're in the converse situation, Klara? That you're scared of going home and that's why you're wandering around in the dark?'

'Yes.'

'Are you afraid of your husband?'

'No.'

Jules knotted his brow in amazement and scratched the back of his neck where the wire headset was chafing uncomfortably. His head was slightly smaller than Caesar's and so the equipment was not the right size for him.

'Haven't you just described a horrific case of marital violence?'

'Yes, but for a while I'm sure I could have gone on living with that on its own,' Klara said. 'Even though I'd never imagined I'd be able to say this. Certainly not after the evening at Le Zen. There's a video of it, by the way, which Martin has uploaded for garnishing on internet forums.'

'Garnishing?'

'That's what the perverts who hang out on such file-sharing sites call it. They watch other women being tortured, take screenshots of scenes they like and print them out. Usually pictures of women with mouths and eyes wide open in fear and pain. Then they masturbate on the photo and upload the result to the site. Martin was delighted with the comments: "Look how I garnished your bruised whore of a wife. Sexy bitch!" That sort of thing.'

Klara's voice now sounded clearer, which wasn't just down to the lack of noises around her. It seemed as if she wasn't outside anymore. Jules had heard something metallic scraping on stone: a door that was stuck. The front door of an apartment block? Then the sound quality of the line changed, but also the register of Klara's voice. It was firmer and more assertive, in contrast to what she now said, which gave Jules the unreal feeling of sitting on shaky ground that might give way beneath him at any moment. 'What I can't live with anymore is what happened after my time at Berger Hof clinic.'

Jules swallowed, but the lump that had formed in his throat wouldn't budge.

Berger. Hof.

The words unleashed a greater feeling of terror in him than Klara's descriptions of her ordeals.

When he closed his eyes, the images from the clinic's brochure, which he'd picked up while looking for the remote control, played on the screen of his mind like a PowerPoint presentation. It took Jules a while to calm down sufficiently to ask his next question. 'How did you end up there?'

The lump in his throat swelled to the size of a tennis ball. Jules couldn't help but think of Dajana, that wonderful woman he'd always introduced as *'my wife'* even though they'd never officially tied the knot. And she too had always ticked the *Married* box on forms, such as the one for admission to the private Berger Hof clinic in the Black Forest, near Baden-Baden.

'Were you undergoing psychiatric treatment?' Jules asked numbly.

Like Dajana...?

'No, I was there for work,' Klara replied. She yawned, to Jules's surprise.

Halfway down the hall he heard the typical sound of an incoming text message. As his own mobile wasn't displaying any notifications, it must have been Klara who'd received the SMS.

'So are you a therapist or psychologist?'

'Why are you whispering?' Klara asked, and only then did Jules realise that he'd lowered his voice.

'I'm an MTA in a psychiatric practice. I was taking part in a research project at Berger Hof.'

'And something happened there?' Jules asked, a little louder again now. The question he was really asking remained unspoken: *What was it that surpassed the horror you experienced with your husband?*

Klara breathed something.

'Sorry, I didn't get that.'

'Yannick,' she repeated.

Jules entered the study again. 'Who is that?'

She sighed heavily and answered with a question of her own, which seemed completely unrelated: 'Have you ever taken desomorphine?'

'You mean krokodil?' No, he told her. It was the most lethal cheap drug in the world, which he'd come across frequently during his time with the emergency services: junkies overdosing on the dreadful cocktail of codeine, iodine and red phosphorus. Usually the paramedics would find them in the loos at a train station, zombielike with green, crocodile-like alterations to the skin where the needle had gone in. In their delirium they often wanted to eat themselves.

'You only need to inject it once,' Klara explained unnecessarily. 'Just one fucking time and it destroys the body's ability to produce endorphins. Do you know what that means?'

'It means a person can never be happy again.'

'Exactly. That's what happened to me with Yannick. I had contact with him just once and he stopped the production of my happiness hormone. Irrevocably, for ever. No matter what happens, I'll never be able to laugh, love or live again.'

When Jules heard a car door shut with a loud thud – that explained the earlier scraping sound.

'You're in a garage,' he remarked, partly because he didn't know what else to say. Her disclosure about Yannick had touched on a topic that required every ounce of his sensitivity. One wrong question, one careless comment, Jules sensed, could terminate this conversation in a flash.

She confirmed his suspicion by starting the engine rather than answering him. Judging by the sound, it was a small car.

'I really want to thank you again,' she said. 'I wouldn't have been able to do it without you.'

Jules was standing between the desk and the television, which was still flickering away silently. The special edition of *Case XY* was over and now talk-show guests – the usual suspects – were arguing over whether short-haul flights and SUVs ought to be banned.

'Why are you thanking me? For escorting you home on the phone?'

'That's a stupid question, Jules, and you know it. We've already established that coming "home" is the last thing on earth I want to do.'

'Because Yannick is waiting for you there?'

'He's waiting for me everywhere.'

'To do what?'

'I already told you. He's going to kill me. And I can't imagine he'll leave you in peace when he finds out you've been trying to help me.'

Jules shook his head at the total role reversal. Never in his time manning the emergency phones had a caller warned him about a danger to his own life.

'Why does he want to kill you?' *And me...?* 'Who is this Yannick? Tell me about him.'

'There's no time for that anymore,' Klara said, and Jules sensed he was in danger of losing her.

Once again she thanked him, and once again he didn't understand why. 'How have I helped you?'

'Do you really not know?'

'No. Please tell me.'

She paused briefly. 'What can you hear right at this moment?' she asked softly, as if in the cinema or theatre, trying not to disturb those around her.

'A voice that sounds confident but tired. And your engine running.'

'And what can't you hear?'

'I...'

He thought about it. There was nothing apart from the monotonous hum of the engine. No squealing of tyres, no hooting, no car radio, no air, no—

Jules stopped in the middle of the living room as if he'd walked into an invisible wall. 'You're stationary. You're not moving.'

Klara gave a sad laugh. 'Exactly.'

But the engine's running. In the garage. Metal on concrete. A closed door.

Jules knew that the mathematics of terror often presented the human brain with perfectly simple calculations, but sometimes the brain refused to accept the result that was as clear as it was shocking. The mind frequently searched for complicated solutions to solve the grisly equation in a less traumatic way. In this instance, however, Jules couldn't put one and one together to make three. A stationary car with its engine running, at night, in a garage. Inside the car, a woman who, propelled by fear, had saved the number of the telephone companion service to her mobile. It could only mean one thing: 'You're going to kill yourself tonight, Klara!'

To get there before Yannick!

With fumes that presumably were filling the car via a tube from the exhaust through a gap in the window.

Have I helped her? Is that the 'way home' I've accompanied her on?

'Spot on,' Klara said, confirming Jules's worst suspicion. 'I'd like to take my life tonight. I hope you won't be offended, but I'll find it easier if I hang up now.'

10

KLARA

The dashboard of her Mini Cooper had always made Klara feel as if she were in an aeroplane. Even now the various different circular aluminium instruments gave off a matt orange glow in the darkness of the garage. Highly appropriate for her final 'departure' into the unknown.

Klara swallowed, but the scratching didn't ease up. She grabbed her throat and beneath the Norwegian sweater felt the chain with the small silver cross she'd worn ever since her First Communion.

The tachometer and speedometer were a blur before her tear-filled eyes. She was coughing and her nose running. The irritation of her mucous membranes had come sooner than she'd expected, although it was a tiny car taking her on her last journey. The air already tasted of coal dust – maybe that was just her imagination – and Klara wondered gratuitously whether Martin would ever be able to sell the Mini if in her death throes she emptied her bowels on the upholstery. Maybe there would even be seepage from her rotting body, depending on how long it took them to discover her remains. It would stink even worse than Dad's Omega which he used to lovingly clean every weekend until one evening Mum threw up in the footwell.

That happened on the way back from a teachers' get-together at Loretta am Wannsee, where the staff at Döblin School held their regular piss-ups, to which spouses were invited once a month. Although Klara's mother couldn't hold her drink, her husband urged her *'not to play the spoilsport'* and leave him *'standing there like an idiot with an uptight bird who didn't know the meaning of fun'*.

Well, her attempt to join in with the 'merry' drinking of the boozy teaching staff ended when, after a single Campari Orange, she emptied the bile-soaked remnants of the cucumber salad onto the foot mat. Klara vividly remembered waking up that night when she heard the front door close shortly after half past ten. She leaped out of bed, opened her bedroom door in the attic and listened out for footsteps. Those were her indicator, the seismographic early-warning system she'd trained since early childhood, and which now, at the age of fourteen, functioned almost to perfection.

Her father's stomping, in the wake of her mother after she'd scurried upstairs, was an especially reliable gauge of his anger. With Dad the creaking of the third step was revealing; sluggish to respond, it needed him to step on it with all his weight to make a noise. The speed was the clear indicator, however. If Dad was seized with uncontrolled rage, he would come upstairs to the bedroom rather sedately. Slowly, like the rumbling of a gathering storm, against which nothing could prevent the inevitable. When Klara heard her father stomping ponderously like this she knew it was too late. It was pointless to go downstairs to her parents' floor and wait outside their closed bedroom door for her mother to groan. Gasp. Retch and throw up. There was nothing Klara could do to prevent *it*. And yet she tried after that evening at Loretta. She plodded barefoot downstairs, past the copy of the Rembrandt soldier with golden helmet, which she hated because his severe gaze reminded her of her father.

On the first floor it smelled permanently of dust, even when it had just been cleaned. The old house seemed to produce dust all the time, as if it were continually shedding its skin. It was on the banisters, in the carpet, even on the walls and especially on the picture that hung between the bathroom and bedroom.

A black-and-white photograph behind glass: a winter shot of the pier in Binz. Nobody about, and the waves that broke against the pier seemed to have frozen to ice as they crested. People often praised her father's keen eye, unaware that his gift didn't end with capturing lovely snapshots of nature on Rügen. His particular talent was his X-ray vision into the human soul. He could identify someone's emotional weaknesses in a trice. But rather than photograph these, he would expose them until they lay before him like an open wound into which he relished pouring salt, acid or something even worse.

'*Everybody has an Achilles' heel,*' he once told Klara in the playground, taking her in his arms. She almost wept for joy; he was so seldom this intimate with her. '*Your weakness is your sensitivity, Klara. You take things too much to heart. You've got to toughen up, or one day life will give you a big kick up the arse.*'

Then he gave her a two-mark coin, which everyone in the family had to pay when they said a bad word, and she laughed.

Later Klara wondered whether he gave Mum anything when he crossed a forbidden boundary. Fifty marks for a black eye? A hundred for knocking out a tooth?

When that evening she stood outside the bedroom door and heard her mother's frantic laughter, that paradoxical displacement activity before he raped her, Klara finally became aware of her father's weakness. She'd grasped the door handle without knowing exactly why, without a plan. But now she knew what she had to do.

Klara went up to the photograph her father was so proud of, grabbed the edges of the glass frame with both hands, and ripped the wave picture from the wall to send it crashing to the floor.

Now there was no need for her to open the bedroom door. Startled by the ear-splitting sound of shattering glass, her father threw it open himself. Bare-chested, with just his suit trousers on, which Mum had laid out for his school day the next morning, he was holding a belt like a dog lead.

'What the hell...?' His eyes grew large when he saw what Klara had done.

'I'm sorry, I...'

She hadn't prepared an explanation. This apparent act of senseless destruction couldn't have possibly been an accident. But her father didn't wait for any plausible excuses; he lashed out. Not for the first time in Klara's life, but definitely the first time with a belt, the first time in the face, and the first time with the desired result: he vented his anger on her. The storm, which had announced its presence with the creaking stair, erupted. But on her rather than her mother's body.

When Klara went to school the following day and told her

best friend how she'd fallen off her bike, bashing one side of her face, she smiled with happiness, but this brought tears to her eyes. *Finally*, she thought, grinning even more broadly. *I've finally found a way to protect Mummy and—*

The beep of an incoming text message wrenched her from what would presumably be her last ever daydream back into the fume-filled reality of the garage.

WHERE ARE YOU????

Martin. Of course. Always reproachful, always with four question marks.
Reliable unto death.

I'VE TRIED CALLING. YOU'RE NOT PICKING UP.

Wiping a tear from the corner of her eye, she read the rest of the message.

OR AREN'T YOU AT HOME????

YOU HAVEN'T LEFT AMELIE AT HOME ALONE, HAVE YOU????

Klara felt sick. Martin had her father's talent. The same psychological X-ray vision.

With unerring accuracy he could poke his finger in her wounds, although it wasn't that great a feat to identify a daughter as a mother's emotional Achilles' heel.

'No, you arsehole,' she whispered. 'I *didn't* leave Amelie alone. Vigo is with her. The babysitter you can't stand because he's gay. Because he's a climate activist, because he rejects mobile phones and cars – in short because he's a good boy and thus the complete opposite of you.'

'*Don't you worry, Frau Vernet,*' the sixteen-year-old said as she was leaving the apartment. '*Amelie is so easy that I ought to be the one paying you money for being able to read my books here. If there's any problem I'll go downstairs and call you from there.*'

Conveniently he lived in the block behind, just across the courtyard, with his mother, who was raising him on her own.

Vigo then added that she needn't rush back; it was the weekend and he had no plans for Sunday. He could lie down in the guest room, right beside Amelie's room. '*I'll wait until you get back.*'

Forever, then.

Klara sobbed and all of a sudden saw her husband's repulsive, aggressive face in her mind again. She screamed at him in her thoughts: '*Do you know why I'm not coming back? Why I'm leaving my daughter on her own? To protect her!*'

To make sure she doesn't get the same idea as me one day. To prevent her from offering herself up as a target and making you so angry you take it out on her rather than me.

For she was sure of one thing: Martin might be the shittiest husband on the planet, but he was a good father. He'd never do anything to his daughter unless she provoked him to act as a vent for his anger, just as Klara had done with her own father during all those lost years of her childhood.

Successfully so. After the 'day of the broken picture' (as she called it in her head) her father never laid a finger on her mother again. Never hit, beat or raped her again, as her mother confirmed years later, long after she'd left home. And why would he? He'd found a new victim. His daughter.

That must never happen in our family, Klara thought.

I'm protecting my child from Martin by leaving her alone with him.

She closed her eyes in the knowledge that this undeniably paradoxical thought was only a half-truth with which she, a former pupil at a Catholic girls' school, was trying to justify her 'mortal sin'. For Martin wasn't the main problem.

Yannick was.

She feared him more than the fire and brimstone which the priest had painted in glowing colours during communion classes.

And yet.

Now that she'd crossed the point of no return, doubts were starting to surface. Obviously. Not about her wishing to die; she was still determined on this point. But more about whether she was right in her assumption that her daughter would grow up in less danger without her.

Without me. And without Yannick.

Klara's head was droning, which she put down to the fumes that must be producing an ever-greater concentration of toxins inside the car. She'd heard that people could hallucinate shortly before passing out, and right now she was indeed experiencing an acoustic delusion. Her husband started speaking. He said her name, softly at first, then louder and louder until she could hear it clearly even though she didn't have her mobile up to her ear.

'Klara?' said her husband, who wasn't her husband and didn't sound like Martin in the slightest, although the voice was strangely familiar.

Jules?

Suddenly the mobile phone in her lap weighed several kilos.

Fuck. She thought she'd cut him off, but clearly the guy from the telephone companion service was still on the line.

She swiped her finger erratically around the touchscreen of her mobile, but instead of turning the thing off she activated the speaker function.

'... already explained,' she heard him say. 'Don't do that to me. I can't take it. Not again.'

Again?

She sighed. *Fuck, why, oh why?* Why did Jules have to say *again*, striking just the right tone once more. His begging had stirred something inside her that neither Martin nor Yannick had been able to eradicate, no matter how much of her they'd destroyed: her curiosity.

God, how inquisitive I used to be. About life, about the journeys it had in store for me. About seeing my child grow up.

'What do you mean by *again*?' she asked in a voice that to her ears sounded husky and thus totally alien.

Klara looked at the clock on the dashboard, but the display swam before her eyes. She couldn't make out if it was 22:59 or 23:09. All she knew was that soon a day would be breaking that she had no intention of living to see. She wouldn't be *allowed* to see it, for the ultimatum would have expired.

'I'll tell you if you switch off the engine,' Jules said.

She shook her head firmly. 'I've got a better idea.' Klara gave a dry cough then said, 'I'll continue to let the fumes come into the car. And you hurry up with what you've got to say, Jules. Maybe you'll manage to tell me your story before I completely lose consciousness.'

She wheezed asthmatically, so loudly that she could barely make out the first few words with which Jules described the most dreadful day of his life.

11

JULES

THREE AND A HALF MONTHS EARLIER

Spandau to Wilmersdorf is generally about thirty minutes in the evening rush hour. Because of an accident on the city motorway it took Jules sixty-five minutes.

A lengthy, agonising hour that felt like an eternity in which he ripped off the headset, sped down the stairs, past the old fire alarm box that stood in the lobby as decoration, and into his car. Foot down to the city motorway, then the short stretch from the Spandauer Damm exit to Halensee and down Westfälische Strasse until he was outside the block in which all his life's dreams would turn to dust.

The stairwell of Prinzregentenstrasse 24 always smelled of food. Over the years, the red sisal carpet that slipped beneath Jules's shoes as he raced up the stairs (even in normal circumstances the cramped, retrofitted two-person lift was a test of your patience) seemed to have sucked up the aromas of gravy, frying oil, wild garlic and grilled fish. Today there was an additional smell in the air, which grew more intense the closer Jules came to his flat: smoke. Asphyxiating smoke.

'Hey, wait…!'

'*What the hell...?*'

'*You can't just...!*'

Jules ran past his colleagues who greeted him with energetic half-finished sentences in the entrance to his soot-covered flat. He had to push one of the two fire officers out of the way, while he evaded a uniformed policeman in the hallway that was flooded with firewater. The postman who discovered the fire had long gone, as had the woman's corpse in the hall.

'Please, this is a crime scene...' the policeman shouted. For a brief moment Jules thought he was losing his mind.

A crime scene? How can my flat be a crime scene?

But when he wrested himself free from a hand that grabbed him from behind as he was being drawn to where the smell of burning was even stronger, he made the mistake of glancing through the open bathroom door.

He looked at the bathtub that both he and Dajana found ugly because the enamel had flaked off in several places and it was stained around the plughole.

The water in the bath reminded him of that sunset at the Scharmützelsee. On one of his last happy days with Dajana, when the blood-red sun disappeared behind the trees of Wendisch Rietz and, with a final flourish, made the surface of the lake shimmer the colour of copper.

A movement from behind impelled him onwards. He had to get to the last room in the hall before the officer overpowered him.

The door was attached only by the top hinge; its cheap wood had been shredded by an axe at head height. It was open, with the inner side facing Jules, allowing him to see something towards the bottom that would prove to be the most horrific sight in his life, one he would never, ever forget.

Scratches.

Deep, bloody, fingernail-wrecking scratches. The body that had produced them had long been taken away. Jules couldn't help coughing and his eyes filled with tears. Because of the stench of burned wood, plastic, cuddly toys...

'Valentin was playing with a candle,' he heard someone say behind him. A man who was crying like him.

'*He must have swiped it from kindergarten,*' Jules apparently replied, but he no longer remembered this. He also said something about the children learning how to deal with fire.

Later he would find out that he'd spoken to the team leader, himself the father of a five-year-old boy. The man who'd chopped through the door to get into Valentin's room. But all Jules could see at that moment were the scratches in the door. Furrows that looked as if they'd been made by a mortally wounded animal trying to escape from a trap.

'... a crime scene?' Klara asked, back in the present. For a moment her voice left Jules no room for memories. Now he was no longer outside the gutted bedroom, but back at his desk in the flat. Wearing the scratchy headset again. His eyes subconsciously fixed on the Berger Hof prospectus.

'My wife had locked the door,' he told her.

'Why did she do that?'

Jules swallowed. 'Dajana didn't want to be disturbed. She didn't want the child to have to see her dead body.'

It wasn't a 'murder–suicide' as the press report had said

in passing. Dajana had only meant to kill herself. Jules was as certain of this as he was of the fact that he'd never forgive Dajana if there were a life after death in which they met again.

Just like I'll never forgive myself...

'The fire brigade thinks that because of the smoke Dajana got out of the bath again after she'd slit her wrists. That's why our flat looked like a slaughterhouse when they found her. The trail of blood went from the bathroom through the hallway and almost to the nursery.'

'You sound as if you've got your doubts.'

'I suspect that she changed her mind at the last second. She was in despair, but in the end her death wish wasn't as strong as her motherly love. It was unfortunate that the fire happened.'

'She couldn't open the door?'

'She probably couldn't find the key and was going to call for help, but collapsed as soon as she'd opened the door to our flat, where the postman found her.'

Jules wiped his dry eyes with the back of his arm. An action he'd repeated so often in his grieving phase, when he'd wept so much that it became a habit, even when the tears no longer flowed. The few friends he had thought it was a good sign he could compose himself in public and no longer sobbed at the merest thought of his family. In truth, however, it was worse, for his tearless grief had migrated inwards where it ate him up.

'Did she leave a suicide note?' Klara asked.

Jules got up and felt an agonising scratching in his throat. He felt for the folded piece of paper he always kept on him. To read it over and over again, whenever he was overcome by grief, which was several times every day.

Today the note was in the breast pocket of his shirt, beneath his jumper and right next to his heart.

My darling Jules...

'Yes.' He cleared his throat. 'On the kitchen table.'

Clearing his throat and swallowing didn't ease the scratching so he headed for the kitchen to fetch a drink.

'May I ask what she wrote?'

I wish I had the strength to go on...

Jules shook his head. 'I don't think it's the content of the note you'd find most interesting, Klara.'

'What do you mean?'

Klara sounded tired and slightly slurry, but she still seemed to be fully conscious.

'What's really of interest as far as you're concerned wasn't what my wife wrote. It's the name on the headed paper she used for her suicide note.'

'What name was that?'

'Berger Hof.'

12

'Whaaaaaaat?'

She drew the word out for what seemed like ages. All that was missing was an ironic laugh, but she was probably too feeble for that.

Jules was quivering with tension. On the way to the kitchen he suddenly felt in a hurry. There was no time to lose; he needed to put Klara under emotional pressure. And so he played his joker; if he could stimulate her curiosity she might regain the will to live. For the time being, at least. 'My partner Dajana had severe psychological problems,' he said, 'and I still don't know what the cause of these was. That's why she was in Berger Hof clinic. In the same psychiatric institution as you, Klara.'

He felt again for the letter whose contents haunted him in his dreams.

Farewell, my darling Jules. Now I'm going to slit my wrists. Maybe I'll manage to call you one last time on 112 before my energies fade. Hear your voice, which used to give me support, confidence and hope. Maybe I'll be able to hold onto it and you can accompany me on my final journey.

A desperate fury flared up in Jules again. He balled his fists.
'When were you there?' he asked Klara.

'End of July.'

At the same time?

'Like my wife.'

Dajana's health insurance had been reluctant to cover
the costs of this luxury clinic. But she'd written a flattering
portrait of the chairman of her insurance company, who
returned the favour by personally approving the funds for
her burnout treatment.

'Her work and family were testing the very limits of
her resilience. She needed some time out with professional
support. Shortly after the treatment Dajana killed herself and
our son Valentin. He was only five.'

And yet his fingers had dug into the wood of his bedroom
door with the desperation of a grown man.

*Did he scream or cry? Or just cough with a rattle in his
throat? Who was he thinking of as he took his last breaths,
choking on soot?*

Jules was now in the kitchen, which was absurdly large,
but in proportion with the rest of the spacious apartment.
Although a huge island with barstools stood in the middle,
there was also a dining table that sat six and there would
have still been space for a sofa opposite the kitchen units.

He opened the chrome double fridge and took a bottle of
orange juice from the drinks compartment.

'Are you still there, Klara?'

He heard a muffled knocking on the line, but couldn't be
sure. Klara was silent. Jules didn't know if she was thinking,
ignoring him or had already lost consciousness.

In the hope that he still had a line to her, he put the juice bottle on the island, pulled up a barstool and placed his private mobile beside it.

It took a moment for the facial recognition to unlock his smartphone, then he typed a short WhatsApp message:

I'LL CALL YOU IN A SEC. ANSWER, BUT DON'T SAY A WORD!

Then he said to Klara, 'I'm asking you, Klara, no, I'm begging you: switch off the engine! Talk to me. And tell me what the hell you did at Berger Hof. What happened to you at that place which destroyed my family?'

Jules opened the bottle of juice, which was two thirds empty, but didn't take a sip.

'My wife took her own life, Klara. And now you want to do the same. After visiting that clinic too. It can't be a coincidence!'

With this unsettling observation he sent the WhatsApp message to his father's phone.

Then he called him and put the other line on speaker so his father could listen in.

13

KLARA

Klara felt as if a blunt gimlet had been driven right between her eyes and was now on the rampage inside her skull. She was sensitive to noise at the best of times; the roar of her engine, amplified by the garage, would have normally been enough to give her a headache, without the need for carbon monoxide in her air. And now this obstinate Jules fellow was polluting the ether with his outrageous, absurd claims.

'You made that up!' she said. 'You don't know the clinic and there's no way your wife was there – if she exists, that is. You're just trying to put me off.' Klara swallowed; her throat was dry. 'Have you diverted this call to the police? Are they on their way?'

'No. With the equipment I've got at home I can't find your location. Besides, that's the last thing I would do.'

'Why?'

'Because the police can't help you, Klara. I know victims of domestic abuse. I used to speak to them all the time on 112. You don't need a doctor, the police or anyone from welfare.'

'You're absolutely right. But what I really don't need is a stranger blathering down the phone because he thinks he can get me out of the car.'

Jules sounded furious. 'I'm not blathering! You're the one who's prattling on and doing nothing. My God, how many women like you did I have on the phone when I worked for the emergency services? Every week I had to send officers to women who'd been beaten to a pulp by their husbands, but the moment they got there it suddenly wasn't so bad and the women would howl, begging, imploring the police not to take the thug away.' Jules groaned. 'All so half-hearted. The cry for help, the desire to escape, even your suicide attempt, Klara – it's just farcical.'

'Farcical?' Klara coughed. She realised he was trying to be provocative to strengthen the emotional bond between them. To make it more difficult for her to stick with her decision.

'Yes. Almost childish. As far as I'm concerned you can sit there in your car for as long as you like. Your death wish isn't that strong.'

Klara was tempted to grab her droning head.

'Not strong? I'm pumping car fumes into my lungs!'

'I bet your car wasn't manufactured before 1999, which means it'll have a catalytic converter and it barely emits any carbon monoxide,' Jules shot back. 'I worked for the emergency services, Klara. My knowledge doesn't come from watching crime series on Sunday evenings. These days it's almost impossible to kill yourself with car fumes. Sure, your car's cold and in winter it takes a little while for the converter to get working, so I was slightly nervous to begin with. But we've been talking for far too long now. I can also hear that you've closed the windows. A widespread fallacy. You ought to have flooded the entire garage with fumes. And if you were really serious about ending your life tonight you would have known all this. Because you'd have done your research. For Christ's sake, Klara, you've got a child! I know you're desperate. I know you're plagued by the darkest thoughts and can't see any way out. But at the bottom of your heart you never want to leave your daughter alone with your husband!'

You fucking arsehole! Klara thought. She stared at the dashboard, where her face was reflected grotesquely in the Plexiglas casing. All of a sudden she found it difficult to argue back.

'Thanks for giving me another reason for ending this conversation,' she whispered, now utterly exhausted. She was totally floored by the possibility that Jules might be right. And yet she said, 'If what you say is true, I need to use the little time I've got left to try something else.'

'Okay, then, let's make a deal,' Jules suggested, sounding placatory.

'What kind of deal?'

'You tell me what happened at Berger Hof. And if you still want to take your life afterwards, I'll let you know about a quick, painless suicide method.'

She slapped the steering wheel in anger and started shouting. 'It's not about *wanting*. I'm *going* to die. Either way.'

Her voice was wobbly, partly because Jules had unsettled her. Nonetheless she sounded defiant: 'I don't see another option. My life is screwed up anyway, but there's no need for me to ruin my daughter's too. The thing is, by ending my life myself, at least I'd have the hope I could do it in a slightly more humane fashion.'

'So you want to commit suicide because you're terrified of a horrific death at the hands of Yannick? Is that right?'

Committing suicide because she's afraid of death.

Klara closed her eyes, which made the droning inside the car seem louder. 'You haven't the slightest idea what you're getting yourself into by talking to me,' she warned him yet again, but Jules wasn't letting up.

'Whatever this Yannick is threatening you with, it can't be worse than what I've been through.'

Klara nodded. 'True. There's probably nothing worse for a parent than having a child die before they do.'

Fuck it, the fumes really do seem to be having no effect. Apart from giving me a migraine and making me feel sick.

Klara switched off the engine and opened the driver's door with numb fingers.

The cold air inside the garage hit her like a torrent of ice water. She greedily inhaled the oxygen with such rapidity that it made her cough.

Jules asked whether everything was okay. Klara said yes, even though she couldn't think of a moment in her life when things were less okay. Apart, perhaps, from the perineal tear she'd suffered after being raped in her marital bed, which couldn't be stitched up because they would have asked too many questions in Casualty. It still hurt sometimes when she peed. Not to mention during sex.

'You're mistaken,' she heard Jules say.

'About what?' Her head was buzzing. All she'd achieved was to wreck her short-term memory. Now she couldn't remember what she'd said ten seconds ago.

'That there's nothing worse as a parent than having a child die before you do.'

'No?'

'What's worse is watching your child die without being able to do anything about it.'

Klara heaved herself out of the car. With her knees feeling as if they might give way at any moment, she had to hold on to the roof of the Mini. The door that connected the garage to the bungalow was right in front of her, only a few steps away. Although 'bungalow' was a rather fancy way to describe the tiny weekend house on the Heerstrasse allotments. Martin was embarrassed to talk about a summer house or dacha and he'd never invited friends here, even though it was the nicest and largest building on the site. It had been upgraded for all-year-round habitation and they'd added a garage, although this had never been approved.

'I've been through both,' Jules said.

'Both?' Klara wanted to know where she was getting the strength to drag herself from the garage into the bungalow. At least the pain in her leg – fortunately the ankle was only injured – stopped her from passing out.

'I don't know what you're getting at.'

Klara closed the connecting door and wondered whether she should switch on the light. They'd so seldom come to this one-bedroom house, renovated in ultramodern fashion with parquet floor, underfloor heating, air conditioning and Italian designer furniture, that it still smelled of paint and moving in. And when they did come, it was without Amelie, who would be left with a babysitter because her daddy didn't want her sullying the light futon sofa with her greasy fingers and drooling mouth. Klara's blood on the upholstery, on the other hand, would have bothered him less.

She hobbled over to the custom-made kitchen table, which divided the tiny open-plan kitchen from the living–dining room, sat on a wooden chair and opted for darkness. Even though it was unlikely that any neighbours would be around at this time of year and up so late, wondering why a light was suddenly on in the Vernets' bungalow, which had stood empty for weeks.

'Valentin wasn't an only child,' Jules said, and as she took in the significance of what he'd just said, the mobile phone in her hand vibrated like an electric razor. She looked at the display and read another message from Martin.

WHERE ARE YOU????

Klara deleted the message and asked him, 'You had a second child?'

'Fabienne, Valentin's sister.'

'And was she…?'

'Yes, she was in the room too. She hid in the cupboard while Valentin tried to open the door. She was still alive when we found her.'

'God, that's awful,' she heard herself say what she was thinking. 'Are you sure that Dajana didn't—'

'—do it on purpose?' Jules asked curtly.

Klara bit her tongue. 'Just forget what I said. I didn't mean to get too personal.'

She heard a sharp intake of breath. 'If I'm being honest, I did wonder that too. I mean, things were quite tense between her and the children. Fabienne had always been a daddy's girl. And when Dajana was hit by burnout, her relationship with Valentin became even more difficult. But all that was perfectly normal. Despite their differences, Dajana wouldn't have done anything to harm the children.'

An awkward silence followed, then Jules asked, 'So? Do we have a deal?'

'My story in exchange for a painless way to kill myself?' Klara nodded. 'Yes, we do.'

She began to sweat in the cool, unheated bungalow. At the same time she felt her heart misappropriating her ribcage as a drum.

'Good.' The tone of Jules's voice was neutral and sober; it was as if he'd offered to take the rubbish out if she did the washing-up.

'In that case I'll up my side of the bargain and tell you what happened to Fabienne. But only if you tell me first who this Yannick is and what he's got on you.'

Klara coughed the last remnants of the fumes from her lungs and then began: 'Yannick has given me until midnight. If by then I haven't ended my marriage to my husband he's going to kill me – very painfully.'

She sniffed and blinked away tears – she had no idea where they were from.

'And if he finds out I've told you everything... no, if he even has the slightest suspicion I might have confided in you, you will suffer the same agonising fate as me, Jules. Is the truth really worth that?'

'Yes.' The answer came like a pistol shot.

'The truth of a stranger who just dialled the wrong number.'

'I'll take that risk.'

'You naive idiot.' She laughed, probably the last laugh of her life. 'My mobile is bugged; he put spyware on it. I imagine Yannick already knows we're talking to each other.'

'You sound paranoid.'

'And you sound like a fool. But, whatever. We've been talking for too long as it is. When he checks the data on my mobile after I'm dead he won't rest until he finds out who I was talking to. And then he'll know we spoke.'

'What then? Tell me.'

'Okay, listen carefully. But do me a favour. In a few hours' time don't curse my name when you're desperate for your torment to stop and wish Yannick would finally put you out of your misery.'

14

KLARA

The needle couldn't find a vein, and so Daniel Kernik had to start again, which wasn't unusual for Klara as her blood vessels were thin. Even experienced nurses had drawn a blank with her arms.

'I'm sorry,' the junior doctor apologised and had another attempt, this time with success. Klara gritted her teeth and concentrated on the print on the wall of the consulting room, where the equipment was as modern as it was expensive. A photograph of a lighthouse being buffeted by the waves of the Pacific Ocean.

Klara felt the second prick, but didn't watch. She was afraid of needles, which in her profession wasn't much of an asset.

'This isn't normally my job. Press on it for a bit.' Kernik handed her a pad for the puncture in the crook of her arm then he pulled over a roller stool. Klara was sitting on the edge of the treatment table right beneath the window that overlooked the clinic's park.

'To what do I owe the honour then, Dr Kernik?' she asked him.

Here in such luxurious surroundings she wouldn't have been surprised if the senior consultant had given her the injection personally. The patients who forked out the price of a top-of-the-range small car for a two-week 'course of treatment' expected to find nothing in this clinic that reminded them of a normal hospital. This was also true of its setting and architecture, which would have made many a five-star hotelier weep with envy.

Half an hour's drive from Baden-Baden, the clinic sat majestically on top of a hill in the Black Forest like an eagle's nest. In between their group and individual therapy sessions the patients, mostly here because of marital crises, burnout or psychosomatic disorders, enjoyed a direct picture-postcard view of the wooded valley from the café terrace, menus prepared by Michelin-starred chefs, and thalassotherapy in the spa.

All the patient rooms were single suites with air conditioning, fireplace, jacuzzi and internet television. But in spite of all the fancy-pants stuff, the clinic had an excellent reputation among experts, which was principally down to its director, Prof. Dr Ivan Corzon.

The Barcelona-born psychiatrist was the editor of the most prestigious textbook on clinical psychiatry and a sought-after speaker at specialist conferences around the world. The fact that Kernik could work under him as a junior doctor here was like a software developer getting a personal reference from Bill Gates.

'I wanted to be alone with you, Frau Vernet,' he said with a curious smile on his lips.

Klara cocked her head and fiddled unconsciously with her wedding ring. Was this guy trying to flirt with her? Kernik had beautiful brown eyes and a disarming smile, but he was anything but her type. With his solarium-tanned face, the La Martina shirt and his tasselled deck shoes, he conformed to the cliché of a golf-playing Porsche driver.

'Why, Dr Kernik?'

'You're not a doctor, Frau Vernet. You don't really understand what's going on here. I fear you need my advice.'

Klara stood up and looked for a bin to throw the pad into. The bleeding had stopped. She wouldn't need a plaster.

Kernik got to his feet too and raised his hand apologetically. 'Please don't get me wrong. The last thing I want to do is disparage your position as a medical–technical assistant. I know you do indispensable work for your practice in Berlin. Your boss thinks you're destined for greater things and wants to encourage your ambition to study psychology. But you must know all this yourself. If you weren't so talented and smart your boss surely wouldn't have approved your application to take part here.'

If he's flirting, he's going about it in a very funny way, Klara thought, surprised by the concern in Kernik's face. She briefly felt angry because the real reason she'd gone along with this visit to a private clinic was to get away from her husband, for a few days at least. Away from all her worries and fears. And now here was another guy unnerving her.

'You have to go,' Kernik said, lowering his voice to an urgent whisper.

'Go? I thought the briefing with Professor Corzon was happening here.'

Klara pointed to a sofa and chairs covered in grey artificial suede. Corzon was a vegan and rejected all animal products, even for furniture.

'You don't understand. You need to get away from here as quickly as possible and—'

At that moment the door opened. Klara felt the draught as a breath of cold on her neck and came out in goose pimples. Or was this because of what Kernik had said?

… get away from here as quickly as possible…

Like a child caught in the act, the doctor hurried over to the man who'd just entered the consultation room.

'Hola, qué tal?'

The Spaniard didn't need a snow-white doctor's coat to demonstrate his authority. Corzon was shorter than you might imagine from the clinic's web site and glossy brochures. Slightly squat with an ample belly, he had a beard with a faint red shimmer that matched the hair on his head, and which ought to have seen a trimmer several days ago to give it shape. Next to him, Kernik looked incredibly smart although the professor gave off a far greater charisma.

'Soy Ivan,' he introduced himself with a broad smile and by first name only, which put Klara at ease. After Kernik's disquieting words, she was longing for some expertise, assurance and trust.

'Muchas gracias por participar en este importante experiment. Con su colaboración está hacienda un servicio extraordinario a la ciencia.'

Klara nodded with a smile. The experiment she'd agreed to take part in was very much out of the ordinary. In addition to her training she'd spent three years learning Spanish, so she basically understood what the doctor was trying to tell her. All the same Klara was pleased when Corzon announced an interpreter with the words: *'Mi colega actuará de intérprete.'*

Her relief turned to disenchantment when she realised that Kernik was going to fill this role.

'He wants us both to sit on the sofa,' the junior doctor said, translating for his boss who left no doubt that this was an order rather than a request. On the coffee table between the sofa and armchair lay a plastic box which Corzon opened. He took out an object that looked like virtual reality glasses for a computer game.

'*Para inducer los delirios, hay que ponerse estas gafas con auriculares, lo que provoca una sobreestimulación por medio de varias señales ópticas y acústicas. Un agente intravenoso adicional refuerza los delirios que causan.*'

'We're going to use these glasses to produce hallucinations,' Kernik translated. 'They will flood you with optical and acoustic stimuli. You've just been intravenously injected with a substance developed by us that will intensify the hallucinations generated by the glasses.'

Klara nodded. That's what it had said in the forms she'd been given at reception when she checked into the clinic. And of course she signed a clause absolving the clinic of any liability in case she became psychotic during her stay. That was, after all, the point of the experiment.

'*No se preocupe, todo se dosifica de tal manera que las halucianaciones persistirán sólamente durante unos minutos después de que las gafas se hayan apagado. Luego seguiremos ampliando el interval lentamente cada día.*'

'This experiment is highly dangerous and could have fatal consequences for you,' she heard Kernik say, completely mistranslating Corzon's words. He'd said that she mustn't worry; the hallucinations would be gone a few minutes after she'd removed the glasses.

'Don't frown. Corzon's now running through the side effects, which he's downplaying,' Kernik said, confusing Klara even more. 'I know I'm putting you in a difficult position,' Kernik continued his phoney translation, trying to sound as objective as possible. 'But you mustn't put on those glasses. Ever. Under no circumstances.'

He waited for Corzon to finish three more sentences then said, 'Please don't look so shocked when I'm speaking. Otherwise the professor will realise I'm warning you. Now give him a nod. Corzon has asked you whether you feel at ease here.'

Klara did as she was told.

'Once again, I know I'm putting you in an impossible situation. And for that I'm very sorry. But like me, you've got a small child.' Klara was no longer able to concentrate on the friendly voice of the head of the clinic. All her attention was focused on Kernik, who now said, 'I beg you, don't put the glasses on. Otherwise something dreadful is going to happen. You might never leave this clinic.'

Never?

Klara unconsciously shook her head, which earned her a disapproving roll of the eyes from Kernik at the very moment that Corzon picked up the glasses again.

Paradoxically, what the junior doctor had just said triggered a tentative feeling of happiness in her.

At Berger Hof forever? Never having to go back to Martin?

Even the fact that she'd be cut off from her child didn't seem so terrible, and she immediately felt ashamed about that. But deep down she was sure that Martin would care lovingly for Amelie.

Or was she deluding herself?

No.

His shortcomings definitely didn't extend to how he treated his child. He'd never lay a finger on his little girl.

'I'm now going to pretend I'm needed on my ward,' Kernik said. 'Follow me in five minutes' time.'

'But...' Klara began, but the stern look in Kernik's eyes made her fall silent.

Corzon went over to his desk and seemed to be looking for something in the top drawer.

'You're going to do this, Klara!' Kernik whispered. 'You're going to say that before the first experiment begins you need to go to the loo. We'll meet in the stairwell at the end of the corridor.'

Kernik's mobile rang and he put his part of the plan into effect. When he said goodbye to Corzon, who nodded back from his desk, Klara found herself alone with the head of the clinic.

'*Comencemos con la primera etapa del experiment*,' he said, pointing to a door that led to an adjoining room he wanted her to enter. Klara understood his words as: '*Let's begin with the first stage of the experiment.*'

15

Klara wasn't in the least bit surprised that she'd followed Kernik's orders. There was a time in the past when she'd regarded herself as confident, emancipated and independent. But this 'past' was long ago and had come to an end at the very latest when she said, 'I do,' entering a marriage in which over the years she'd become programmed to obey men.

Unconditionally.

After explaining to Corzon in broken Spanish that she wanted to freshen up before putting on the glasses, Klara went down the corridor towards the lavatories, feeling as if she were being pulled by an invisible dog lead. Because it had become second nature to follow a dominant man, she gave scant consideration to the absurdity of the situation in which Kernik had put her. She'd travelled all the way to Berger Hof to take part in a scientific experiment under the auspices of an expert with a lofty global reputation, and already on the second day she was being bossed around by a junior doctor.

Why? she wondered as she turned away from the loos and opened the door to the stairwell. The key question that summed up her entire, miserable existence: *Why?*

In the eyes of friends and colleagues she came across as a strong woman: a fairly powerful physique with curves in the right places. Her poise too – the expressive chin, the shining eyes and maybe her slightly dark complexion, which she owed to her mother's Italian roots – made people believe she was strong-willed and unflappable. Not a woman you could easily push around. And indeed she hadn't been pushed around for ages; Martin preferred to hit her straight up. On her liver, so hard and so often that she would shake on the edge of the bed as if suffering a bout of fever, unable to move.

The door to the stairwell closed behind her with a loud bang, which made Klara flinch as if she'd just been hit again.

Beatings.

Klara had read a lot about abused women. She'd even consulted an advice centre *('I'm asking for a friend')* and learned that domestic violence wasn't a class problem, but one that tainted all sections of society. And it crept up on you. Almost unnoticed, it poisoned what had once begun as a great, blinding love. First with radioactive compliments *('You're so beautiful, I'm never going to let you out of my life')*, then compulsive demands for proof of love (*'Let's pick a shared password for all our email accounts and mobiles')* and feigned self-pity (*'You know how badly I was hurt by my ex')*, until the verbal blows below the belt were replaced by physical ones. And while the outside world continued to shower you with compliments (*'How lucky you are to have found each other, you're such a great match. Your husband is a real diamond')*, you clung to the hope that everything would return to how it was before the first swollen eye. But as you waited, your shame grew into self-loathing and made it impossible to trust others. Even though Klara had tried, calling her mother when she thought she could take it no longer.

Klara had sobbed so fervently down the line that she wasn't sure her mum had understood anything to begin with. Her voice trembled with sheer terror as she said that Martin might come home early from tennis and find her sitting so distraught by the phone. Some of the tear-choked torrent of words must have got through to her mother, however, as all she said to her daughter – which left Klara holding the receiver, her open mouth contorted in distress – was the following:

'You mustn't annoy men, darling. Make a bit more of an effort. Think of how hard Martin has to work for you.'

Then she changed the subject and told her about a rude employee at the garden centre who'd refused to take back a pot of orchids infested with aphids.

What now?

Klara was alone in the stairwell, which seemed to have been recently mopped. It smelled of disinfectant and tile cleaner.

'Hello?' she called out pointlessly, at which her mobile ringtone mingled with the echo of her voice in the stairwell.

'What did you think you were taking part in here, Klara?'

Kernik.

She'd thought she'd be meeting him in person, but instead he was calling her. He came straight to the point, without bothering to explain his odd behaviour. For a moment she wondered how he'd got hold of her number, but as a doctor he obviously had access to the information she'd provided on admission.

'I'm not going to answer any of your questions before you tell me—'

'Quiet! We're running out of time and soon I won't be able to save you anymore.'

Save me? From what?

Klara wanted to make it clear to Kernik that he couldn't speak to her like that, but of course he'd struck exactly the right tone to make her obey.

And so she replied, 'Along with other participants I'm going to experience what it's like to be mentally ill. I think it's a perfectly logical and necessary approach.'

According to Corzon there was a fundamental problem in the treatment of psychotic illnesses, which were essentially different from physical complaints: virtually every psychiatrist had suffered from a physical ailment at some point in their life. But very few of them had any experience of the symptoms described by, or observed in, mentally ill patients. Even someone who 'only' suffered from toothache could imagine the effect of a painkiller for tumours. A doctor who'd never had a hallucination, however, could prescribe psychotropic drugs without knowing, based on their own experience, anything of the effect the prescription might have on a schizophrenic patient.

This, in a nutshell, was the problem. And that's why Klara was here. So that under controlled test conditions, psychotic symptoms could be activated artificially and temporarily, which the subjects could suppress themselves with psychotropic drugs.

'Where are you?' she asked Kernik.

And what the hell do you want from me?

Ignoring her question, the junior doctor asked, 'What sort of symptoms are you supposed to suffer from, Klara?'

'Paranoia. Persecution complex.'

She went down some stairs to a wide, double window that gave onto the clinic's car park, where she couldn't see a vehicle worth less than eighty thousand euros, not including extras. Porsche, AMG, BMW 9 series, Touareg, and even a metallic-blue Ferrari, which was parked next to a luxury convertible Klara didn't recognise.

The only blemish on this beauty parade was a white plumber's van in the entrance directly below the window, two floors down.

'And so as soon as the hallucinations come on, you'll be given a remedy?'

Klara sighed. 'Unless I'm in the placebo control group. What's all this about? If you've got ethical concerns, why don't you report your boss to the relevant supervisory authority? I did plenty of research beforehand.'

Which was a lie. Several weeks ago she'd fished the leaflet out of the wastepaper basket at work, which her boss had thrown away with other advertising material. After which she'd made two telephone calls and was told that non-qualified individuals could take part too. When she found out that she'd have to give up a whole week for the experiment, that was that. She knew that Martin wouldn't let her go away for the weekend with friends, but strangely he never put obstacles in the way of her professional life. He would even look after Amelie if he knew she were away for 'training'. Klara would put up with anything for a few days without him. Including artificially induced hallucinations.

'Frau Vernet, please don't believe what you've been told. Berger Hof isn't a normal clinic. The risks—'

'—fill two pages of the application form, I know.'

'Oh, for goodness' sake, forget what's in the documentation. The real risks aren't listed there.'

'So what are they?'

She heard a fluttering, as if a pigeon were flapping its wings wildly down the line.

'I can't tell you,' Kernik replied. 'But I can show you. Please go over to the window.'

'I'm already there.'

'Good. Have you eaten yet?'

Is he having me on? 'Do you want to have lunch with me?' Klara asked, baffled.

Kernik gave a bleak laugh. 'No. I just wanted to know if you've got an empty stomach.'

'But why?'

For a moment there was silence. Then Kernik asked, 'Are you looking outside?'

'Yes.'

'At the white van?'

'Exactly.'

Klara wondered whether the van's sliding doors were now going to open and reveal a dreadful secret.

'Okay. Do me a favour. Everyone in this place is condemned to death. Please promise me that you'll leave here once you've seen what's about to happen.'

'*What's* going to happen?'

'This,' Kernik said.

Then she saw a shadow. Right in front of the window. Just for the fraction of a second, although in her nightmares it kept appearing as an endless stretch of time.

A never-ending moment in which she slapped both hands

over her mouth and started crying and screaming, just when the shadow turned into a metal-splintering thud. With a loud crash the van shook and the roof suddenly looked as if a giant had thrust a fist through it. But it wasn't a fist; this destruction had been caused by the impact of a human body plummeting from the top floor of the modern building.

Klara screamed and then couldn't help but vomit when she saw who'd leaped to his death from the roof. She recognised him by the La Martina shirt, now stained blood red. And by his tasselled deck shoes, one of which had come off and was lying in the gravel beside the van.

And by the fact that the phone line was as dead as Daniel Kernik on the roof of the white van.

16

JULES

Klara brought her monologue to an abrupt end. As concerned as she was confused, she asked Jules, 'What on earth is going on there?'

'I'm sorry, I just dropped something.'

Jules had been getting a glass to pour himself some juice, but it had slipped from his grasp.

The glass had shattered with the noise of a falling tree. The crash was amplified by the silence in the apartment as well as his concentration on Klara's story, which was as horrific as it was bizarre. If the glass had toppled from the cupboard into the sink during the daytime, this would have barely registered among the noise of everyday life. But it had torn into the night like an alarm and sent his pulse racing.

'I'm sorry,' he repeated, and tried to return to the subject. 'Everyone in this place is condemned to death?'

'Those were pretty much his last words.'

'Do you have any idea why Kernik did it?' he said, picking up on her description of the doctor's suicide. Her melodramatic performance didn't match any known suicide pattern, and

Jules knew what he was talking about; in his work he'd been confronted with almost every method. Although, when he thought about it, Klara's suicidal behaviour didn't correspond to the norm either. For the moment, at any rate, he was relieved to have talked her out of her plan, even though he knew he was merely buying time.

'Corzon claimed it was an accident. Kernik had often gone up to the roof, he said, to get around the clinic's smoking ban.'

'How did you react to the lie?'

'My first impulse was to get out of there.'

'You were going to follow Kernik's advice.'

'Exactly. Get away from the clinic as soon as I could.'

'But?'

'But then I thought about the alternative. And that meant going back to my husband. And then it seemed to me that Kernik had done the right thing. I mean, he'd put an end to his life rather than give it up to someone else.'

Jules took a large shard of glass from the sink and opened the bin beneath it.

'But why did he do it? Did it have anything to do with the experiment?'

'Yes.'

'But then you aborted it, surely.'

'No.'

'No?' Jules asked in disbelief.

'Once again, what should I have done? Gone back to Martin and listen to him tell me on the first evening just what a loser I was? *"Too cowardly to do something important for science, just because some limp-wristed poofter threw himself out of the window."'*

Jules paused to think. As far as her personality was concerned, Klara was a weird, almost schizophrenic mixture. On the one hand confident, which was probably her determined, professional side. Privately, however, she was quick to surrender to her fate.

'How did the experiment go?' Jules asked, then winced. One of the smaller shards he'd tried to throw in the bin had got caught in his finger.

'I remember putting the glasses on. They were as bulky as a large pair of binoculars and almost covered my entire head. I had to wear headphones too. In retrospect I can barely recall any details. Only that at the start I felt as if I were in an MRI scanner. With a techno-like drone and booming that was replaced by high frequencies while a strobe storm assaulted my eyes. I know now, at any rate, what it must feel like when someone gets an epileptic fit in front of the telly, triggered by extreme light stimulus. I lost consciousness after a few minutes.'

'And then?' Jules stuck his little finger in his mouth and stopped the blood with his tongue. At the same time he glanced at his mobile, on which he'd called his father earlier. It lay right beside the laptop, which he'd taken from the study into the kitchen. He'd removed the headset and was now conducting the conversation via the computer's speaker so his father could listen in.

'There's no "and then". Professor Corzon told me I was too sensitive a test subject and therefore unsuitable for the experiment. The side effects would be too strong and not justifiable ethically.'

'So you did go home early after all?' Jules tore some kitchen paper from a roll and wrapped it around his finger.

'No, first I had to recover from the side effects. It took a long time for me to get over them. Unfortunately.'

'Why unfortunately?'

'Because in hindsight I wish I'd left immediately, Martin or no Martin.'

'Why?'

'Because then I'd never have met Dr Kiefer.'

'Who is this Dr Kiefer all of a sudden?'

I thought we were talking about Yannick, Jules thought, but kept this to himself to avoid unsettling Klara. The longer she kept talking, the less likely it was she'd spontaneously choose another way of ending her life.

'Jo. A senior doctor. His real name is Johannes, but everyone called him Jo.'

'You too?' Jules asked. The fact that she confirmed this with a sad sigh said everything about the relationship that must have developed between the two of them. Intense and tragic.

'Where exactly did you meet Dr Johannes Kiefer?'

'In the clinic park. I was sitting on a bench at the bottom of the café terrace. You get a wonderful view of the valley from there. Suddenly he was standing beside me. I hadn't heard him approach even though the gravel crunched loudly beneath people's feet.'

At that moment there was a ping and Jules cursed not having muted his mobile for incoming messages. His father had sent him a WhatsApp. Before Klara could ask what the sound was, he said, 'What did Dr Kiefer have to do with your experiment?'

'Nothing directly. He said he was a pathologist and was working behind the scenes – for example he'd analysed my haemogram.'

Jules flicked the switch on the side of his mobile, putting it on silent and smearing the screen with his bloody finger in the process.

'I found him incredibly nice and friendly. I thought he must be in his mid-forties, which was mainly down to the youthful way he dressed – jeans, trainers and a hoodie. As he confessed later, he was over fifty, which was almost unbelievable. I mean how many people do you know of that age with wrinkle-free skin that's as smooth as a baby's and jet-black hair that's not dyed?'

'None,' Jules said, trying to open his father's WhatsApp message.

'When he sat down beside me, my first question was whether he was also the clinic's fitness trainer.'

The timbre of her voice changed from minor to major; she was evidently relating a happy memory.

'Most of all I was taken by his self-deprecating, boyish smile. I think that's what drew me. Just as some fish are attracted to the light at night, I was bewitched by his smile that sparkled from the corners of his mouth to his deep, dark eyes.'

'What did he want from you?'

'He didn't really say much to begin with. Unlike Kernik, he wasn't immediately talkative.'

Jules said nothing, certain that Klara would tell him what had made the meeting with this Dr Kiefer so extraordinary, whether he asked or not. Even after a failed suicide attempt she wanted to talk about it at length.

'After some small talk the subject turned to Kernik, and I remember Jo gazing into the distance. Until that point he'd been looking me in the eye all the time, but he couldn't anymore. I asked him what he thought had really happened, and he hummed and hawed, saying he wasn't allowed to discuss my case with me.'

'Your *case?*'

'That's what I thought too. *"What do you mean, my* case?*"* I asked him, and Jo nodded like someone who'd just taken an incredibly difficult decision. Then he said… I can remember it word for word, and the quiver in his voice.'

'What did he say?' Jules asked as he read his father's WhatsApp message:

WHAT THE DEVIL'S GOING ON THERE?

At the same time Klara repeated Dr Kiefer's words verbatim, the words that must have completely cut the ground from under her feet, and which now made Jules shiver all over:

'When Corzon came to your bed the day after the experiment was aborted he didn't tell you the truth. You weren't unconscious for five minutes. You were dead for five minutes.'

17

KLARA

She was now speaking very softly, as she often did when her surroundings were familiar. It was a habit she'd developed as an overanxious mother. As soon as Amelie was in bed she'd tiptoe through the apartment, turn the volume of the television down to a whisper and even refrain from flushing the loo if she'd only done a pee. All of this in spite of the fact that her daughter slept soundly the moment she slipped into the realm of dragons and unicorns. But Klara couldn't bear the thought that she might wake with a fright and toddle over to her father. He was quick to anger when disturbed, but would never have taken out his ire on Amelie. Klara would be the one to feel the full force of his fury.

Martin pretended he was processing patient bills, but Klara knew that he'd contracted an agency to do this work. She'd never dared say a single word to him while he was at his desk. If she had, the minimum penalty would be a long night of torment. And doubtlessly the same would happen if Amelie disturbed him, so Klara got used to whispering and gliding across the creaky parquet floor almost silently in thick socks.

At some point it must have become second nature to her to whisper within her own four walls, as she was doing now, even though her husband wasn't anywhere nearby.

And hopefully never would be again.

'I was clinically dead,' she said, repeating the shocking revelation, as if she still couldn't believe it herself.

'Do you think Dr Kiefer told you the truth?'

'Why would I have had any reason to doubt him?'

She felt certain Jules knew she was avoiding his question with this answer.

And once again her inadvertent companion was sensitive enough not to delve any deeper. 'Did he say what the cause was of your cardiac arrest?' Jules asked. It sounded as if he was in a large room with a tall ceiling.

'He said it was a type of anaphylactic shock, a severe reaction to the drug that was supposed to trigger the hallucinations.'

'So you went five minutes without any vital signs? Did that leave you with any lasting damage?'

'Lasting damage?' Klara parroted back his words. She only just managed to stifle a laugh. 'Are you seriously asking that question of a woman who's just tried to kill herself with exhaust fumes?' Ironically, Klara was desperate for a cigarette for the first time in years. Before her pregnancy she'd been a casual smoker, never having her own cigarettes and always bumming off friends and colleagues, and cadging them at parties. This had been a thorn in the eye as far as Martin was concerned. He would criticise Klara for her 'ashtray mouth', even though her teeth were no less white than those of her dentist husband. Sometimes Klara thought Martin had only got her pregnant to make her stop smoking. For he knew how conscientious she was and that she would never expect a defenceless creature to have to undergo nicotine withdrawal directly after birth.

'But yes, immediately when I woke I felt as if I'd been kissed by a wrecking ball,' she said, answering Jules's question as to whether she'd felt the consequences of having been resuscitated. 'For the first few days after I almost died I suffered from bad night sweats. I could have mopped the entire clinic floor with my nightshirt, no joke. It was Jo who explained that this was a sign my heart was totally out of rhythm.'

'Hmm.'

It seemed as if Jules had to digest what he'd just heard.

Or is he distracted?

Again Klara was nagged by the suspicion that her companion might be playing a double game. It was obvious he was trying to stop her from committing suicide. But how far would Jules go to achieve this? And what means did he have of discovering her location, if any?

'Why did Corzon not tell you that you were clinically dead?' Jules asked. 'Were they worried you might sue the clinic?'

'I suspect so. If word had got out, Berger Hof would never have found any more guinea pigs for their tests.'

There was a crash behind her and Klara got such a fright that she whipped around and leaped to her feet, jabbing the mobile phone at the imaginary intruder as if it were a knife. But nobody was there. It was just the double fridge in the niche beside the pantry, which had started making ice again.

Christ you're so jumpy. A scaredy-cat to the grave.

Klara put the phone back to her ear and made out the end of what must have been quite a lengthy question from Jules.

'... connection between Dr Kiefer and Yannick?'

Yannick.

Klara's stomach tightened. 'You'll soon find out,' she whispered, and waited for another torrent of ice cubes to be dumped into the storage case. She closed her eyes. Concentrating very hard, she managed to recall the senior doctor's face. The intelligence and clarity in those large eyes surrounded by laughter lines. And how she had to watch those warm-hearted eyes vanish from one moment to the next.

Klara shuddered with disgust. 'Before I reveal the gruesome details, I'd like to tell you about the wonderful experience I had just before that.'

'With Dr Kiefer?'

'Exactly. I realise you don't get the connection yet. But if you give me five minutes you'll understand why Yannick has this power of death over me. And why you've got no choice but to stick to your part of the deal.'

'Help you depart this world,' Jules said, and Klara was pleased to hear him say it openly; clearly he *was* going to stick to it.

'But don't worry,' she said. 'The memories I wallow in and which I'm about to share with you only sound like a romantic love story between me and Dr Kiefer at the start. In truth, I enjoyed my brief time with him.'

Despite the subjects of our conversations.

To begin with she'd tried to deceive Kiefer, as she had all those others who'd asked about the blue marks on her arms or neck, or about other injuries. But Jo hadn't been satisfied by her standard excuse that she bruised easily. Ultimately it was less his obstinacy that breached her dam than a single sentence of his. They were still in the park when he said, '*I can't unrape you; that's impossible, Klara.'* Although he didn't need to say any more, he added, *'But I can listen to you and I am bound by patient confidentiality.'*

With this, Jo had given her a gift. He hadn't palmed her off with the false hope that he could change anything to do with her situation. He hadn't acted like a knight in shining armour. But he had given her the sense that he wasn't judging her for what she'd allowed herself to undergo. Such as in Le Zen hotel. When, on only their second meeting in the clinic park, Klara told him about the group abuse disguised as a 'game', he was the sole person in her life who knew about the darkest hour of her existence to date.

The man with the mask.

The cable ties.

The gag in her mouth.

And the men. All those men.

'Did you fall in love with Dr Kiefer?' she heard Jules say.

'Head over heels.'

'And then Yannick came into your life?'

Klara opened her eyes, and around her everything was engulfed by a thick, pervading blackness – the very thing she'd longed for when she suddenly found Yannick standing in front of her. Tall. Naked. And psychotic.

'Exactly,' she replied to Jules, then repeated his words: 'Until Yannick came into my life and sparked my desire to take leave of this world in which something so dreadful as what I had to suffer with him could happen.'

18

KLARA

A FEW WEEKS EARLIER

Only a few seconds before Yannick appeared on the screen of her life and destroyed it for good, Klara felt happier than she had in years.

The sex was awesome, she thought as she lay in the semi-darkness on the bed, from which Jo Kiefer had got up to go to the bathroom.

Not that she had much to compare him with. Prior to her husband she'd only had two lovers, but all that seemed an age ago. The negative experiences of the present had long buried the positive ones in her past. For years now, she'd associated what happened in the bedroom merely with pain and humiliation.

And now I'm lying here. Breathing the scent of a new man in my life and wishing our night of passion could begin all over again.

She turned over on the waterbed and giggled at the pleasant gurgle made by the movement of her naked body. For her taste the bed was a touch too modern, seeing as the apartment was otherwise kitted out with solid leather and wooden furniture.

Jo lectured in psychiatric pathology at the Free University, and a year ago he'd rented a place to live in Berlin so he didn't have to keep staying in hotels when he travelled from Berger Hof to give seminars and lectures. Like today.

I'm in Berlin. 3 p.m. Debrief? he'd messaged early that morning. Without the slightest hesitation Klara lied to Martin that she had to do some research for a course in the Berlin State Library and told him that Vigo would look after Amelie after kindergarten. Then she accepted the doctor's invitation.

'I shouldn't have told you,' she said, beginning their 'date' with an apology as she alluded to the admission she'd made to Jo back in the clinic. 'I don't know what came over me that day.'

Klara was astonished at how quickly she'd put her trust in him and revealed to him the violence she suffered in her marriage. But she'd felt drawn to Jo from the very first moment she heard his deep voice and gazed into those warm, dark eyes that looked at her in a way her husband never had: openly, honestly and affectionately.

She'd almost told him about the Le Zen video that Martin had put up online.

With her and the men.

Lots of men who'd abused and humiliated her.

It's hard to believe that I've willingly surrendered to a member of the 'stronger' sex again, Klara thought, as she listened to the whoosh from the bathroom where Jo was taking a shower.

Usually it was she who spent hours trying to scrub the disgust from her body after being 'used' by Martin, but now she was savouring Jo's tangy scent on her skin and wanted to preserve it so she could remember forever how she'd bid 'farewell' to him in the dark restaurant in Prenzlauer Berg. It was Jo's perceptive idea to meet in a place where, in total darkness and served by blind waiters, they would have no distractions and be forced to concentrate on each other. And talk.

'Thanks for listening to me,' she said, still in the dark and feeling timidly for his hand.

'*I'm* the one who should be thanking *you*,' Jo countered.

'For what?'

'First: thanks for accepting my invitation to meet so spontaneously.' He began stroking her hand.

'Second: thanks for being so frank and telling me about your private problems. And third: thanks for allowing me to kiss you.'

Kiss? she thought, but before she could say it out loud, she'd already felt his lips on hers. This sensation alone was unbelievable. Quite apart from what happened later, here in the bedroom.

Unbelievable.

Although Klara hadn't climaxed, she'd been so close to an orgasm for the first time in an eternity. She could hardly comprehend how open-minded, indeed frivolous, she'd been only a few minutes earlier. Even yesterday, the idea that she might not recoil at a man's touch would have seemed inconceivable, if not ludicrous. Not to mention the idea of opening up to a man so voluntarily.

And yet that's precisely what I've done. She felt the sheet beside her again, which in her undreamed-of passion had loosened from the bed and was stained with their bodily fluids. Her cheeks turned red and Klara could sense her face glowing. Unfortunately the positive feeling of excitement was swamped by a dreadful shame, because she couldn't help think of the last bedsheet which had been so stained with her blood that she'd had to throw it away after Martin had—

Fuck! Martin!

The sheet beneath her body shifted even further when she turned to the bedside table and reached for her mobile.

Thank God!

It was a miracle that her husband hadn't sent any messages, nor tried to call to check up on her.

The relief spread through her body like the warmth from a tot of brandy. At that moment the noise of the shower stopped and it was suddenly silent in the apartment.

'Fancy doing something now?' she heard Jo call from the bathroom a few moments later. The door wasn't closed – it had taken several months for Martin and her to be so intimate in this regard.

'Love to,' she replied, even though she had no idea what to say to Martin if she stayed out longer. And it was already...

She looked at her watch, but it was too dark to make out the face. Apart from the narrow opening in the bathroom door, the only other light came from a faintly lit work of art. A slightly curved samurai dagger with a mother-of-pearl hilt hung on the bedroom wall, its green shimmer picked out by two dimmed LED spots which were as muted as nightlights. As she reached for her mobile she noticed a strip of light switches embedded in the bedside table.

'How about we go for a cocktail?'

She pressed the outer button on the strip and couldn't help giggling, as it clearly had a different function. The sheet below her shimmered in a halogen-blue colour that made it look as if she were on a lilo in a swimming pool.

'Your waterbed has even got lights inside,' Klara called out in amazement, pulling the sheet back even further. 'I never knew you could get see-through mattresses.'

'It was custom-made,' Jo told her. She could tell he was smiling without seeing his face. Klara sat up cross-legged on the mattress, in which the water shone brightly and as luminescent as a glow stick. It also changed colour. From azure blue to phosphorous yellow to dazzling white *to...*

'What's that?' she asked. Softly. More to herself, for at first glance she was totally surprised. She leaned forwards and found herself peering through the diamond formed by her legs and crotch, into the inside of the mattress. For a brief moment she was convinced it must be a reflection.

I don't look like that, do I?

Surely my eye is still in its socket?

Absurdly, Klara even touched the corresponding spot on her face; everything was fine, of course. Her cheekbones were still covered with skin, and her lips weren't as bloated as those on the face that had suddenly appeared between her legs.

Beneath her.

In the illuminated water of the bed she was lying on.

In which a few minutes earlier she'd been making love with a man she would never see again after he went to the bathroom.

'You found it, then,' a voice to her left said, which wasn't so unlike Jo's but it lacked all his warmth.

And as if the stranger were holding a remote control to operate the terror, Klara suddenly saw a torso and a severed leg swimming in the water that glowed blood red. She screamed more loudly than ever before, and yet still couldn't turn her gaze from the dismembered body beneath her.

'I assume I'm right in thinking this is the first time you've fucked on top of a corpse?'

Klara felt the urge to throw up, but she also wanted to tear out her eyes so as not to have to look at the mattress anymore.

'Where is Jo? What have you done with him?' she screamed at the stranger, even though at that moment she knew that her question was verging on madness. For the man before her still looked like Johannes Kiefer, but nothing of the Johannes she knew was present anymore – all those endearing features that marked his sensitive personality had gone. Standing before her now was merely his body which seemed to have been possessed by an evil spirit. It seemed quite logical, therefore, when the monster said, 'Please forget your lover for the moment, Klara. I think it's time you got to know *me*.'

Grinning smugly, he came closer. 'My name is not Johannes Kiefer. Nor am I a doctor. The media know me as the Calendar Killer. But you can call me Yannick. I've come to give you your date.'

At that second, Klara was stung by a bee for the second time in her life. The first occasion – at her uncle's wedding – had been more painful; her windpipe had swollen almost as soon as she'd dropped her plate at the buffet. This time the throbbing beneath her skin was less intense, but she blacked out... *probably because this time it's a needle rather than a bee.*

With the syringe still in his hand, the smiling and bare-chested Yannick pushed Klara back onto the bed, and she lost consciousness.

19

All-over cramping.

That's how her best friend Anne once described the most severe phase of acute food poisoning after she'd eaten some bad sushi. Klara fancied she understood how Anne must have felt when the germs that had entered her organism ordered her body to turn completely inside out.

(Good God, Anne, I wish we hadn't lost touch after you moved to Saarlouis with your great love.)

The term 'all-over cramping' was also an excellent reflection of her condition, except that it was far too harmless. The disgust she now felt, having woken up, was greater and more intense than any other negative sensation she'd had in her life so far. This was in part down to the anaesthetic but more a result of the realisation that she'd leaped straight from purgatory into hell.

In her attempt to escape the ordeal of her marriage for a few hours at least, Klara had ended up in the clutches of a sadist who could teach her husband a thing or two about 'perversion and violence'. And his first lesson would probably begin with a screening of the video she was now forced to watch.

'Watch carefully,' she heard the man beside her say, who'd undergone a reverse metamorphosis. From lovely butterfly into ugly caterpillar.

From Kiefer to Yannick.

He stood beside her, the Japanese dagger from the bedroom wall in his hand.

She sat on a kitchen chair, her fingernails digging into the wooden arms to prevent her from tumbling forwards into the television, where she was currently being beaten up by three men in masks.

The Le Zen video. Another reason why she wished she could pass out again.

At least her fall would be soft; a thick rug with silver fibres lay on the parquet at her feet. Klara froze when she realised she was naked and Yannick must have carried her into the sitting room from the bed.

The bed!

Far too quickly, she jerked around, back to the bedroom, even though the last thing she wanted to do was to look at the illuminated waterbed again and what was floating inside it. What actually made Klara turn her head was the hope that she'd just imagined the body parts in the see-through mattress.

But then Yannick gave her a slap, which flipped her chin in the opposite direction, back to the television set. There she basically watched her reflection, because just like in the video, now she was naked and being tortured again, and no longer had the will to live.

'Why?' she said, asking the all-encompassing question.

Why are you doing this to me?

Why did you make me believe you were someone else?

Why do I have to watch that disgusting, humiliating video again?

Why do you have me at your mercy?

'As you might imagine, Klara, none of this is any coincidence. I've spent a long time researching your case. I know I'm not telling you anything new, but your husband Martin is an arsehole.'

Klara didn't dare nod. She didn't know if any reaction was permitted, nor if another movement of her head would bring on a stronger swell of nausea, causing her to vomit. It would be unbearable to have to debase herself even further – not just sitting naked beside this madman, but covered in sick too.

'He's distributing this video of you on the internet, uploading it to the relevant sites. Easy to find for someone who knows what they're looking for.'

Without moving her head, Klara shifted her eyes so far to the side that she could see parts of Yannick's face. He still looked as attractive as the man she'd spoken to at the clinic. And she was certain he smelled just as good as the lover who'd been on top of and inside her only minutes earlier. But he'd swapped his soft, warm voice for that of a devil.

'And even though he does this to you, Klara, even though Martin abuses you and shares his crimes with the world to humiliate you time after time, you won't leave him. On the contrary, you come back home punctually, today being an exception. You cook him his favourite meal, wash his socks, iron his shirts, satisfy his desires.'

Yannick paused, then asked her the question she'd just posed herself.

'Why?'

He moved right in front of her chair, blocking the view of

the television (a relief) and kneeled. He showed her the blade of the samurai dagger, making her go cross-eyed. 'No matter how hard he hits you, no matter how often he rapes you, you keep going back to him. Why?'

Now Klara did nod; she couldn't help it.

'Dunedin,' she said with a dry voice. She was desperate for a glass of water, almost as desperate as she was to wake up from this nightmare.

'What was that?'

'I did the calculation. Dunedin is the second-largest city on the South Island of New Zealand. And the place on earth that's the furthest away from Berlin: more than eighteen thousand kilometres.' She couldn't put a greater distance between her and Martin. 'I really wanted to go there.'

'So why didn't you?'

Klara shook her head. Yannick knew the answer; he wasn't so stupid that it wouldn't occur to him. But she obliged him and answered his rhetorical question. 'Amelie,' she whispered. Her be-all and end-all. The only reason she hadn't sought a way out from her miserable life ages ago.

'An excuse!' Yannick barked. 'And a really cheap one at that!'

'But...' Klara stammered.

She had no idea how to talk to this individual, who was either a talented actor or indeed a multiple personality. Kiefer, the sensitive, loveable man had disappeared. Before her was a monster, an it.

'My husband's strong. He's got money, power and friends. It's not that easy to leave him.'

'Oh, yes, it is. *You* can. You just have to stop playing the role of the victim. Or do you enjoy that?'

Klara shook her head.

'So why do you take it on without raising the slightest objection? For God's sake, this victim role that you women always assume is the fount of all evil.'

Yannick stood up and took deep breaths, as if preparing for a dive without any apparatus. 'Forget emancipation. Most children are brought up by women: mothers, then teachers at nursery and primary school. In their most important, formative years children almost always encounter women. Do you know how many male kindergarten teachers there are?' He gave a grim laugh. 'Three per cent. What a joke. A risibly small number of men take parental leave, which means the children are still a woman's concern. Although it's all in your hands; you mollycoddle your girls and then complain later that you're being oppressed by men. But it's you. *You're* the ones who buy your girls pink clothes and dolls. *You're* the ones who sign them up for ballet rather than martial arts. And so you're teaching them, if not consciously then subliminally, to fall in line, to put up with everything. Because boys will be boys, isn't that right?'

Klara shook her head, wanting to object, but even if she'd been in a position to find the right words, Yannick wouldn't have allowed her an opening.

'You spend years poisoning their self-confidence, until your girls have completely internalised their role as the weaker sex. So much so that they can no longer summon the courage or will to follow their own head. In the end they seek out the most unsavoury arsehole for a husband and keep on going back to him, just like you.'

'Please, I don't understand.' Klara was shivering as she crossed her arms in front of her chest. Her feeling of shame had returned and now she was trying to cover it as best she could. 'What do you want from me?'

Yannick gave her the answer with the dagger, the tip of which entered her left nostril in a flash. And shredded it.

'Put your hands down,' Yannick bellowed in competition with Klara's cries of pain. She'd instinctively put both hands in front of her face in a useless attempt to stop the bleeding.

'I swear I'll slice your tits off if you don't sit still.'

He pointed a finger at her like a schoolmaster might to a naughty child.

'Please, please don't kill me,' Klara begged him.

'That isn't my plan. Not yet.' He stepped closer. 'Right now I just need a tiny amount of your blood. That's why I gave you an insignificant, harmless injury, to make something clear to you.'

Klara shuddered when Yannick touched her almost gently and held his fingers beneath her cut nostril in the stream of blood that was dripping down her chin, neck, breasts and stomach as far as her pubic hair. One after the other, he allowed his fingers to be covered in blood, from his thumb to his pinkie.

Then he went over to the wall and used his fingers as a brush for the blood. With rapid movements he wrote four numbers in red on the white plaster beside the television, the digits thinning out at the ends.

30/11

Then, turning back to Klara, he handed her a cloth handkerchief, which she immediately pressed on her nose, and asked, 'Do you know what I'm getting at?'

She closed her eyes and shook her head for the umpteenth time. The shock, the cold, and maybe the loss of blood made her shiver all over.

'It's a date. Remember it. If, by 30 November, you haven't managed to end your marriage to your husband, I will kill you the moment day breaks. And in a more agonising way than you could possibly imagine.'

Klara laughed despite the pain and her impotence. A laugh of despair and helplessness in which the anger that the lunatic's impossible demand had prompted was clearly audible.

'You can't end a marriage to Martin Vernet as simply as that. The women's refuge in which I'd be safe from him hasn't been built yet. And the country where I could hide from him and an army of highly paid private detectives hasn't got a flag yet. Martin's got far too much money, power and energy. Once something's taken root in his head he carries it through. And he never lets anything get taken from him that he regards as his property. Certainly not his wife.'

'You weren't listening to me. I wasn't talking about a separation, divorce or escape.'

'What were you talking about, then?'

'The end. End it with your husband. In the only way that's possible in cases like yours. Using the only language that cowardly arseholes who torture their wives understand.'

'And what's that?'

'Murder.'

Klara choked on her own breath and had to cough. 'You mean...?'

'That's right. Kill your husband. You've still got a few weeks to do it. But if you don't manage to kill him by 30 November, you know what will happen.'

'You'll kill me.'

'Precisely. And don't get any ideas about contacting the police or getting any other sort of help. If you speak to anyone about this evening you'll be handing them a death sentence. Do you understand?'

Klara nodded.

'It's in your hands. Do the right thing! Otherwise you'll end up like all the other women who were too weak to do it.'

Yannick pointed towards the bedroom.

'You've seen parts of them in my bed.'

20

JULES

No words, no murmuring, no coughing. Jules had put the headset back on, taken off his shoes and during the conversation crept into the bathroom in his socks. He'd taken a small plaster from the cupboard with the mirror and attended to the cut on his finger.

Then he'd returned to the kitchen and sat at the island on a stool, trying his best to avoid making any distracting noises while listening. Only occasionally did a deep breath or a slight clearing of the throat signal to Klara that he was still on the line and that she wasn't talking to thin air. He was fairly sure, however, that in describing her gruesome experiences Klara had been returned to the scene of the crime as if under hypnosis, and had stopped being aware of his presence on the other end of the line.

'I hope you *did* go to the police?' he asked after the first lengthy pause, his eyes fixed on the tear-off calendar with sayings beside the fridge. It showed 26 November. The wisdom for today read:

> *The adventure of a close relationship*
> *is the search for the right distance.*

The calendar hadn't been touched for three days. Today was 29 November. The ultimatum that the killer had set for Klara would expire in a few minutes' time.

'You reported the man?'

'Of course.'

'And?'

'Yannick's still at large. Clearly my statement to the police didn't do much.'

'How is that possible?'

After all, she had a description, convincing injuries on her body and she knew where the culprit lived. This ought to have led to a search of the property at least.

'Yannick was very shrewd. We arranged for him to pick me up from Potsdamer Platz and then we drove to Mitte for dinner. I didn't know beforehand that he'd booked a restaurant where we'd be served in complete darkness by blind people. We went for a little walk, then on the way to the underground carpark he asked if he might surprise me. He wanted to abduct me and I absolutely mustn't see the surprise beforehand. I found it a bit sinister to begin with and I was about to break off the date there and then. But he was so gentle and I thought I couldn't experience anything worse than what I'd already been through. What won out in the end was my hope for an unusually exciting evening.' She laughed as someone might at their own stupidity. 'Full of anticipation, therefore, I agreed to be blindfolded with a silk scarf. Then he led me into the restaurant he'd booked for us, and when we sat down he asked me to take the blindfold off.'

'And when you opened your eyes you still couldn't see anything.'

'Yes, and although I find it really hard to admit this, it really was an amazing sensual experience. Unable to see, my other senses were sharpened. The food literally exploded in my mouth and every time he touched me it felt like a power surge giving me a positive charge, exciting me. When we finished our meal Yannick said he'd prepared a second surprise for me at home. At that moment I'd already fallen for him and I felt unbelievably secure in his presence.'

'Let me guess: he blindfolded you on the way to his apartment?'

She sighed in acquiescence. 'Which is why I don't know where he took me to torture me, that's right.'

Klara paused briefly, then added, 'After Yannick had spelled out the ultimatum he gave me another injection and I ended up back outside my apartment block where neighbours discovered me. Which was lucky, as these witnesses were the only thing that stopped Martin from beating me up there and then in the front garden. I lied to him, saying I'd been mugged – what should I have told him? This led to my initial victim statement, which I was going to retract a day later. Secretly of course, without Martin's knowledge.'

Jules nodded. Gradually he was realising just how messy Klara's situation was.

Reaching for the bottle of orange juice, he faltered. It was still almost one third full. He thought he'd taken several gulps in the meantime, though he wasn't sure anymore. His conversation with Klara had claimed all his attention. Besides, he felt a scratch in his throat again, so he couldn't have drunk much.

'The only thing I could have said for certain is that it was a period apartment, of the sort you'd find in Charlottenburg, Steglitz, Schöneberg, Prenzlauer Berg, Kreuzberg, Wedding,

Friedrichshain and in virtually every other district of Berlin.'

He took a big gulp of juice and put the plastic bottle back down. 'No helpful markers that might narrow it down.'

'No, but if they'd taken my statement more seriously I'd have had a name for them at least. But the moment they found out where I'd met Johannes Kiefer, who turned out to be Yannick, the Calendar Killer, they were convinced they were dealing with an attention-seeking madwoman. It's pointless to mention that no one at Berger Hof has heard of a Yannick or a Dr Kiefer.'

'I understand.' Klara was a classic example of what you'd call an unreliable witness. A former patient of a psychiatric clinic who'd taken part in an experiment that generated artificial hallucinations, now trying to correct her initial statement to the effect that she actually had contact with the Calendar Killer. And in an apartment she entered blindfolded.

'I literally had to force them to make a photofit, but so far it hasn't been made public. One of the investigators told me quite openly that they got statements like mine almost every day, as well as potential death dates people claimed had been smeared on walls. And there was something else.'

'What?'

'Something which made me doubt myself.' Rather than badger Klara with another question, Jules gave her a chance to compose herself. Then she went on: 'They interrogated me in detail about the features of his handwriting, but I couldn't give them any information.'

Jules thought back to the *Case XY* reportage he'd been watching at the beginning of their conversation.

'*... there's a squiggle at the top of the number 1. With a*

*little imagination the figure which the killer wrote on the wall
at the scene of the first murder looks a bit like a seahorse.'*

'You didn't have a clue?'

'No. I was so upset and terrified, how could I have paid
any attention to details of the Calendar Killer's handwriting?'

Jules nodded and suddenly felt hungry. He realised he
hadn't eaten anything for hours.

As he talked he focused on the knife block beside the
cooker, right next to the coffee machine. Four knives with
brown wooden handles, their blades in the block. One of
them, the longest, was from a different collection and didn't
belong with the others. Its serrated blade stuck a little way
out of the wood. How he'd love to grab that knife, cut a thick
slice of crusty bread and slather butter all over it.

'After my statement I was completely rattled and didn't
know if...'

Jules raised his eyebrows when Klara abruptly stopped.

'Is everything okay?' he asked into the silence. 'Are you still
there?'

All of a sudden the background noise at his end changed.

What the hell...?

He heard scratching.

Just a few metres away, down the hall.

Like an animal with claws. Or another creature dragging a
sharp tool on metal.

21

'Stay on the line. Whatever happens, don't hang up,' Jules whispered, muting the conversation via a switch on his left earphone.

Would she do as he said?

Or had he lost the connection to her already? *And perhaps for ever?*

Jules's heart was in his mouth, but he didn't have a choice.

He recalled Klara's words at the beginning of their conversation: *'He won't believe that it was just an accident. That I dialled the wrong number. Christ, if he finds out I've called you he'll come to see you as well.'*

The scratching was now a clinking, like coins in a ceramic bowl. The sound had briefly become louder; Jules even fancied he'd heard someone coughing in the hallway. But now there was silence again in the apartment.

He reached for the mobile he'd called his father with, so he could listen too.

'Are you still there?' he asked quietly, leaving the kitchen.

'No, I hung up.'

In the hallway his shadow was cast onto the wall by the

nightlight, creating the impression that Jules was a gigantic stilt walker.

'Cut the jokes. Are you sober?'

'Now you're the one making the wisecracks.'

'Touché.'

It was way past six o'clock; his father would have had a skinful by now. In truth, this was a good thing; the old pisshead functioned better when running on high percentage fuel.

'Did you get all that?'

The parquet groaned under his feet, even though his footsteps were muffled by a thick rug. The noises, wherever they'd been coming from, had not returned.

'No, what in God's name was that? Why on earth did you make me listen in?'

'The woman's being threatened by the Calendar Killer.'

'Okay, my boy. You know you can always count on me, but—'

'Spare me all that,' Jules interrupted his father. 'I'll say it again: just because I call you from time to time, doesn't mean that I've forgiven you.'

'But it probably does mean you need my help.'

For a split second Jules wondered whether he ought to have a bad conscience. Whenever they spoke on the phone, and that must have been a dozen times since Dajana's death, he'd never wanted to talk to his biological father, but only ever to Hans-Christian Tannberg, the most successful insurance detective of his trade. H.C., as he was called by his colleagues, worked freelance for the largest companies like Axa, Allianz and HUK. Over the past decade nobody had uncovered as many insurance fraudsters as Hans-Christian Tannberg.

'Why are you whispering all the time? And what exactly do you want from me?'

'I want you to stay right where you are, stay well away from your bottles and keep the line free. I'll call again in ten minutes.'

Without wasting time on goodbyes, he ended the call and then suddenly realised what he'd heard, because he was standing right by the source of the noise. The clinking came from a bunch of keys hanging from the lock of the front door. The ring was still swinging back and forth; the individual keys had knocked into each other. He could only think of one explanation for this:

Someone was trying to get in from outside.

22

Very few people get onto a rollercoaster in the hope of being flung from the cart during the ride. Most embark on this hellish escapade because they like bathing in the endorphin rush of relief that washes over them after surviving the near-death experience.

Jules too preferred controlled exposure to fear rather than a direct, real confrontation with death. Whatever was on the other side of the door, he had to face it. As hot-headed as he always was when his reason was drowned in a flood of adrenaline, his instinct was to immediately wrench open the door. But he put his eye to the spyhole and saw something far more unsettling than a man with a gun. Which was: *nothing!*

Darkness, an all-embracing blackness. Not even a shadow, and so the jangling of the keys was now tantamount to a supernatural experience. Who had moved them? What physical entity had been in a position to go up the stairs and stick a key (wherever they'd got that from), a picklock or another tool into the lock from the outside, without activating the motion sensor in the hallway?

His head pressed against the door, Jules closed his eyes.

In an irrational, almost transcendental moment, Jules had

the fear of being completely alone in the world and of seeing that darkness all around him when he opened his eyes again. And so it was partly the concern that his crazed train of thoughts might correspond to reality that made him reconnect to his conversation with Klara. Touching the switch on the headset, he asked, 'Are you still there?'

A crackling, followed by static, then finally: 'Yes, I am. But don't ask me why.'

Thank God.

Jules blinked, then opened his right eye wide. The dark corridor still lay beyond the spyhole, but the light in the kitchen was on, illuminating the hallway where he was, which was as real as the chest of drawers, the drawing of chalk cliffs above it and the keyring in the door, which wasn't moving anymore.

Was I merely imagining it all?

23

KLARA

Trembling hands, racing heart, sweats. If Klara had googled her symptoms she'd have probably come to the conclusion that she needn't bother going to the effort of committing suicide as she was on the verge of a fatal heart attack. But she knew her body and realised that she was simply hypoglycaemic and urgently needed something to eat, preferably something sweet.

Luckily there were still a few indestructible muesli bars in the kitchen cupboard. Although they tasted dry, they brought her blood sugar level back to normal for the time being.

'I only stayed on the line because you still have to fulfil your part of the bargain.'

'The painless method of suicide?' Jules asked.

Klara cleared her throat, which was still hurting.

'Yes.'

'If I tell you now, you won't be able to do anything about it.'

'Because you think I'm too weak?'

'Because the DIY stores are closed. What you need for your suicide only costs a few euros, but you won't be able to get hold of it in the middle of the night.'

'You're such an arsehole.'

'And you are what the Calendar Killer called you to your face.'

'What?'

'Weak. You're a weak woman, Klara. I don't mean that as a criticism, because I'm weak too. My weakness cost me the most important thing in my life.'

Your family, Klara thought without saying it, although maybe she ought to because then her companion might spare her the lectures.

'Many people have a tendency to betray their principles and try to please everybody. My mother, for example, put up with my father's capers for years. When he came home pissed from work she'd give him his dinner with a smile. When he complained that it had been warmed up she failed to point out that he'd come home three hours late because he'd been hanging around in the pub. And whenever he hit her, she explained to us – her children – that it was her own fault. She should have known that after such an exhausting day he couldn't take the perfume she'd put on specially for him. Lots of people are like my mother. They're so prepared to bend over backwards that in the end they'd rather risk their own lives than take action.'

Klara gave a sigh of irritation. 'Let me explain again: my husband's got money, power and influence. His best friend is the police chief's right-hand man. He plays squash with the mayor once a week. And he's so popular and charming in public – not even my friends can believe that he's got a dark side. A dark side which isn't always apparent. Sometimes after his bouts of excessive behaviour he'll spend weeks being the most caring, sensitive husband on earth. So lovely that I could almost forget what he's really like.'

'The honeymoon phase,' Jules said. It was common for wife-beating to be followed by apologies and gifts.

'Exactly. And in that sort of honeymoon phase he's more charismatic than George Clooney. If Martin can fool my entire group of friends, how am I to convince a family judge who's a complete stranger?'

'But don't you ever think about the effect this is having on your child? Especially in their younger years children pick up far more than you might think. It's going to leave its mark on – what's she called again?'

'Amelie.'

'It's going to leave its mark on Amelie for life. Do you really want to leave her alone with that monster?'

'But I don't have a choice! I can't leave Martin and take Amelie with me. No matter how I choose to go, Amelie will stay with Martin. It's what she'll say she wants too, if a judge asks her. You see, Martin's never been a monster to her.'

'You don't know that.'

'Oh, I do. What exists between Martin and me is a very particular power balance. At the beginning of our relationship I was far too strong and confident for his liking. He won't get anything out of dominating a little child. Martin gets his kicks from breaking a strong, grown-up woman.'

'Which he's managed to do,' Jules said.

As is quite plain, Klara thought in resignation. Once again she fought back the tears. 'I've only got one thing left up my sleeve and that's my death. Look, my life is hell as it is. Suicide is the lesser evil with the same result that I lose my child. Only without the persistent, uninterrupted agony I'd feel viscerally if he took Amelie away from me, allowing me to suffer all my life because I dared to rebel against him.'

'That's rubbish and you know it. Just the excuses of a weak woman. You don't have the choice only between suicide and a women's refuge.'

'What other options are open to me?' she snapped back.

'I'd advise you to think about your anger. It's eating you up, am I right?'

'Yes.'

'Then imagine you're playing tennis. Play a volley. Use the strength of your opponent. Don't back off, but hold out the racket and direct his power straight back at him, unfiltered. Destroy him.'

Klara sounded shocked, really detached when she said to Jules, 'Are you being serious? Is that your advice? So like Yannick you think I should kill Martin?'

She heard a rustling on the line as the companion shook his head. 'Your husband is not your greatest opponent at the moment. He wants to torment you, but someone else wants to kill you.'

Yannick…

'Stop being so passive, Klara. What have you got to lose? You've already factored in your own death. Reclaim your life. A life with your daughter. Without fear. But you'll only succeed if you set priorities and deal first with the greater danger to your life.'

Klara shook her head. She'd run this thought through her head many times before, always coming to the conclusion that her life was long over and couldn't be 'reclaimed'.

'What precisely do you suggest I should do?' she asked, without really hoping for an answer.

'First you have to pre-empt Yannick. You can't wait like a rabbit in its burrow for the predator. You have to work out who he is.'

'I've already told you I don't know where he lives!'

'But if everything you've told me is true, he apparently knows where you're hiding. Tell me where you are; I'll try to protect you the moment he turns up.'

'Such bollocks. How do you intend to do that? Do you think you're a match for a man who keeps dismembered bodies inside his waterbed?'

'Not me, but the police.'

'Who won't do a thing until I've got proof.'

Klara's already dry throat felt very sore from talking. She went to the fridge to get some water.

'If Yannick, or whatever this guy is called, is caught in the act, that'll be proof enough,' Jules stated.

'What if he just shoots me? How do you know you'll have enough time to help me when he appears on the scene?'

Blinded by the internal light when she opened the fridge door, she closed her eyes, but that didn't help banish the images that had entered her mind as an answer to her own question. If Yannick really was the Calendar Killer – which she didn't doubt in the slightest – he would stab her and write the date of her death on the wall in her blood.

'The police will intervene in time if they know where to go.'

'And if they don't? If they step in too early? Then they won't have anything on him. I've been through it all a thousand times. It's pointless.'

'You're mistaken...' Jules began, but she took the phone from her ear when she heard the noises outside the house.

The crunching and humming.

Klara immediately closed the fridge again, too late in all likelihood. From the darkness outside, the light must have appeared like the flare of a ship in distress.

She automatically lowered her voice and hunched her shoulders as if already having to cower from the danger that was approaching the house.

'We're wasting our time. There's nothing more to discuss,' she whispered.

'Klara, please listen to me.'

'No, you listen to me. It's too late. I've got a visitor.'

Klara pointed her mobile to face the window which, hit by a beam of light, flashed a matt silver colour. A few seconds later the car stopped.

'Who?' she heard Jules ask unnecessarily.

'It's just past midnight.'

30/11.

'The ultimatum has expired. We both know who the visitor is,' Klara whispered. 'And what his plans are for me. And then for you, when he's finished with me.'

24

Klara was about to hang up, but then hesitated. She sensed that ending the conversation would be cutting her only lifeline. Even though the moment she heard a car door shut heavily outside she wondered what sort of life she wanted to save.

Just because Jules has told you that everything's going to change? Rubbish, Klara!

Instead of going to the door with her head raised to meet her fate, she backed away, in the process hurting her swollen foot so badly that she wanted to scream.

'*Why don't you just hobble towards your end? I mean you don't want any more of this!*' said the dark inner voice that had been nagging away at her for the past few days and had reinforced her planned suicide.

'*Because it's no longer your decision,*' the brighter voice inside her head said, responding to the dark devil. It was one thing to take the final step, but a completely different one to surrender to someone else. Especially to a man who took pleasure in torturing women and who wouldn't ensure her a painless death.

How did he find me so quickly?

She'd had her phone checked for spyware at a mobile shop

in Kreuzberg, where the greasy-haired student ensured her it was clean. But she didn't believe him. Her fear was stronger than her belief in the technical understanding of a mobile phone nerd.

Or is it Jules who located me?

Outside, heavy footsteps made the boards creak. Purposefully they approached the door of the weekend house – a simple door from a DIY store, slightly more robust than the chipboard doors of the other cabins, but not an insurmountable obstacle for a violent intruder.

'Hello?'

The male voice sounded muffled – was he wearing a mask? – but that wasn't as menacing as the direction from which it was coming. For the killer wasn't on the other side of the door; he was right beside her.

Klara spun around, and in the darkness of the hut bit her lip to avoid screaming in terror. She was already bleeding when she realised that the tension had played a trick on her.

It wasn't the intruder who'd managed by some miracle to get into the hut through the locked door. It was Jules whose voice she heard; her phone was still on speaker.

'Talk to me, Klara!'

Fortunately the mobile wasn't on the table anymore, but in her trouser pocket, and the lining muffled Jules's voice. Although Klara was still worried the killer might have heard it.

Any moment now she was expecting steel-capped boots to kick the door in, but to her amazement it opened without any visible or audible force. As if being pushed by a magic hand it swung towards her, and along with the light from the vehicle parked outside, a cold, snow-filled wind poured in.

The killer stood in the doorway like an actor making an important stage entrance. His face was completely in the dark and his physique looked larger than life from the shadow it cast on the wooden floorboards. He didn't say a word, not even when Klara stirred from her paralysis and ran away, despite the sharp pain in her leg.

To the door to the garden, behind the dining area.

She immediately realised that this was a mistake. Maybe she'd have had a chance had she raced in the other direction, back to the garage, before Yannick could catch her. Instead she stood by the locked back entrance, with no escape car waiting for her on the other side if she managed to open the door with its glass window.

No, no, no...

Her sweaty hand slipped on the round doorknob, which wouldn't budge a millimetre. By the time she remembered that you had to press a tiny button in the centre to undo the lock, it was too late.

The cold was piercing, her clothes seemed to be drenched in sweat, she felt a bony, icy hand on her neck, yanking her back with great force. Smelled the foul breath of the Grim Reaper...

Only in her head, thank goodness.

For the time being.

Klara heard a panting and, unlike her vision of death, this was very real and extremely close. She heard the footsteps of the intruder who was still yet to say a word, and who must enjoy seeing his victims in such distress. Perhaps he was entertained by the fact that although she'd managed to finally open the back door, she stumbled on the wooden steps and fell into the snowdrift.

Klara saw flashes before her eyes like welding sparks.

'*Aaaaagh!*'

She bit her hand to avoid screaming her pain into the night. For a moment she perched there in total darkness. The headlights of the car parked outside, its engine still running, didn't reach into the vegetable garden.

All the same Klara thought she could sense the shadow hovering above her as she tried to stand up again from all fours.

When she'd managed it and turned her head back to the house the snow was so thick she could hardly see a thing.

Thick, damp flakes that seemed to explode into ice crystals when they touched her face. Lit by a torch, with which the killer was scouring the area outside. She felt the beam of light like a bullet. Hit by it, she dropped to the ground, even though this was ridiculous and totally pointless.

Like a child who thinks they can't be seen if they close their eyes.

To cap it all she'd thrown herself into a puddle covered in a very thin layer of ice. Her clothes soaked up the dampness like a sponge. The cold stabbed her with a thousand needles. Then, when she raised her head and looked back at the torch beam, something unbelievable happened.

The killer's shadow appeared to nod to her, although she couldn't be sure. But then he didn't come outside, nor did he aim a gun at her. No, he closed the door.

From the inside!

A second later he switched off the torch, and the silhouette in the glass window vanished too.

The darkness made Klara acutely aware of the cold, this time with merciless force.

Good God, please...

She'd forgotten something vital.

My coat!

It was still hanging over the chair in the kitchen. With her purse and keys.

Christ!

No wonder the killer could now sit back and relax. She was injured, in a panic and already hypothermic. And she only had two options: go back into the house, into the lair of the predator that murdered women; or brave the driving snow despite being underdressed, and hobble with her gammy ankle into the woods that bordered the garden. If Klara succeeded in making it through the woods, she'd come out at Teufelssee: an insurmountable obstacle. In the water she would be dead within minutes, and the lakeside path was much too far away.

Besides, as soon as the killer realised she'd opted to flee through the woods he'd simply wait to scoop her up, given how deathly tired she was.

I'm in a trap, Klara thought.

And fell even deeper into it.

25

JULES

Jules was back into the living room, trying desperately to make sense of the rustling and static on the line, when he remembered Klara's words.

'I'm sorry to have said that, but it's the truth. As soon as he finds out we've been in contact, he'll want to come looking for you and get rid of you too.'

The bunch of keys started preying on his mind again. *Now you're becoming paranoid as well.*

Shaking his head, Jules went back to the front door and removed the keys. Just to be on the safe side.

In the inconceivable scenario that someone had actually managed to break into the apartment, he didn't want to give that person the opportunity to lock the two of them in together. The bunch of keys felt heavy and cold in his hand, with far too many keys for a flat like this. He was overcome by a painful memory: Dajana always teasing him for going around like a caretaker. He put the keys in his trouser pocket and returned to the desk.

'Hello?'

No reply. He thought he'd heard Klara groan, then she seemed to be moving. But the creaking and rattling could mean anything, especially as the reception appeared to be getting worse by the minute.

He sat on the desk chair and pulled open the drawer containing the leads for small electrical items. Jules searched in vain for a charging lead to connect the plug with his mobile, which was beginning to run low on battery. He muted the microphone, moved the left headphone from his ear and used his mobile to call his father, who picked up before Jules heard it ring.

'Would you finally tell me whassup?'

Jules rolled his eyes. Hans-Christian Tannberg didn't realise how ridiculous he sounded when he said things he thought were cool, but which no one apart from him had used for years. Even if they had been current youth slang, they'd have still sounded utterly silly coming from his mouth.

'You've got to find something out for me,'

'Hmm, I was actually going to say no, but seeing as you're asking so nicely.'

'Cut the crap, we've got no time to waste. You heard what this is about.'

'Life and death, apparently.'

'Precisely. The woman I'm talking to—'

'What I don't understand,' his father cut in, ignoring what Jules had just told him, 'is that you're not working for 112 anymore, are you?'

Jules had to restrain himself from hurling the paperweight at the television. His father had the gift of being able to make him livid within seconds.

'I've taken over Caesar's shift at the telephone companion service,' he hissed.

'What's that?'

Jules explained as concisely as possible.

'Okay, I got that. But who the hell is Caesar?'

'My old schoolmate, he used to live in the house next door. Before we moved to the city. You ought to remember him. He often heard you shouting when you came home.'

'I remember the Kaisers very well: a family of total arseholes. They always had new cars and holidays to the Maldives on credit. And that lanky, pimply Magnus was the most irritating of them all. He's the one with the silly paragraph tattoo on his middle finger, right? I still don't understand why you had to seek out such losers as friends, I—'

'Enough! Listen to me: the woman who called me claims to have had contact with the Calendar Killer. She's terrified she's going to be his next victim. Find out everything you can about her from the staff at Berger Hof. Her name is Klara.'

'Surname?'

'She won't say.'

'Great.'

'But I do have other names for you: Daniel Kernik, Johannes Kiefer and Ivan Corzon. Supposedly they're doctors and the director of Berger Hof.'

Jules pulled a pad of squared paper towards him, tore off the top sheet that had already been used and tried out the black refill of his ballpoint pen. While he briefly explained to his father that Klara had taken part in a psychiatric experiment to generate artificial hallucinations, he noted down a few things for himself:

*Klara, not a medic, probably a medical–technical
assistant, paranoia???*

'I know Corzon,' his father stated. 'I vetted him after Dajana's death. He's clean.'

Jules nodded. He had recognised the name too. Right after Dajana's suicide his father had done some research into Berger Hof on his own initiative, leaving no stone unturned in case the clinic had something to do with her death. But by his own account H.C. Tannberg hadn't been able to find anything. No irregularities, no misconduct by doctors and carers, even though he'd set the best people in his team on the case.

'Kiefer and Kernik don't ring a bell, but I'll get on the blower tomorrow.'

'Are you deaf and blind? What makes you think this can wait till tomorrow?'

'What makes you think you can speak to me like that?'

Jules gave a bitter laugh. 'Maybe because I've got a video showing you beating the shit out of Mum?'

That was a lie. The only film proving how violent Hans-Christian Tannberg had been towards his wife was the one that played on an endless loop in Jules's nightmares. Ever since he could remember.

'Why can't you be like your sister and forgive me?'

'Becci hasn't forgiven you; she's just more polite than I am.'

The violence at home had almost broken Rebecca, Jules's sister. There had been one decisive event. Their father had come back blind drunk from the tennis club in broad daylight, having lost an early-morning match against a substantially poorer player, then been teased about it in the club bar. It occurred to him that the correct way to boost his self-esteem was to serve up his loved ones a very special 'one-pot creation' that lunchtime.

Sunday was the only day of the week when all the family

ate together. Just as Rebecca and Jules were each trying their first spoonful, surprised by the salty taste, their father started laughing like a madman. 'Look at your mother – what a wreck of a woman. So weak and cowardly.'

Jules's mother did look paler than usual and her eyes that sat deep in their sockets were jittery. She hadn't helped herself to a bowl yet, which wasn't unusual; she rarely had much of an appetite and often didn't eat a morsel all day long.

'*Look at her!*' Hans-Christian Tannberg screamed, pointing his fork at the miserable figure who'd weighed twenty kilos more in the wedding photograph on the mantelpiece.

'She'd rather poison her children than dare protest.'

Then he confessed to what he'd done. No sooner had he got home than he'd grabbed the pot from the cooker, peed in it and forced his wife to serve the 'lunch'.

This was three days before Rebecca's twelfth birthday. The day when she started wetting the bed again. It didn't stop until one night her mother disappeared, depriving Hans-Christian Tannberg of his victim to bully.

'Can you really not forgive me?' he now asked his son, decades later.

'I'll think about it when you've become a better person.'

Without weekend benders. Without one affair after another. When Jules thought about it, he was almost certain that it wasn't just the beatings which had made his mother age prematurely. There was also the humiliation of regularly being cheated on by her husband, whose handsomeness was preserved by all the alcohol in his blood. As the years went on, H.C. drank more and more, and kept sleeping around, but he didn't get a day older, whereas Mum fell to pieces.

'And yet she was tough enough to up sticks and abandon

us. Heaven knows where the old bag washed up,' his father once told him as a 'goodnight story'. That was six months after she'd left. Unlike Becci, Jules hadn't wept tears over her. Of course the whole affair had broken his heart too, but unlike his younger sister he understood that it was the only way of escaping the spiral of violence. He was also convinced today that Becci would never have become a confident, life-affirming woman if their mother hadn't left. Children try to ape their parents, especially in those formative years. Up until the day she disappeared, Becci hadn't seen her mother as a role model, only as a weak, spineless woman. When she never returned, Rebecca learned that this wasn't a law of nature you had to comply with, but that a woman can break out and go her own way too. A way that took Rebecca to Malaga where now she lived happily married with two children by the sea, pursuing a stellar career as a property lawyer.

'Call me as soon as you've found something,' Jules told his father. 'I have to know where this Klara lives. She's got a daughter, about seven years old, called Amelie. Her husband is rich, and that's about all I know.'

Jules had got to his feet subconsciously, then the thought of something to eat directed him towards the kitchen. By now not even the tension of his conversation with Klara could distract him from the grumbling of his stomach. With his mobile by his left ear and the headset by his right – as if he were the caricature of a crazed manager – Jules wandered down the hallway. On the line to Klara all he could still hear was static, and his father wasn't saying anything either. He was probably making a note of Jules's instructions.

'Did you get all that?'

'I think so. There's not much to go on.'

'Please do your best.'

'Oh, you said "please",' Hans-Christian observed. This time he hung up before his son could retort. The sudden silence in his ears felt uncomfortable. The memories that every conversation with his father evoked left a dull pain.

When Jules entered the kitchen he felt as if he'd been beaten up, which complemented the sounds he could now hear at Klara's end.

26

KLARA

'You have to understand that cold is the norm in the universe and heat is the absolute exception.'

The day when her father spoke these words to Klara, she thought she'd never be as freezing again for the rest of her life.

She was eight years old and on the way back from tobogganing on the Teufelsberg. In a tantrum just before they'd left home, Klara refused to put on her mittens, insisting on her thin knitted gloves instead. She made a similar mistake with regard to her choice of trousers, preferring a pair of jeans to the ski suit Mum recommended. Figuring that she had to learn the hard way, Dad was unforgiving that day; he kept marching up to the top of the northern hill for another descent, even though after an hour a shivering Klara was begging to go home.

'All fire is extinguished, all warm life seeps into the grave, and at some point our sun will burn out. Only the cold that ensues will outlive eternity.'

Klara had never understood the lesson her father was trying to teach her that day. At any rate he couldn't have been preparing her for the torture she was currently undergoing.

The frost is tearing the skin from my flesh, she thought, now barely able to bend her fingers to push away the branches lashing her face as she slogged her way through the woods. As if they were malicious opponents aiming to punish her for this pointless attempt at escape.

The wind too seemed to be whispering a sort of farewell to her pitiful life into her burning ears: 'You didn't deserve any better. You tried to kill yourself and failed – now we out here will make sure you die.'

Klara's good foot tripped over a root as thick as her arm. Like all the other obstacles she hadn't been able to see it. Normally the ball of light from inner Berlin washed over the outskirts of the city, but today the snowstorm filtered out every ray and laid an impenetrable cloche over the woods.

Klara could hear her own breathing, throaty and raw like an old woman. On the other hand she wasn't crying like she usually did when the profound feeling of hopelessness threatened to hurl her into the abyss. But maybe after all these years of marriage her tears had simply dried up. Or maybe she just couldn't feel anything on her skin that was numbed by cold.

Another searing pain that shot from her ankle to her knee forced her to stop. She had no idea how much distance she'd put between herself and the hut, but she needed to rest, if only on account of the stitch she could no longer ignore.

Is my companion still on the line?

She was certain she'd lost the connection to Jules, but if her mobile still had any battery then at least she could use it as a torch. To find out she first had to get hold of the phone, which was stuck as if frozen in her front trouser pocket.

Shit.

Klara leaned against a thick tree trunk and resisted the temptation to slide down so she could sit in the undergrowth. Her eyes gradually got attuned to the darkness; shadows became contours. And from the contours, three-dimensional objects took shape.

If she weren't mistaken she was standing on the edge of a path, but probably not an official one as it was too narrow. She recalled how as a child she'd loved to beat secret paths through the woods with her friends, although 'beat' was much too martial a word for a ten-year-old. They'd trodden down the undergrowth and cut back twigs with Dad's secateurs, but only for a few metres until a tree finally blocked their way. There they would pitch their 'secret camp' and use sticks, branches and leaves to create a tipi-like tent.

Although sure she would stumble upon some useless children's den, Klara hurried to the right, along the path, simply because she had no other choice.

This path would lead to the shore of the lake too, where Yannick would be waiting for her. That was if she didn't get lost and woefully freeze to death, which right now was a highly likely prospect.

'It's no surprise that in their death throes people often say how cold they feel. It's because they're becoming one with the only constant of the universe.'

How unfortunate that in these last moments of Klara's life her father, himself festering in the cold earth – having gone to sleep peacefully one night and never woken up again – should live on as a ghostly voice in her head. She would have wished for something nicer now that she was running towards the final light at the end of her life's tunnel.

Although Klara was confused that the narrow track before her eyes actually did appear to be getting brighter. And wider.

Christ, am I at the lake already?

She thought she could hear the rushing of the water treatment plant at the nature conservation centre, which of course was complete nonsense at this time of year. But her brain refused to accept that Yannick had found her here so quickly.

How did he know that I would step onto the path to the lake precisely from this narrow track?

She dragged herself out of the woods and to her right suddenly saw two lights bobbing up and down, like two outsized torches in the hands of an out-of-control giant. And even as she realised her mistake and was about to retreat, she sustained a powerful blow as if from a sledgehammer. Klara flew through the air, spun all the way around and tried to shield herself with both hands.

In vain. The darkness met her with bone-crunching force.

27

JULES

A continual gurgling in the kitchen signalled that the radiator beneath the window hadn't been bled in ages. Jules turned down the thermostat and then the only sound he heard was from the iPhone up to his ear.

Now that his father was no longer on the line he could activate the headset microphone again.

'Klara, can you hear me?'

Still no reaction. If he wasn't mistaken, she was still outside of a protected space, judging by the ambient noise. Jules opened the fridge, took out some butter and slices of salami, and put them on a wooden board beside the breadbox, in which there was a wholewheat sourdough loaf.

As he hunted for a knife, his eyes alighted on the wooden block by the sink and it took him a moment to realise why he was confused.

The knife!

The one that didn't fit in the block. The one with the serrated blade that stuck out.

It's gone!

Jules felt for the keys in his trouser pocket: still there. But the knife...

He gaped in astonishment at the knife block as a believer might at a bleeding figure of the Virgin Mary.

His hunger was forgotten; he wouldn't be able to eat a single mouthful now. Not just because he realised he was no longer alone.

But also because an agonising scream rang out through the hallway.

It was coming from the nursery.

28

KLARA

It was the wet that woke her. The sleet on her face. *Blood* – was her first thought because it seemed to match the pain that wasn't restricted to her ankle and leg anymore, but had spread to the entire left-hand side of her body.

The frozen sand path she was lying on, face-up, wouldn't be in any official street directory – it was far too narrow for that – and yet there was no way she'd been run over by a forestry vehicle on this unpaved mogul field. More like a really small car, a Smart or Mini probably. The frozen bumps on the ground had made the car judder so much that it had come bobbing towards her like a nutshell on the waves.

But what did she care about the make of car? All that mattered, what her life depended on, was what sort of monster was getting out of it right now.

Yannick?

In her recollection he was shorter and slimmer, but maybe the huge shadow was just an optical illusion.

Maybe all of this is an illusion?

Klara weighed up whether she could cope sufficiently with her pain to stand up and run back into the woods, but these deliberations were robbing her of time to react. The shadow above her was growing. Footsteps getting closer.

She managed to roll to the side and make it to her feet, and was even able to shake off the hand that grabbed her upper arm. But then she stumbled over a mound of earth or a branch or her own feet – she couldn't tell anymore. At a stroke her body felt strangely numb and even her tongue was sluggish when she cried out – now lying on her back again – 'Leave me alone, Yannick! Fuck off! You fucking bastard.'

But the killer didn't oblige; he didn't move back an inch. Instead he bent down and seemed to be looking at her in the beam of the headlights. Blinded, she screwed up her eyes.

'At least make it quick,' Klara begged, opening her eyes again as best she could.

What she saw hovering above her face finally made her doubt her sanity.

29

Klara knew the theory of Occam's razor; she knew that the simplest explanation was often the right one.

That's to say: if a whinnying animal gallops past the front door it's more likely to be a horse than a zebra. But the theory that went back to the English philosopher William of Ockham didn't help Klara as she tried to make sense of who was bending over her.

Big conk, bushy white beard, red cloak…?

Not even the simplest of all explanations made sense.

But if she stuck with the most probable theory, then looming over her was a kind-looking, chubby-faced Father Christmas.

I'm hallucinating, she thought, closing her eyes. *The aftereffects of the failed experiment at Berger Hof.*

As it grew darker, so did her conviction that she was indeed at the mercy of Yannick, who'd allowed himself to play a macabre joke on her.

'Just get on with it!' she urged the fake Santa. The cold of the woodland floor she lay on crept further up her body. She tensed like a patient in a dentist's chair just before the drill touches the nerve. Klara knew the pain would come, and she knew it would be unbearable, but even more unbearable were the seconds before, in which her final enemy seemed to be playing a perverse cat-and-mouse game.

'You alright, love? Bloody hell. What are you doing out here?' she heard the costumed man say in his Berlin brogue. His words stank of alcohol and smoke, and even speaking seemed to be quite an effort for this fat individual, for he was wheezing like a postman after a delivery on the fifth floor.

Klara opened her eyes again. 'You're not Yannick,' she declared.

'Who am I not?'

He's not Martin either. Her snob of a husband hated dialects and would rather rip his tongue out than talk *'in the unmistakeable vernacular of the lower class'*, as he described the Berlin accent. But the guy was trying his best to speak high German and only slipped into dialect when it came to certain words.

'Jeez, it looked like you really went flying. Is anything broken?'

Klara managed to lift her head. Her thoughts danced like the confetti of snow in the headlights of the car the man had just got out of. She guessed he was in his mid-fifties.

'No, don't move. I've heard things can get uncomfortable if there's something wrong with your spine.'

Klara felt like laughing out loud. 'Uncomfortable' corresponded accurately with her overall situation – and, in truth, not just this evening. What didn't correspond at all, on the other hand, was the Father Christmas now putting a mobile phone to his ear.

'Stop!' she barked at him, more powerfully than she'd thought herself capable of.

'Sweetheart, we need to call an ambulance, even if I have no idea how it'll get in here. For Christ's sake, what did you think you were doing, hopping out of the woods straight in front of my car like Bambi?'

'It's not a problem, I'm fine,' Klara lied. 'There's nothing broken,' she said, hoping that this at least was the truth. She gritted her teeth and shifted herself into a sitting position.

'Seriously? That was quite a bang.'

'Yes, seriously. Who are you?' she asked the man whose face seemed to consist of nothing but hair and beard. What she really wanted to say was: *Are you real? Or an aftereffect of my psychotic experiment?*

To her own ears she sounded totally unintelligible, but she did get an answer.

'I'm Hendrik, from Jimmy Hendrik Entertainment. Normally I give people I meet my card. But without wishing to be impolite, you don't look like you'll be booking me anytime in the near future.'

Klara gave an incredulous laugh and tried to get up further. 'You're just pretending?'

'No, I really am Santa Claus.' The man turned away, shaking his head, and muttered to himself, 'Man, she must have smacked into one too many fir trees even before the accident.'

He looked at his car and scratched the back of his head.

'Jeez, jeez, jeez. I thought nobody could top those crazy women in the Forsthaus, but this one is off the scale. Although… hang on a sec.' He must have remembered he wasn't alone and he turned back to Klara. 'Are you one of the lumberjacks?'

'What?'

'They've commandeered the Forsthaus and are putting on a bash that makes Lollapalooza look like a kids' birthday party, I swear. One of the girls seriously asked me if she could drink her glühwein from my boot. You look like you were there showing them all what to do before launching yourself in front of my motor.'

Klara reached for his outstretched hand and pulled herself up. 'I'm not drunk,' she slurred, then was unable to stifle a sharp cry when she put her weight on her leg.

'Yeah, right, and I'm here with my reindeers. Hey, wait.'

Step by step Klara teetered towards the headlights of the car which, from the logo turned out to be a Japanese or Korean make – Klara wasn't much of an expert in this area.

'Where are you off to?'

Klara didn't respond, for in truth she didn't have a clue. Her frozen trousers chafed her groin, and her body shivered as much from exhaustion as it did from the cold. The only thing she was used to was the pain from the collision. She felt as if she'd been beaten up. All that managed to pass her lips was a brief 'I'm cold'. Then she wrenched open the passenger door and fell onto the seat inside.

'Alright, sure. No problem. Make yourself at home seeing as we're such good mates now,' she heard Hendrik call from behind her. 'What on earth next? No one's going to believe a word of this.'

He followed her, opened the driver's door and manoeuvred himself into the car beside her like a screw. 'Right, I'm taking you straight to A&E.'

Amazing given his size that he fitted in the driver's seat at all.

'No, couldn't you please...' Klara stopped mid-sentence

because she had no idea where the costumed stranger could take her instead. At any rate he made no moves to start the engine.

'I'm not moving a millimetre before you tell me what's going on. Who are you, love? And what are you doing at this time of night in the middle of nowhere?'

'It's a long story,' she mumbled.

'I've got time.'

Klara couldn't help smile in spite of the wretched state she was in. When she considered how the truth would sound to her costumed saviour she had to watch she didn't burst out laughing like a lunatic.

'I'm being forced to kill either my husband or myself. As I'm a weak woman, something that was just confirmed to me by my telephone companion, I opted for suicide but was too stupid to leap from the climbing wall on the Teufelsberg. I didn't manage it with the car exhaust either. Which is why now, trying to escape the Calendar Killer, I fled from my summer house and ran slap bang into Father Christmas's car.'

As Klara kept her thoughts to herself, Santa–Hendrik did the talking for her. 'Do you have any idea what a mess you're in, young lady? I've got a special permit. Normally no one's allowed to drive along here, and anyway, only those who work in the woods know this track.'

Her mobile buzzed a battery-level warning, reminding her that she had maximum twenty per cent left.

Klara took it from her trouser pocket and saw to her astonishment that she was still on the line to Jules.

'Hello? Can you hear me?'

The reply came almost instantly, albeit very softly.

'Yes, I'm still here. Everything alright?'

'Hmm, depends on your point of view.'

She glanced at Hendrik, who gave her a sceptical look, probably wondering why this crazed woman had been wandering frozen in the woods rather than calling for help on her mobile.

'I feel weak and cold. I don't know where to go.'

Hendrik shook his head in consternation, as if with every second that passed he had less of a grip on the situation he'd slid into. All the same he switched on the engine and with it the heating.

Jules was speaking so softly now, almost in a whisper. 'Tell me where you are, Klara. I'll come and pick you up.'

'I don't know where I am. I'm sitting in a car.'

'Your car?'

'No, I'm getting a lift.'

'From whom?'

'Father Christmas.' She laughed hysterically. God, Jules too must think she was drunk. 'It's no joke; next to me, I've got Santa in full gear. Boots, coat, wig and beard.'

Oddly enough, it was the absurdity of his get-up that made her less frightened of the stranger than might be advisable. But it wasn't the first time in her life that she'd fallen for a man's likeable outward appearance.

'Put me on to the guy,' Jules told her.

She was going to protest, but to what end? She didn't have a plan anymore that her companion could thwart.

'Hold on.'

Klara was about to pass Hendrik the phone when she heard an extremely unsettling sound.

'What was that?'

She put the phone back to her ear in the hope that she was mistaken.

Clipped, distorted and yet unmistakeable.

Klara wondered whether it could be true. Jules had told her his children had died in the fire at their flat.

Valentin immediately, then supposedly he'd watched Fabienne die.

And yet that was without doubt a little girl she'd just heard crying for help on the other end of the line.

30

JULES

'Help me, help!'

This cry was much softer than the first one that had echoed down the hallway and into the kitchen. But loud enough for Klara to hear it down the phone.

'What was that?' she asked again.

Her voice sounded as worried as Jules felt, even though he had a gun in his hand. A 9mm CZ he used to practise with on the shooting range once a month. It wasn't loaded; there was no way he wanted access to a functioning weapon, having in his time sent far too many ambulances to shooting victims. But he was reassured by the weight in his hand, which was why he'd fetched it before making for the nursery even though he couldn't imagine the sort of potential opponent he might find in there.

'Who was that screaming?'

Jules wondered whether he ought to lie to Klara, wondered what he could tell her.

'*Only small talk on the companion service, nothing about your private life,*' Caesar had cautioned him. '*There are enough stalkers out there. You don't know what they might do with any information you give them if they think they've forged a personal connection to you. Believe me. It's best if they don't even find out your real name.'*

Wise words. But how could you forge a connection without giving away something of yourself?

'My daughter has nightmares,' he said finally.

When he entered the room at the end of the hall he was briefly expecting to find the seven-year-old gone. His gaze would fall on an unmade bed, while the wrinkled sheet, crumpled pillow and half-full water bottle on the bedside table would be mere souvenirs she'd left for him.

Reminders of a present that was gone for ever.

As he opened the door to the nursery, in his mind he had again the vivid image of Fabienne wrestling with death for the umpteenth time. But when the light from the hallway angled into the girl's pastel-coloured realm, Jules saw to his immense relief that she was still there.

Thank God.

And breathing.

Still.

Jules's pulse relaxed, even though the sight of the girl was anything but reassuring. Her eyes were wide open, the lids unblinking, and the pupils seemed to impale the darkness in the room. Her lips moved like a carp's; judging by the pale-blue colour of her face they must have been doing this for a while.

Dajana! he implored inside his head. *Help me!*

His wife would have known what to do in case of a fit like this. Once when Fabienne had been running a high temperature, they'd taken her to A&E, where a permed assistant at reception rolled her eyes in irritation and muttered something about parents who didn't want to take their children to see a paediatrician during the day and instead burdened the hospitals with minor ailments in the evening.

At that very moment Fabienne stopped breathing. Still in Dajana's arms she turned blue, at which her mother didn't panic or rush around screaming, but just shouted to a passing nurse, 'We need ventilation immediately', hotfooted it into the nearest treatment room, laid Fabienne on a stretcher and began resuscitation herself until a qualified medic arrived.

When it came to other people, Dajana was calmness personified, able to solve problems with a cool head.

She just wasn't able to tame her own demons.

'Your daughter?' Klara asked suspiciously. 'Didn't you tell me she'd died?'

Jules heard something that sounded like the squeaky suspension of a vehicle. She must be moving again.

'No, you misunderstood me. I said I had to watch her die. Fabienne survived in the wardrobe, but since that day her mum and brother passed away, she too has been dying bit by bit every day. She's only seven, but she's eaten up by grief. And there's nothing I can do to help her.'

Jules placed the gun on the floor, sat on the edge of the bed and stroked a strand of hair from the girl's forehead. She curled her lips angrily and hissed something unintelligible. But she did close her eyes again.

'I'm sorry, Klara. I've got to look after her now.'

'What's wrong?'

Jules laid his hand on her brow and eyes, and felt them spin wildly beneath the closed lids, like tiny little wheels in a cog.

She'd developed a sudden temperature, which wasn't unusual for someone her age. When he'd checked on the girl earlier her head was quite cool; now it was glowing.

'She barely eats a thing, just sleeps and doesn't want to go to school anymore. The child psychologist says it's typical post-traumatic stress disorder.'

Jules took the gun back into the study and shut it in the bottom drawer of the desk.

'She has to deal with the fact that her brother's dead and that by some miracle she survived in the wardrobe,' he told Klara. 'Albeit with serious smoke poisoning which the doctors warn might have repercussions in the future.'

He went into the bathroom and had to open three drawers before he remembered where he'd seen the Nurofen only an hour ago. In the mirrored cabinet above the sink.

Jules drew ten millilitres into the syringe and went back. Klara had asked him something that he didn't understand because of interference on the line.

'Hold on, I've got to give Fabienne something.' He gently squirted the medicine between the girl's lips. As she sucked it, her eyes briefly fluttered open before closing again.

'What did you just ask me?'

'Did you give up your job to look after her?'

'Partly. But also because I was too involved. You need a distance from your cases. You can't go driving the streets of Berlin after work, knocking on strangers' doors just to find out whether the resuscitation was successful or if the premature baby survived.'

'And that's what you used to do?' This was more of a statement than a question.

'The cases shattered me even before Dajana's suicide,' Jules now confessed. 'Afterwards it just got worse. I couldn't take any emergency calls and so I resigned. There was no other way. I felt like an impostor. How could I help other people if I couldn't even save my own family?'

'And yet you're talking to me.'

'We don't normally have emergencies like yours on the telephone companion service. Or at least that's what everyone assured me.'

'Then you've got bad luck tonight.'

'Or you have. I'm not the right person for you. You ought to be talking to a psychologist.'

'To be honest, I didn't want to talk to any—'

The conversation was interrupted by a tormented, feverish scream.

'Was that your daughter again?'

'I'm sorry,' Jules whispered, not to Klara, but to the seven-year-old he mustn't lose in any circumstances. After everything he'd had to sacrifice already.

'Is she awake now?'

'More like dozing. I've just given her some Nurofen.'

The girl's lids were half closed and her eyes were darting around even more wildly than before.

'But it hasn't started working yet.'

'I know that only too well. Amelie also picks up infections easily. When it's been stressful. Which it often has been recently.'

Because she senses something, probably. Children are like seismographic early-warning systems. They have the most sensitive antennae.

Jules heard Klara say something. It sounded as if she was covering the microphone on her mobile with her hand; she must be talking to the driver. Then there was a rustling and he heard her voice clearly again.

'You must know a lullaby?'

'You mean like "Twinkle, Twinkle, Little Star"?'

'Sing it to her. That's what I always do for Amelie. It calms her down.'

'I can't sing,' Jules admitted.

I can only telephone. Put myself into other people's souls. Feel their pain, their worries, their fears. But the most important thing is to take these away from them, and in this I've failed time and again.

And even if he could sing, he wouldn't have had the balls to do it now. As well as the concern for his little girl, he was also worried about the potential intruder and the danger this posed to both of them.

'Then put me on speaker,' Klara demanded.

Are you being serious? Jules thought with a shrug. Basically he was against this, but perhaps Klara's voice might at least help with the feverish dreams.

'Wait a sec.'

He took the laptop from the kitchen, disconnected the headset and put it on speaker. Then he held the computer close to the bed.

'All yours,' he said, handing her the audio platform, which she made use of at once. Her singing voice was as clear as a bell, albeit untrained, and yet with its very warm timbre it was even soothing for Jules.

Twinkle, twinkle, little star.
How I wonder what you are.
Up above the world so high,

Like a diamond in the sky.
Twinkle, twinkle, little star.
How I wonder what you are.

Even after the first verse, the miracle that music can produce happened. Chemists and neuroscientists might have a scientific explanation for the explosion of feelings that a succession of sounds and beats can trigger in the human brain. But for Jules it always verged on a miracle to feel the effect of music.

'Is Fabienne a little calmer?' Klara asked after the second verse.

'She is,' he said, almost regretfully. He felt like lying beside her and listening to Klara sing for hours. 'You were right. It works.'

Her eyes were no longer spinning beneath his hand. Her breathing was regular. Only the back of her neck was damp from her sweaty nightmares.

Jules waited a while longer until he was certain that she was over the worst. Then he tiptoed out of the room and closed the door as quietly as he could. 'Thank you.'

'You're welcome.'

Now that he no longer had to whisper, the noise of Klara's surroundings suddenly seemed much louder. At any rate she was still sitting in a car that was accelerating substantially.

'Where are you going?' Jules asked.

'Home. The song did something to me too.'

'I get it. You want to see your daughter.'

'Exactly.'

'I think it's the right decision,' Jules said, then considered his next words very carefully. If he made a mistake now he would give Klara such a fright that he'd lose her for good.

He felt for the keys in his pocket, thought about the missing knife in the block and asked, 'Have you got something to write with?'

'Of course not. But hang on, there's a biro by the gearstick here.'

'Help yourself, please,' he heard the driver say beside her, sounding both amused and irritated.

'Okay, Klara, now pretend you're back at school. Make a note of my mobile number on your hand.'

'What's the point of that? We're already on the phone to each other.'

'Via the companion service. If the connection goes and you try calling again it's quite possible you'll end up with another volunteer. So I'm giving you my private number.'

'You're well aware that I've been trying to hang up for hours and so I'm certainly not going to call you on your private number.'

With every minute Klara was audibly gaining energy. Now it was time to steer this energy in the right direction. *And sometimes*, Jules thought, *an implicit threat is quite useful for this.*

'You do realise that your situation has changed dramatically?'

'In what way?'

'Klara, please don't panic, but a few minutes ago you described the driver whose car you've got into.'

'And?'

'Just explain one thing for me...'

He paused for dramatic effect.

'... If the Father Christmas beside you is coming back from a party – and at this time of night his work must be finished – why is he still wearing his beard?'

31

Nothing. Not even any static.

Klara's reply, assuming there had been one, was stranded somewhere in the ether.

Dead spot?

According to his display, they were still connected, even though she hadn't said a word since his last question. The clock measuring the length of their conversation was burrowing its way forwards by the second into an uncertain, menacing future. And not just for Klara, who as a result of her nocturnal wanderings now possibly faced, after Martin and Yannick, another male source of danger: the driver beside her. Jules too felt threatened by an invisible force. A person who'd managed to enter the apartment unnoticed. Who, given the wooden block beside the sink, might be armed.

And who Jules had locked in here.

The bunch of keys in his trouser pocket felt as if it had been sitting on the barbeque. On his way to the kitchen Jules thought he could feel it eating through his trousers, like a piece of red-hot wrought iron.

Go back into the nursery?
Lock all the doors?
Call the police?

Jules pondered what a normal person would do in this
situation and decided on the most obvious solution. Before
he called for help he had to make sure himself and give the
apartment a thorough search. Quite apart from the fact that
no police officer would respond to a call that went: '*Come
quickly, my daughter and I are in danger. I heard a bunch of
keys jangling and one of my kitchen knives is missing.*' On
a weekend like this, when even the weather put the city in a
state of alert, there might be three patrol cars for the entire
district, and they would have to follow up more serious
calls.

Jules was just wondering where to begin his search when
his mobile vibrated.

No greeting, no introductory words. His father came
straight to the point: 'Right, I've pulled a few strings, which
isn't that easy at this time of might, as you might imagine, my
boy. But I've got a premium contact with a top-notch nurse.'

Aha. Premium contact.

So that was how he described his sexual escapades these
days. Jules, now back in the kitchen, was amazed that there
were still sufficient young and mostly good-looking women
who fell for the private detective ploys of this long-in-the-
tooth playboy. Maybe they were attracted by his dark
streak that sometimes shimmered through, like wrinkles
beneath crumbly make-up. One Christmas his father, flowing
with tears, had insisted how much he regretted his violent

behaviour of the past. And was deeply sorry for taking out his screwed-up life on his son, having beaten Mum out of the family. But Jules had never believed this regret. For him it had felt like the protestations of an alcoholic who tells everyone that he intends to stay sober once and for all, while seeking out a withdrawal clinic near his favourite pub.

'What have you got for me?' Jules asked, whipping around. In the matt mirror of the chrome fridge he thought he'd glimpsed a shadow behind him, but the kitchen was empty.

'Two words: forget it!'

'Nothing at all?'

'What I mean is, you need to forget the woman. She's not completely kosher. Yes, she was undergoing treatment at Berger Hof, but not as a participant in an experiment. She suffers from a dissociative disorder – or whatever you call it when people can't distinguish between madness and reality.'

'And?'

'And? What else do you need to understand that you've got carried away? Put your saviour complex on hold. If you want to save the world, focus on real people. Nobody had heard of that Johannes Kiefer guy either. There wasn't and isn't a doctor there by that name.'

Jules pulled up a barstool and sat by the chopping board on the kitchen island. This gave him a good view down the hallway through the open kitchen door. If anybody went near Fabienne's room he would see and hear them.

'Run another check under the name Yannick. And what about Kernik?'

'Oh, yes, this is the real bombshell. I spoke to him personally on the phone.'

'He's alive?'

'Full of beans. Which probably means that the junior doctor didn't jump out of the window like your fairy tale merchant would have it.'

'Strange.'

Jules opened the top drawer of the kitchen island. From the baking implements he could see (moulds, rolling pin, baking paper) he couldn't fashion a useful weapon against any intruder, assuming there was one.

'Not strange, but mad. Just hang up and put her out of your mind. I'm going back to bed.'

'No, you're not.' Jules had to admit that his father's conclusion was obvious: he'd got carried away. But just out of principle he wasn't going to let him off that easily. 'Did you find out Klara's surname?'

'No. Nor an address.'

What?

'So how did the nurse you've been talking about know her?'

'Because all of them remember the mad bat screaming her head off at the clinic, claiming a doctor had killed himself. Doesn't happen often, not even there.'

Jules shook his head. That version of events couldn't be right. His father was tired and just couldn't be bothered to do the proper research. 'Let me guess: in the middle of the night your source doesn't have any access to the patient database?'

'Bingo!'

'Well then, stay on the case. I want to know who I'm talking to. Oh, and you have to go to Le Zen for me.'

'The hotel?'

'That's right.'

'To do what?'

Jules squinted, which was pointless as it wasn't a visual stimulus that had startled him, but a cracking sound. Although that could be from the old windows. It was still sleeting outside and the gusts of wind were shaking everything in their path. No wonder that inside the apartment he should hear the odd groan from the beams and masonry.

'I'll tell you when you're in the lobby in thirty minutes,' he said to his father.

He voiced his protest at once: 'Have you seen the time and glanced out of the window? I can't be arsed to leave my warm shack in this weather.'

'But you will.'

'What if I don't?'

'I'll never exchange another word with you again.'

The final threat. Jules knew that however much he kept insulting him, he was the only really important person left in his father's life. At first glance H.C. Tannberg looked like the trunk of a powerful oak. What remained hidden to the outsider, however, was that only a few roots in the ground were still holding this tree upright. He'd lost the strongest ones with his wife, and he had but few friends. If the connection to his son were now lost too, he'd topple and fall in the next storm.

'Okay, okay, I'll do it,' came the prompt reply. 'But if you ask me, you ought to be thinking about something completely different.'

Jules couldn't help blink. 'And what's that?'

'Look, you're talking to this Klara bird via a laptop, right?'

'Correct.'

'And you got the laptop from this Caesar chap today?'

'Yes.' What was his father getting at?

'And the first call you got after taking on his shift, just happened to be from a suicide case who like Dajana was treated in Berger Hof?' His father clicked his tongue. 'Well, if that isn't an unbelievable coincidence, then I don't know.'

You're right. None of this can be a coincidence, Jules thought, cocking his head once more. Again he closed his eyes, which was pointless because it didn't sharpen his senses. On the contrary, they were probably playing tricks on him.

Unsure whether he was merely a victim of his own imagination, Jules hung up on his father, picked up the silent mobile with which he was hoping to maintain the line to Klara, and followed the sound of a dripping tap.

Wherever that was suddenly coming from.

32

KLARA

Thirty monsters, most of them asleep.

To keep her daughter entertained on long car journeys Klara had explained that the navigation system was a monsternav. As soon as it got dark it would show the number of ghosts on their route and what they were up to. Dark-green areas on the map represented sleeping monsters, lighters colours those on the move. The speed indicator stood for the total number of monsters, but Amelie mustn't be afraid. Evil spirits couldn't penetrate the car's bodywork, so she would always be safe inside the car, Klara promised.

All lies, Klara thought, as the car left the bumpy track and turned onto Teufelsseechaussee. Her mobile was between her thighs, which like the rest of her body were slowly thawing.

'*Why is he still wearing his beard?*'

Ever since Jules had asked her this question, Klara had wished that the tale she'd regaled Amelie with about the monsternav was true on one point at least, but in real life, of course, there were no barriers impenetrable to beasts. And in all probability she was sitting next to one right now.

The fact was: Hendrik (if that was his real name) was still

in his full Father Christmas outfit and he hadn't taken his beard off yet.

In all the chaos she hadn't considered how preposterous this was. The heating alone, which was on full blast, would have made her tear the white felt from her face (although unlike her, Hendrik hadn't been wandering aimlessly in the cold), but he was even wearing the gloves that were apparently obligatory for the perfect Santa outfit (she'd read this in a women's magazine) because gloves were the best way to disguise the age of the person beneath the costume.

No jewellery, no watch, no white socks, no cheap jeans – nothing that could destroy the illusion of children, who by nature were suspicious.

'I think the nearest one is Pauline Hospital on Heerstrasse, but I'm not sure if they have an A&E.'

There was a crunch as Hendrik shifted up a gear. The wind was gusting so violently now that sometimes the tiny car was slowed as if an invisible giant had sat on the roof.

The monsternav had moved up from thirty to fifty. Klara's anxiety grew.

Even the fact that Hendrik was still out and about at this time of night was proof enough that she was at the mercy of a liar, who in the best-case scenario was just an eccentric, but who in all likelihood was far more dangerous. Father Christmases were booked to appear in the afternoons in people's living rooms, not at the witching hour in the middle of the Grunewald.

'Won't you tell me what's going on? I mean, first you throw yourself in front of my car, then on the way to hospital you're singing lullabies down the phone. Forgive me for saying this, but normally my first dates go slightly differently.'

Oh really? With Rohypnol, cable ties and packing tape?

Klara wondered whether to do the most obvious thing and just quiz him about his outfit, but what sort of answer might she expect? 'Yes, I am a fucking pervert who likes dressing up before abducting and raping women. I'm sorry, I ought to have told you that at the start.'

No, now that they'd left the woods and had put some distance between themselves and the summer house, she had to get out of this car as fast as possible. Basically she didn't care whether Hendrik was a psychopath or a harmless nutter. Either way she wasn't going to let him know her home address, and that was where she wanted to be – and needed to be – as soon as possible. With Amelie. Jules had stirred this desire in her. Klara wanted at least to see her daughter's face one last time, hold her hand, kiss her, before Yannick or Martin brought the matter to an end. Each in his own way.

'I've changed my mind,' Klara said, as they were passing the Friedenskirche on their left. 'Please let me out up there at Heerstrasse station.'

Hendrik's answer was as she'd expected: 'No way.'

He turned the heating down a notch and the windscreen wipers up, but made no move to take the beard off.

'A mate of mine, Jürgen, was once rammed by another bloke. A harmless prang at a junction. He had a pain in his neck and didn't want it X-rayed at first. Luckily his old man persuaded him to, because end of the story is, he'd broken two vertebrae.'

'Please, I want to get out.'

'And I don't want no public prosecutor asking me what I thought I was doing abandoning a seriously injured woman in the middle of the night.'

'I'm not seriously injured.'

'That's what Jürgen thought too and... Oi! What d'you think you're doing?'

Following her instinct, Klara had opened the glove box. And as the contents spilled out, she found the answer to her question of whether Hendrik was a harmless nutter or dangerous psycho. For glinting among the condoms, handcuffs and latex gloves were a long, serrated knife as well as a nine-millimetre handgun.

33

'Stop!' Klara screamed, pointing the gun at Hendrik's chest. She'd never fired a pistol before, but at a distance of twenty centimetres she was unlikely to miss the huge target behind the wheel.

'Are you smashed?'

'I said—'

'Yes, yes. I'm not deaf.'

Hendrik hit the brakes, which made the car skid on the fresh layer of snow.

'Stop!'

'I can't!'

Finally the car came to a stop at an angle, the bonnet slanting right to a cycle path connected to the woods they'd just left behind.

From the frying pan into the fire.

'Nice and calm, okay?' Although Klara was threatening him with a lethal weapon, Hendrik didn't seem to be losing his cool. On the contrary, he appeared to be enjoying this; she thought she saw him grinning beneath the beard.

Klara was going to ask him to remove it and show his true face, but in fact it made little difference as far as she was concerned. She'd never see him again. So long as she managed to get out of this car.

Or, *even better…*

'Get out!'

'What?'

'Get out of here!'

'Are you going to nick my Hyundai?'

'Borrow. Afterwards I'll park it by Heerstrasse station. That's just ten minutes' walk from here.'

'Listen, I don't know what you've been smoking, but I can't be arsed to hoof it in the cold and the wet out there!'

'Out!'

She pressed the gun right to his chest. A mistake.

With a speed she'd never have credited to this hulk of a man, he threw up his forearm, whipping the pistol against Klara's nose. The blood flowed immediately, as if a tap had been turned on. Assailed by pain, she allowed the gun to be wrested from her hand before she could think of clenching her fingers which, seeing as the barrel was briefly pointing at her own chin, was probably a blessing in disguise.

There was a time delay, then Klara felt a tiny charge detonate behind her eyes and with the pressure wave came the pain, from the inside to out. It changed from a white-hot burning in her head to a piercing scream that escaped from her mouth as she felt her arm moving. As if gripped by a ghost, her right hand was raised aloft – she wanted to stop the flow of blood by pinching her nose. Then she heard a click and Hendrik had incapacitated her for good by handcuffing her right wrist to the handle above the passenger door.

'Fuck's sake,' he bawled at her. Klara was in so much pain she couldn't open her eyes and all she could taste was blood.

'Why did you have to do that? Why couldn't you just sit still?'

His voice had changed. Now louder and angrier, the pitch was higher and it sounded younger, almost like that of a young adult.

'I didn't want any of this, d'you get me? I just wanted to go home. No more trouble. And now this. Fucking hell!'

Klara heard his growing desperation. She heard the windscreen wipers scratch the glass as if idling, heard her inner voice tell her that she'd now found a way to die without having to do it herself, because the lunatic with the Santa costume would do it for her. And yet she begged him, 'Please, let me go!'

'You should've thought about that earlier, for fuck's sake. I can't let you go now.'

'Why not? I won't tell anyone about you.'

I mean, I don't even know what you look like.

'You expect me to believe that? I'm on probation, see? You go running to the cops and they'll bang me up. No, no way...'

Klara, who'd pressed her left forearm to her bleeding nose as if she were going to sneeze into it, shook her head as circumspectly as possible. 'I don't even know what you look like. Please unshackle me and let me go. I just want to get out.'

'Fuck!'

With a cry of anguish, he wrenched open the car door and the courtesy light came on. On this stretch of the road, the Teufelssee lay in total darkness; there were no houses or street lamps, and of course no other car came towards them or overtook from behind. The wide road led to bathing ponds, toboggan runs and viewing points; in winter the visitors came during the day, if at all.

Unless, perhaps, you're planning to leap at night from the climbing wall, but even then you'd take the train and walk the rest of the way.

Klara was shivering. Without the engine running, the cold ate into the interior of the car like a hungry animal, even though Hendrik closed the door again at once.

Probation?

Even though his costume, his weapons and the handcuffs were proof enough, she'd now heard it from his own mouth. She was sitting in the car of a criminal. Handcuffed and injured.

Every time during these last few days that she'd visualised the hours prior to her death, this was the state she'd found herself in: helpless, unconscious and bleeding. And that was exactly what she'd wanted to avoid.

In her escape from two mortal dangers she'd run into the clutches of a third.

In a ludicrous attempt to set herself free she shook at the handcuff, which was as firm as the handle above the passenger door. How quickly he'd managed to shackle her! Clearly he had practice.

Experience at killing...

Klara gave a start when the passenger door opened and Hendrik was suddenly standing beside her. He held onto the roof of the car and bent down to her.

Like a prostitute on Kurfürstenstrasse sweet-talking a punter on her patch, Klara thought.

'That's what you get for being nice,' he grumbled.

She saw the gun he'd snatched from her gleam in his hands, the barrel reflecting the courtesy light as he brandished it in front of her face.

'Fucking hell, I didn't want this.'

'Then let me go!' she implored once more. 'Please!'

Hendrik moved his hand as if he were going to slap her. As she turned her head away she glanced at the dashboard, which in one respect was similar to that of her Mini.

No key.

Like with her car, Hendrik didn't need to put a key in the lock and turn it. You just had to press the START button beside the gearstick and the engine sprang to life, so long as the electronic smart key was inside the vehicle. *Or on the person of the driver while they were touching the car!*

Without questioning her desperate thoughts for a second, Klara drew up her left leg then pushed it into the footwell below the driver's seat. Fortunately the car was so small that she could reach the brake with her foot. Which was necessary to start the ignition with the button. Before Hendrik could react and let go of the roof, contact was established between the on-board electronics and the transmitter on his body, and the engine roared into life. A wave of euphoria unleashed by this minor success gave Klara renewed strength. Now, with her right hand gripping the handle, she switched her foot from the brake to the accelerator. The car jumped forwards, taking Hendrik with it for a while. It stuttered as if driving over cobbles, but Hendrik's cry of pain told her that she'd run over his foot.

Amid the whine of the whirring engine she heard something from inside fly against the windscreen and drop into the footwell. At almost the same time the passenger door that Hendrik had pulled open closed again in the wind, but not so hard that it clicked shut.

So what?

She just had to put enough distance between her and the madman.

With the back wheels spinning and her left hand on the wheel, she sped the howling car through the snowstorm. Fifty, one hundred, two hundred metres until...

Oh, my God! No!

The engine cut out, and if there had been a bang, Klara would have thought it had exploded from overload. But now she knew she'd simply made a mistake and squandered her last chance.

She frantically pressed the START button again. Over and over again. To no avail.

The engine was dead and couldn't be restarted. Only the headlights and dashboard were lit up.

That's it, then...

She'd hoped that the car, once started, wouldn't stop again. But the system must have realised that the key wasn't in the vehicle any longer.

Or, more likely, Hendrik had used his radio key as a remote control and activated the anti-theft device.

Either way she was still trapped. Unable to move another metre.

Klara glanced in the rear-view mirror, then turned around to check on Hendrik.

Who was approaching slowly. The sight that met her eyes was so bizarre and unnerving that she felt like screaming: a Father Christmas on an icy road, limping through the snow with a weapon in his hand. Yelling curses and insults that were drowned by the noise of the storm outside and the fear inside her head.

With her eyes Klara made a desperate search of the

Hyundai, during which she discovered the object that had hit the windscreen and now lay just a few centimetres from her. It must have fallen from his hand, and certainly involuntarily because the metal object was a ring with two tiny keys which, if she wasn't completely mistaken in her confused panic, must be for the handcuffs. However, the keys lay between the upholstery and the hard plastic cover on the rail for adjusting the seat. Klara could touch them, just like the stale chips and one-cent coin that must have slipped down there too at some point. But she needed some wire, a little stick or – *for Christ's sake* – both hands to get hold of the keys. Besides, Hendrik was far too close now. Soon he'd open the car door, get behind the wheel again and beat her black and blue. Or even worse, now that she'd injured him and tried to escape.

Nonetheless she attempted the impossible. Reached her hand as far as it would go between the seat and...

Dear God, please help me...

The tips of her fingers brushed the keys, nudging them further into the footwell, albeit just a few centimetres. Klara could smell her own fear, the sweat soaking her clothing. Yanking her head up again, she looked behind her and saw Hendrik only ten metres away at most. Nowhere near enough time to grab the keys, unlock and remove the cuffs with her left hand, get out of the car and run away.

But because she had no other option, she made one last try. She bent forwards, pulling at her wrist as hard as she could, throwing all her bodyweight into it, felt the skin tear under the handcuff at the most sensitive spot on her artery that she'd never have dared slit (if only to spare the person finding her body the sight of all that blood) and finally managed to clamp a bit of the key between two of her fingers. Once more she glanced back, convinced that she'd see Hendrik almost at the boot. But she was wrong. To her great astonishment she was gazing at a dark road. Hendrik, or whatever the criminal who'd shackled her to the inside of his car was really called, had vanished.

Klara looked right, in the dreadful expectation of seeing him beside the passenger door, but here too she was staring into space. *Nothing.* Apart from the fir trees at the edge of the woods with their frosted branches, which would not be able to hold the snow much longer in these high winds.

She glimpsed a movement behind her. Had he stumbled? *What the hell...?*

Klara forgot to open her mouth to scream, for her brain was too preoccupied with the question of how come Hendrik's shadow was suddenly so much longer and thinner, and why he'd taken off the hat to wave at her with it. Nor could she scream when she had the answer to all these questions. Because the man who'd appeared as if from nowhere and was now grinning demonically beside the car, brandishing the Santa hat like a trophy, wasn't Hendrik.

'I've found you, you fucking whore!' he greeted her.

Klara recoiled in horror. She tried to grab the mobile between her thighs, but in all that shifting around it had fallen into the footwell. To her dismay she saw that the screen was dark; the connection to Jules must have been cut. She'd lost contact with him and probably would never speak to him again in her life. The same was true of Hendrik, who'd vanished.

The only man who would be with her in her final hours was the monster with the gun he must have pinched from

Hendrik, pointing it at her head through the side window: Martin.

Her husband hurled a saliva-spattered threat in her face, the full, ghastly significance of which she couldn't yet understand.

'That's what you get, Klara. I'm taking you to the stables, you piece of shit!'

34

JULES

I've found you, you fucking whore...

Had he just heard a man scream those words down the phone?

Jules turned up the volume on his headset, but the line was dead.

Shit!

He'd lost her.

The emotionally and acoustically fragile connection to Klara no longer existed, and it was highly unlikely that she'd call him again, even though he'd given her his private number earlier.

Whore...?

He suspected that Klara was in greater danger than at any point that evening, right when he couldn't throw her a digital lifeline. As he put his headset down on the edge of the sink he felt like a failure.

The dripping tap that had lured him into the bathroom was smeared with dried toothpaste, typical of a household with small children.

Before the fire in Prinzregentenstrasse, when Valentin and Fabienne still romped together around the flat that was far too small for a family of four, the froth that ought to have landed in the sink after brushing made its way onto the most unlikely surfaces and into the most improbable crevices. Spread by tiny hands – poorly washed or not washed at all – that never tired of discovering a world full of secrets, hiding places and adventure.

And lethal dangers.

Even in your own flat.

Following the move there was far more space in Jules's current apartment, but no more romping around after that fateful, deadly day when Dajana locked her children in and forever extinguished the light that burned inside her, a light he'd thought strong enough to show others the way and even bright enough for others to warm themselves by.

How could I be so wrong?

Jules avoided the mirror above the sink because he knew how exhausted and dishevelled he looked, with the dark rings around his eyes and the dry skin in the T-zone between forehead, nose and mouth. He wondered how often he'd been wrong in the last few hours alone.

Was Klara really in danger? Was she a victim of domestic violence? Or did a large part of what she'd told him exist only inside her head, as his father claimed.

'You need to forget the woman. She's not completely kosher. Yes, she was undergoing treatment at Berger Hof, but not as a participant in an experiment. She suffers from a dissociative disorder – or whatever you call it when people can't distinguish between madness and reality.'

Had she really sat in her car and tried to take her own life tonight? Was she right now driving through the night beside a stranger dressed as Father Christmas?

And has this tap been dripping the whole time?

Jules had sensitive ears. The whole apartment had to be quiet for him to get to sleep. Dajana loved teasing him about his bat-like, ultrasonic hearing when he searched the bedroom for a device beeping in standby mode, or bled the radiators for the umpteenth time because the gurgling was driving him mad. It was hard to believe that he should have failed to hear the plopping coming from the bathroom. Besides, there were splashes on the enamel sink, a sign that the tap had recently been used and not turned off again properly.

Or maybe not?

As he reached for the valve to turn it off, Jules felt his heartbeat, which was quicker than normal. He thought of the keys in his trouser pocket, the missing knife from the block and the words of his instructor at the fire brigade: *'Always listen to your intuition, chaps. No helmet, uniform or any equipment in the world can protect you as well as your inner voice, trained as it is by experience. If it tells you "Something here isn't right", then usually it isn't.'*

Jules nodded involuntarily. Something wasn't right here. His inner voice wasn't telling him, it was screaming at his cadaverous face: 'YOU ARE NOT ALONE!'

Not even pressing both hands to his temples helped; he couldn't silence the voice. On the contrary, the pressure against the side of his head only seemed to make it louder: 'THE TWO OF YOU ARE NOT ALONE. YOU AND THAT WONDERFUL SLEEPING CREATURE YOU WERE GOING TO PROTECT FROM NIGHTMARES, BUT NOW HAVE PUT IN DANGER!'

Because he didn't listen to Klara. Because he didn't hang up when she asked him to.

'He won't believe that it was just an accident. That I dialled the wrong number. Christ, if he finds out I've called you he'll come to see you as well.'

'THAT'S ENOUGH!' Jules cried, hammering his fist against the mirror, which cracked in its wooden frame. This unpleasant sound of irreparable destruction succeeded in stopping the carousel of Jules's thoughts and silencing the voice inside his head.

'Such rubbish!'

There weren't any demons out to take Klara's life and, after completing this mission, ready to hunt him down.

Jules shook his head and laughed at his own stupidity, at his irrational worries, triggered by the jangling of keys that could have been caused by a draught or heavy footsteps in the neighbouring apartment. He realised his thoughts were as absurd as the fear of his own reflection. Which he was now gazing at. The crack in the mirror divided his head into two asymmetrical halves, but of course there was no shadow disappearing behind his back, no face grinning diabolically at him, and nor did he feel a breathing down his neck.

Instead the tap started dripping again. It must simply be broken, and no matter how tightly he turned it, it wouldn't close properly. Jules tried closing the valve again, but it was pointless. It looked as if the pipes needed seeing to as well. The water had taken on a strange, dirty colour.

And while Jules wondered why he suddenly felt so weak, more of the viscous liquid that had a whiff of iron dripped into the sink. Now he realised it wasn't coming from the tap.

It was falling in thick, rusty drops from his nostrils.

35

KLARA

Tor-ture

A-buse

Dis-tress

Many two-syllable words in Klara's life had horrible meanings. But none as blood-curdling as: Mar-tin. There wasn't any other she hated more. Not a single one she'd learned to fear as much over the years. Not one that had changed so much over time. From beloved to sa-dist. From tenderness to tor-ment.

… more of which I'm going to have to suffer tonight, Klara thought, turning away from Martin. He'd sat behind the wheel, of course without unshackling her from the handle. Martin had already fished her mobile from the footwell and slipped it into his jacket. The gun, which he'd taken off Hendrik along with his hat, was in the side pocket of the driver's door, out of Klara's reach.

Without looking she could sense Martin's sadistic smile.

But he hadn't said another word. Not when he started the engine, nor when he drove off, the tyres skidding. He must have stolen Hendrik's key too, and thus the car he was now abducting her with.

To wherever it was they were heading.

All she knew about their destination was his cryptic comment: *'I'm taking you to the stables, you piece of shit!'*

Where are we going? And what have you done with Hendrik? Klara wanted to ask, but she knew she'd just get a punch or even worse by way of an answer. Despite her fear she was still able to think logically. It wasn't Yannick she'd fled from at the summer house, but her husband.

Martin followed me. As I was getting lost in the woods he must have been waiting for me in his car on Teufelsseechaussee, the only way back from the forest to civilisation. Keeping a careful distance he followed the only vehicle around, which emerged on a hidden track from the woods, with me in the passenger seat. He watched as I argued with the driver in the strange costume and tried to escape. And taking advantage of the situation, he knocked Hendrik out in the middle of the road.

This was the only explanation Klara could come up with for how Hendrik had seemingly vanished off the face of the earth just as she was desperately trying to free herself from the handcuff.

He was probably lying unconscious on the icy road, exposed to two dangers simultaneously: either freezing to death or being run over by another car in the darkness. Once again in her life Klara had the impression of being caught in an endless loop, slipping from one disaster into an even greater one, which seemed to make what she had just been through appear less perilous.

Given the choice, she'd rather be at the mercy of the stranger than facing her husband's brutality. Despite the sheer wrath in his eyes, he looked just as outrageously handsome as that very first day she'd fallen for him. Martin's three-day beard was neatly trimmed, his thick hair perfectly coiffed thanks to the fortnightly hundred-euro cut, the fingernails of his shapely hands freshly manicured. Not even the sleet was able to dent his style. With the tailored suit that closely traced the contours of his muscular body and the white shirt with double cuffs beneath the dark jacket and its pink handkerchief, he looked like a model advertising middle-aged men's luxury goods: wristwatches, sports cars, yachts. His voice, however, made him sound like a contract killer. 'Who was that?' he asked Klara. Coldly. Harshly. And mercilessly.

'I don't know.'

The blow was hard, but not unexpected, followed by that all-too-familiar taste of blood dripping from a cut lip.

'This really has been a fucking awful day. First I see my car's been broken into. But my wife couldn't care less, I can't get hold of her, she won't answer the phone. Oh...' Now he started shouting again: 'And then she fucks a stranger!'

Drops of spittle flew in her face.

'No, I—'

'Have you been shagging him in our summer house?'

'No, I haven't, I—'

'Sure, sure, it's not what it looks like,' Martin sneered and hit her again, this time in the pit of her stomach with the side of his hand. Klara tried to double up, but her shackled wrist prevented her. When Martin changed lanes she was hurled to the left.

'Costume and handcuffs?' he said, giving her a scornful look. 'I thought you didn't like roleplay.'

Klara gasped, unable to get sufficient oxygen for an answer. Besides, she needed to focus all her concentration on not emptying her bladder on the seat. The pain that followed the blow had buried itself into her stomach like a pickaxe and was now running riot with no less force around her insides.

Martin accelerated to catch an amber light on Heerstrasse, probably wanting to avoid the risk of stopping beside a car whose driver would give Klara strange looks in the passenger seat, although from behind a misted-up window they would at most make out an anxious-looking woman clutching onto the handle.

'I've been thinking about us,' Martin said, abruptly changing the tone as well as the subject. This was his talent or his illness, depending on how you viewed it. Klara hated this ability to switch from aggressive to patriarchal at the drop of a hat.

'Or, more precisely, I've been thinking about what you asked me.'

He turned onto the roundabout at Theodor-Heuss-Platz and Klara pressed her forehead against the window.

Which of my questions do you mean? Why you threw the tree stand at me on Christmas Eve and broke my big toe? Why you poured boiling-hot water over me so I couldn't go to work for a week and after that had to feign a 'solarium' accident?

But of course she didn't ask these questions.

She'd learned to keep quiet. Not to fill even long silences in conversation with questions. For no matter how hard she tried to sound interested, there was always the danger that she might interrupt Martin's thought processes, earning her another bruise on the back.

'Do you remember last year when I drove you to A&E in Potsdam?'

*She nodded. Because we'd been to all the ones in Berlin
and you were worried someone might notice that your wife,
'the silly moo', had 'fallen down the stairs' a bit too often.*

That day he'd gone through her mobile (for years he'd
forbidden her to have a PIN to lock it) and had found the
chat with Toni: *Lunch tomorrow, honey?*

Those three words and Martin's refusal to believe her
protestations that Toni wasn't a man, but that the name was
an abbreviation of Antonia (her work colleague) had secured
Klara a cervical fracture when he'd slammed her head against
the wall.

'When we were back and I cooked you your favourite dish
you asked me for what must have been the thousandth time
why I didn't have therapy if I always felt so sorry after our
altercations.' He cleared his throat and drove through an
amber light again.

'Do you know what the truth is? I *was* in therapy. I went
to see a shrink who wasn't bad. His name is Haberland. He's
old and hardly works anymore. And when he does, he only
takes on very specific cases that interest him. He rejected me.'

She ventured a glance at him.

'Because I was too normal. The standard offender, so to
speak, when it comes to domestic violence.' Martin laughed.
'You see, I don't have a problem saying it. If there were a self-
help group like Alcoholics Anonymous where you have to
introduce yourself to the others, I would do it. I would get up
and say, "Hello, my name is Martin Vernet. I'm forty-eight,
I'm a dentist and I beat my wife."'

She looked at him.

*Wrong, Martin. You don't beat her. You're killing her.
Maybe not in the strictly criminal sense. But those blows*

break your wife's soul, and without a soul she's nothing but a lifeless shell.

'I had just a single session with Haberland, then he referred me to another quack. But he too only told me what I already knew: that domestic violence is nothing but a lack of self-confidence. And that it's virtually inevitable in men like me.'

'Men like you?' The words slipped out.

Remarkably he didn't punish her for this interjection. Indeed he even responded to it.

'I told you how hurt my father was when my mother left him.'

Klara nodded. At the beginning of their relationship she'd taken it as a sign of trust that Martin had confided this secret in her. She'd felt sorry for him when she found out how much he'd suffered from the separation.

What mother abandoned her only child?

At the time she wasn't able to come up with an answer. Today she knew better, even though her situation wasn't comparable to Martin's mother's. Whereas Klara couldn't, in all honesty, continue to conceive of a life that consisted only of worry, fear and pain, in Martin's mother's case she had merely found the prison of marriage – something she'd chosen herself – too claustrophobic. It was Martin's father who'd wanted a child, not her. And unfortunately she'd given in to the pressure, shortly before she was accepted as a dancer by the Friedrichsstadt-Palast.

With the result that from day one she was overwhelmed by her existence as a housewife and mother, and from that point on mourned her life as an artiste on the stage. Looking back, it was a miracle that she'd stuck it out for ten years before meeting a man far better suited to her, an unconventional, creative director with whom she embarked on a new life. Penniless and without a fixed income, she left her ten-year-old boy with his father, who earned a good enough salary as the manager of a wholesale drinks firm to guarantee his son a decent standard of living. He didn't, however, have what Martin needed most of all at the time: a loving heart. Devoured by self-pity, Martin's father refused to consider that he might be to blame for the separation. He disregarded his irascibility and the marital prison in which he'd tried to lock his determined wife by forbidding her from appearing with the jazz band and keeping her so short with housekeeping money that she could no longer afford piano lessons. Instead he blamed the failure of their marriage on the fact that he'd given her 'far too long a leash', which ultimately meant that 'the wickedness which naturally occurs in the female sex' could develop unimpeded.

'*Women are like flames,*' Martin's father once said in the presence of his son, and Martin had repeated these words so often that Klara now knew them off by heart. '*So beautiful to look at and full of warmth, wonderfully enticing. But woe betide you let your guard down and get too close to them. For then they'll burn you. Women use men's bodies and souls as fuel. And when they've devoured you, when as a man you're utterly burned out, they spread even further. Bigger, brighter and warmer than before, they lure new victims.*'

Klara closed her eyes, but the words Martin's father had poisoned him with as a child didn't get any quieter inside her head:

'*The only thing you can do to protect yourself from women is to keep their fire small. Don't give them too much space or too much oxygen. Always have something at hand to beat down the flames or, if necessary, to smother them, if you see what I mean.'*

When Martin took a bend her body was flung to the right; she opened her eyes and found she'd completely lost her orientation. The street was far smaller and more upmarket than the main roads they'd been driving down. They were in a residential area with cafés, boutiques and wholefood shops on the ground floors of old apartment buildings.

'I only ever nodded, without understanding the full significance of what he was telling me,' Martin said. 'Only now has his lesson become totally clear: women must be kept down. If necessary I have to break their confidence so as not to be broken by them. I was conditioned to be like this from when I was a child.'

Klara closed her eyes so that Martin didn't see her rolling them.

If you're now trying to tell me that as a man you can no longer find your bearings in a changing society then I'm going to throw up.

Martin laughed out loud; his mood had turned again. There was more of a strain in his voice, more hissing, which lent his words an undertone of aggression.

'Do you know what? My old man was right. I've been restrained these past few weeks. I let you leave town, take part in an experiment. Without grumbling I managed the double burden of work and Amelie. When you were back I let you spend longer in the library. And then at some point I thought: *Hmm. I wonder if she's exploiting your generosity.'*

He looked at her. 'No, I thought. Not my Klara. Not my wife who I've trained so well. I've resisted the temptation to examine your phone, even though I sensed you'd changed.

Like when you started putting your mobile face down on the table. Did you worry you were going to be called by this Christmas clown?'

She shook her head.

No, even if you don't believe me, I don't know him.

'Even after you tried to serve me up that cock-and-bull story about an accident when to our shame I found you totally dishevelled in the front garden, I held back and only gave you a mild punishment with the belt. But of course I took precautions, in keeping with what my old man told me: *"Control every step your wife takes or you'll lose control over your own steps."'*

They stopped beneath a railway bridge and now Klara recognised where they were. Amelie loved the playground on Savignyplatz, but at this hour, long after midnight, she wouldn't dream of coming here with her child. The wide pavement beneath the arch of the bridge was lined with filthy, sodden mattresses on which a host of homeless people had set up camp for the night.

Why are we stopping here? she wondered anxiously, but didn't dare say it out loud because she was fearful about the answer. She tried distracting Martin by keeping him talking.

'Did you bug my mobile?' She wondered whether it was actually possible that, independently of each other, both Yannick and her own husband could have installed different spyware programmes on her mobile without the computer nerd at the phone shop finding anything.

Martin shook his head. 'Too complicated for me. You've got a GPS transmitter on your car. You can get them for next to nothing online and the magnet sticks perfectly to the undercarriage.'

As he was saying this, the window on Klara's side lowered and the tiny car was immediately filled with icy air. Her heart hammered against her ribcage. Sticking two fingers in his mouth, Martin whistled loudly. 'Hey, Professor!'

To Klara's horror, one of the figures on the mattresses started moving.

A man pushed a plastic cover from his body and struggled out of his makeshift bed.

'Come on, come on, Professor. I haven't got all night.'

The homeless man shuffled towards them. He was stooped, but not because of the sleet lashing his face. Everything about him suggested that he'd been broken by life on the street.

'Who's that?' Klara whispered. She didn't really want an answer to this question either.

The closer the old man came, the more pathetic a figure he cut. Everything that at a distance she'd only been able to see in outline in the dim glow of the street lamp, now looked so awful that Klara could only find one word to describe it: ill.

His dull-grey hair was like that of a patient undergoing radiotherapy. It looked loose, as if it might fall out if the man shook his head. His skin had the greenish-grey hue of a drowned body and matched the colour of the parka he wore like a rain poncho, his arms not in the sleeves that hung down loosely.

'Dr Vernet?' the man asked politely when he was just a couple of paces away from Klara's window. The smell that accompanied his words went with the putrid yellow of his teeth. Only in his upper jaw did he have most of them left; in his lower jaw she saw the flash of a single, lonely incisor.

'Fancy earning a few euros?' Martin asked the homeless

man, who nodded as keenly as if he'd been asked if he'd like to spend the rest of his life in the suite of a luxury hotel.

Again Klara felt the pickaxe in her guts, for she suspected what was coming. And indeed, Martin said to the man who reeked of shit, piss and decay, 'Then get in and put this on.'

He threw the Santa hat he'd nicked from Hendrik onto the back seat.

'My wife fancies some perverted roleplay tonight.'

36

JULES

Whatever you do, don't put your head back.

Most people who had little experience of nosebleeds did this wrongly. Jules had been afflicted by them so often in the last few months that he now knew the correct way of dealing with a nosebleed according to Dr Google: sit up and hang your head as far forwards as possible to avoid being sick or blood blocking your airwaves.

'Where are you?' he asked, a wad of damp kitchen paper on the back of his neck.

'I'm where you ordered me to go,' said his father, who'd rung the moment Jules was back in the kitchen.

'In the lobby of Le Zen. Very swanky. A bit too sterile for my liking, but the loos are wicked. I urgently needed to take a dump, and there's nowhere better for that than a five-star hotel. I don't understand those people who go to McDonald's to do their business, when next door—'

'Enough!' Jules rudely interrupted his father. 'Now, listen carefully. You need to work all your charm on the lady at reception, assuming there is one, and do some research for me.'

'Jules?'

Amazed that his father had suddenly called him by his first name and then so hesitantly, Jules took his mobile from his ear and checked the signal strength. Four bars: almost perfect reception.

'Can you hear me?'

'Exceptionally well, and it's precisely that which worries me.'

Jules screwed up his eyes. 'Why?'

Now his father sounded really concerned. 'What's going on there, my boy?'

'What do you imagine?' Jules looked down the hallway through the open kitchen door. Just to be on the safe side he'd left the door to the nursery ajar; he'd hear if someone crept in.

'Everything's fine here,' Jules said, earning an irritated clicking of the tongue from his father.

'You're as bad a liar as you ever were, my boy. Half an hour ago you were completely chipper. Now you sound like Kermit with a cold. Have you had another nosebleed?'

Another?

Jules was tempted to check the kitchen ceiling for hidden cameras. How could his father know?

He hadn't seen him in months, and in any case he never discussed anything personal with him.

'I'm not stupid,' his father said. 'Don't you remember? That time I had to call out the locksmith for you because your neighbour below thought you had a burst pipe.'

Jules nodded. The only thing that prevented him from snapping at his father was the fear of aggravating his nose again, the bleeding only just having stopped.

Jules suspected that his father had used the false alarm to have a good poke around his apartment. Besides, long ago the place had been the seat of the Tannberg family and on paper a share of it still belonged to him.

'I admit, I was curious,' his father explained frankly. 'I wanted to see how you'd settled in. I mean, you never invite me over. Once a snooper, always a snooper.'

'You went rummaging through my things?'

After a brief pause, during which Jules heard Japanese-sounding relaxation music on the other end of the line, which must be coming from the Le Zen lobby, his father confessed, 'It was when I saw the bloody tissues in the bin. Those medicines in the bathroom—'

'That's none of your business...'

'How long have you been taking that stuff?'

The bag under Jules's left eye began to twitch like the skin of a drum being struck at irregular intervals.

'What stuff?'

Had he googled the contents of Jules's medicine cabinet?

'Come on. Your antidepressants. I looked them up. Those serotonin reuptake inhibitors can cause serious bleeding. You have to let the doctor know if you ever need surgery.'

Citalopram. 10 mg. The pills were just about smaller than pinheads and Jules couldn't believe that such a tiny speck of dust could have any effect on his body. Unfortunately for him the side effects were unusually severe and stronger than the intended, positive effects.

'Have you been taking this psycho shit since Dajana died?'

'What of *That's none of your business* don't you understand?'

'All I'm saying is that, well, perhaps depression isn't your only problem.'

'What are you getting at?'

'Look, you send me in the middle of the night to a luxury hotel, prattling on about some Klara who's being threatened by the Calendar Killer. I can hear you falling apart—'

'What do you mean *prattling*?' Jules interrupted him harshly. 'You heard my conversation with her.'

'No, I didn't.'

'What?'

He screwed up his eyes pointlessly, as if this might help him understand his father better.

'Earlier you asked me if I'd understood anything and I said no. For minutes there was just static and crackling down the line, the odd murmur, but the only thing I heard was you, my boy, and that worried me.'

'You're talking bollocks!'

What was his father trying to tell him? That he'd merely been imagining his conversation with Klara?

'Wait, wait!' Something occurred to Jules. 'You said yourself that they remembered Klara at the clinic.'

'They remembered a woman who flipped out, yes.' His father coughed awkwardly. Softly, as if he were embarrassed to imply his son was suffering from a psychological perceptual disorder, he said, 'But Dajana could have told you that if she'd been at Berger Hof at the same time as this person. Anyway, the clinic couldn't confirm her name for me.'

'That's absurd.'

'All I find absurd, my boy, is this conversation. I haven't been able to confirm anything you wanted me to find out for you. Let's talk frankly, please. Since you started taking these psychotropic drugs, have you been suffering from other symptoms apart from nosebleeds?'

'No.'

'What about your senses playing disturbing tricks on you?'

You mean like the fear of a jangling bunch of keys? A knife missing from the kitchen and dripping taps?

'I'm not having hallucinations,' Jules hissed, noticing the plastic bottle on the island. He put a hand to his throat, which felt as if an invisible noose were being tightened around it.

What the hell…?

He lifted the bottle, now almost empty, and held it up to the light at an angle.

Was that…?

He tipped the bottle carefully so the orange liquid slowly ran up to the neck. If he'd been looking for a harmless explanation before, now it was beyond doubt.

What he'd seen swimming in the juice wasn't lumps of fruit. But pills!

Flat, white pills, dissolved on the surface, but easy to identify as medicine.

How did they get in there?

'… to this Klara woman,' his father said. Jules was so distracted he had to ask him to start from the beginning again.

'I said, then let me speak to this Klara woman. I want to get my own picture of her. Hook me up to your conversation.'

Jules swallowed heavily, his eyes fixed on the headset lying on the edge of the sink.

'I can't,' he admitted to his father.

'Then at least turn the volume up.'

Jules closed his eyes for a two-second blink. He knew how it would sound to his father if he said, 'I've lost her. She hung up.'

'Hmm.' The mistrust in Hans-Christian's voice was deafening.

Jules was starting to doubt himself. The ground beneath his feet, the foundation on which he'd built all his certainties, was crumbling. And while the fear of plunging into a terrible self-realisation was intensifying, a single thought formed in his mind, which he grabbed onto at the last second:

'The lift!'

'What about it?'

'Where you are, in Le Zen. Do you see a fourth lift there? Slightly hidden beside the other three in the lobby. At first glance it looks like the door to a room, a door covered in tissue paper.'

His father said no at first, but then seemed to take a few steps through the lobby until he said with excitement, 'You're right, my boy! There *is* another lift.'

So he hadn't made it all up!

Thank God!

Jules breathed a sigh of relief. 'Get in. Go up to the twentieth floor.'

37

KLARA

In his global bestseller, *The Cafe on the Edge of the World*, John Strelecky asks the key philosophical question that has kept billions of people before him awake at night: 'Why are you here?'

Cooped up in the tiny confines of a stolen Hyundai, abducted by her sadistic husband, with a tramp on the back seat who, judging by his smell, must be close to death, parked beneath the railway arch on Savignyplatz, Klara could no longer think of an answer to the reason for her existence.

If God weren't a psychopath who'd created a bizarre orgy of violence called the universe as a reality show he could watch for relaxation and his perverse pleasure, Klara was certain he would have abandoned all of them here long ago.

In all probability God didn't exist. No good, omnipotent power could sanction Martin turning to the tramp and handing him a silver pair of pliers which, for whatever reason, he'd had in his inner coat pocket.

'What am I supposed to do with those?' the homeless man asked. He sounded ashamed, not just because Martin had forced him to put on Hendrik's ridiculous Father Christmas hat, but because the whole situation was embarrassing. Klara could see this from the uncertain glances those sad eyes gave her from the middle of the back seat. The poor soul didn't dare look at her anymore and was probably avoiding staring at her shackled arm too. Part of him was no doubt keen to get out again, but the warmth of the car and prospect of cash were just too enticing.

'I'd like to buy something from you, Professor.' Martin turned to Klara. 'He used to teach computer studies at the Technical University; I gave him fillings years ago. This was before his wife left him, of course, fleecing him for everything in the divorce and leaving him plenty of time to drown his sorrows with Lidl wine – losing his job and his mind in the process.'

He turned to the tramp again. 'I'll give you two hundred euros.'

'But what for? I haven't got anything to sell.'

Martin gave a knowing nod. 'Strictly speaking you're right. In truth I just want something back that I gave you a number of years ago.'

With a jittery movement of his forearm the professor wiped some raindrops from his bushy eyebrows. 'You gave me something?'

'I want your upper right four.'

'I'm sorry?'

He didn't say 'Eh?' or 'What?'; in spite of his life on the street, which had turned him into a living corpse, the homeless man remained polite, even now when Martin's aggression was as palpable as the rumbling of a volcano shortly before an eruption.

'Your upper right four, you fool.'

'I'm really very sorry, but I'm afraid I don't understand what you're saying.'

Martin groaned and pointed at the man's mouth, which was surrounded by a beard, presumably home to a diverse array of tiny creatures.

'It must be ten years ago – I gave you a ceramic filling in your first molar. Right upper jaw.'

Klara stared in horror at the pliers that started shaking in the dirt-encrusted hand of the homeless man.

'Please I—'

'Stop yakking! With every word you're contaminating the air inside this car, so hurry up!'

Now the professor did look at Klara again. The supplication in his face brought tears of anger to her eyes. She was furious with Martin.

'Leave him alone, you bastard!' she hissed at her husband. A moment later her head smashed against the window. This time she hadn't even seen Martin's rapid fist coming. Fresh blood ran over her lips, and yet she told the old man, 'You don't have to do this. Get out.'

Martin laughed. 'No, this isn't about "having" to do anything. It's about two hundred euros!'

Her husband had to shift to the side slightly to reach the clip of money in his trouser pocket. With relish Martin counted out four fifty-euro notes and held them in front of the tramp's nose.

'This here in exchange for your molar. How about it? Do we have a deal?'

Now it was Klara's turn to plead with her eyes as the homeless man actually moved the pliers up to his mouth.

'No, don't do that. Please.'

'Two hundred euros will keep me going for several weeks,' the professor said, who unlike Klara clearly saw a point in his wretched existence.

'Exactly. It's a good deal. You've only got a few teeth left in your grotty gob anyway. They probably only hurt like hell when you're on the sauce, don't they?'

'Martin, please. Let it out on me. He's done nothing to you...'

Clenching his teeth, her husband hissed, 'Oh, we're back in "Klara saves the world" mode, are we? You don't understand. This tramp has to be grateful. Nobody else is going to make him such a good offer. I mean, there's not even any gold in his rotten teeth.'

Appalled, Klara forgot to look away.

'You have to twist rather than pull,' Martin said, audibly excited when he saw the professor obeying his sadistic order and putting the pliers inside his mouth.

Almost nothing turned him on more than wielding power over other people.

Klara closed her eyes and thought she heard a cracking and crunching, as loud as when she visited the dentist aged sixteen and her wisdom tooth broke into two as it was being extracted. But all that reached her ears was the man's pained whimper, followed by a shrill cry, which faded into Martin's applause.

'There you go. Wasn't that hard after all, was it?'

When Klara opened her eyes she saw Martin take the pliers from the man and study the bloody molar in the glow of the car's interior light.

'It hurts,' the professor groaned as milky-brown blood seeped into his beard.

Martin, who'd lost interest in the extraction, chucked the tooth, along with the pliers, into the side pocket of the driver's door.

'I'd like to go now,' the professor said.

Klara couldn't and didn't want to look at the heap of misery who was talking as if he had a hot potato in his mouth. Disgust welled inside her. Not at the humiliated and tormented man, but at Martin. She wouldn't have thought it possible that her antagonism towards him could get even stronger, but was soon put right on that score when her husband snatched back the two hundred euros from the homeless man's grasp and waved the notes in Klara's direction.

'First you have to kiss her.'

You fucking arsehole!

'That wasn't part of the deal,' the despondent professor muttered, as Klara, now beside herself with rage, tugged at the handcuff again.

'But of course it was,' Martin countered. 'When you got in the car I said, *"My wife fancies some perverted roleplay tonight"*, didn't I?'

He looked at Klara, then the professor.

'Please, I can't, I—'

'Oh, I'm sure you'll manage to stick your tongue inside the sluttish mouth of my whore of a wife. Because that's what she is. A whore – look at her. Half an hour ago I caught her being shackled in the car for crazy sex games with her lover. Can you believe that?'

'That's not how it was, you fool!' Klara shouted. Yet she turned in her seat to the homeless man behind her. In her eyes the professor deserved far more respect and consideration than her husband. Grabbing him by the collar of his matted coat, she pulled the flyweight closer.

'Please, you don't have to do this.' The roles were now reversed. Now it was the professor trying to stop her from doing something against her will.

Klara looked into his profoundly sad face, which may not have been handsome once upon a time, but with its large, dark eyes would have certainly been intelligent and kind.

'He's not going to give you the money otherwise.' She pointed her free hand at his bleeding mouth. 'And that would have been in vain.'

'Exactly right. My wife may be a slut, but she's a clever slut. No kiss, no cash.'

The tramp's breathing was heavy and smelled musty. Klara braced herself.

She thought of the men who'd tortured her in Le Zen, of the video Martin had put on the internet. Everything else he'd 'tried out' on her, the 'toys' that were hard to find even in DIY stores. And the thought that she'd been subjected to far more repulsive individuals than this psychological and physical wreck of an academic helped her do it.

Helped her close her eyes and open her mouth.

Helped her suppress the nausea, keep down the lunch that was threatening to make a reappearance, and put her lips to something that stank of pus, blood and alcohol, and felt like a mouldy rag. It helped her ignore her revulsion at his matted, foetid beard, as well as the idea of maggots wriggling in the gums of his toothless lower jaw as she touched the professor's tongue with hers.

The pain she felt soon afterwards came as something of a deliverance.

'You are such a revolting bitch!' Martin roared with laughter, yanking her away from the tramp by her hair. 'You'll fuck anything with a cock, won't you?'

He spat in her face.

'Right, and now piss off!' Martin bellowed at the homeless man.

'Yes, but my money…' the professor said, putting out his hand like a beggar. Martin spat at that too.

'I told you to piss off!'

'Please, Dr Vernet. I did everything you wanted me to.'

'Then keep on like that and get out of the car.'

'Please, I…'

Tears flooded Klara's eyes and ran down her cheeks, combining with the spittle on her chin. She should have known. Martin hadn't got his satisfaction in making a desperate man remove a tooth from his own mouth. Nor had he got his kick from forcing her to kiss a tramp stinking of piss and decay. No, his real pleasure came, after humiliating the professor, from extinguishing the last spark of hope he might harbour.

'Just piss off, or I'll call the police and tell them you tried to rob me.'

He leaned back and opened the door.

'FUCK OFF!' he screamed into the professor's ear, and the man accepted his fate in resignation.

With these words the poor soul was driven back to the rest of the forsaken group. Back out into the cold, to his damp mattress. Klara watched him go; despite his humiliation he still closed the car door behind him. On the pavement he grabbed the tarpaulin as a blanket to bed down for the night in which he'd lost not only a tooth, but perhaps the last ounce of his dignity.

'You are pure evil,' she said to Martin, who started the engine and turned around under the railway bridge.

Yannick was right. It was your life I should have put an end to, not mine.

'Ooh, are you feeling sorry for him? Don't bother. I mean, no one's going to help you either.'

At the lights he indicated to turn onto Kantstrasse, to head towards the zoo.

'Where are you taking me?'

'Is nobody listening to a word I say tonight? I told you ages ago: I'm taking you to the stables.'

38

JULES

Please hold! This is the Berlin police emergency number. All our lines are currently busy. Please do not hang up...

Feeling edgy, Jules drummed his fingers on the kitchen island and wondered whether he should hang up. At this time of night it could be ages before he got through to an operator.

The early hours of Sunday morning were a peak time for the police, when the capital's residents, fired up by their Saturday-night binge, prowled the streets like vandals under the cover of darkness. All manner of offences were reported during these chronically understaffed shifts, and the weather tonight would no doubt add a large number of road accidents to the alcohol-fuelled excesses. A bespoke emergency number could probably be set up just to cater for incidents around Alexanderplatz and Warschauer Brücke. Jules was pleased, therefore, to have got through at all. If more than thirty-four people called the police at the same time, the system was brought to its knees.

The police's aim was to answer every caller in less than twelve seconds. Last year this happened in only seventy-five per cent of cases, and even now it took thirty seconds before the recorded male voice was interrupted by a childish-sounding female operator: 'Berlin police, good morning!'

Jules arched his back and sat up straighter to put a bit of tension in his body, hoping to lend his tired voice a little more weight.

'My name is Jules Tannberg and I live in 14057 Charlottenburg. I'm calling about an intruder at Lietzenseeufer 9A, third floor.'

He heard the clicking of a keyboard, accompanied by the murmuring of other operators sitting nearby. The typical soundtrack of a control room.

'Is the intruder still in the flat?'

From experience Jules knew that he was now in command of the situation. The young woman would classify the emergency according to how he reported it. If, for example, he mentioned the word 'gun', a task force would be there at once. If he stuck to the truth, however, he'd have to reckon on a waiting time of several hours before a patrol car came past. In spite of this he decided for now to describe the situation as honestly as possible. 'I've got the worrying feeling that there's a stranger in our apartment. I haven't seen anyone yet, but there are signs that my daughter and I are in danger.'

'What sort of signs?'

The ice maker in the fridge rattled, complementing the driving snow outside that continued unabated. Jules tried to fix his gaze on individual flakes lit up by the street lamp before they splatted on the glass, turning the kitchen window into a distorting mirror.

'I feel like someone's been meddling with the front door. There are also items missing from the kitchen. I think someone has used the sink in the bathroom and...' Jules didn't finish his sentence for fear of the operator putting him into the 'my neighbour is pumping poisonous gas into my flat' category of lunatics. What he was going to say was, '... *and all of a sudden there are some pills floating in my orange juice. Maybe that's why I had a nosebleed?*'

'You live with your daughter at Lietzenseeufer 9A?' the operator repeated.

'Yes.'

'How old is she?'

'Seven.'

'Could your daughter be the reason for the missing items?' the policewoman asked.

Because she's a sleepwalker with a weakness for kitchen knives?

Turning away from the windows, Jules peered through the kitchen door down the hallway, as he was now doing every three minutes. From his vantage point at the kitchen island he had the perfect view. If there were a danger lurking in the apartment, it wouldn't be able to slip unnoticed into Fabienne's room. The door, still slightly ajar, hadn't moved a millimetre.

'No, she's sleeping deeply and soundly.'

Unfortunately she's got a bit of a temperature and isn't really with it today.

The operator stopped typing briefly. 'Have I understood you right? You haven't seen or heard the potential intruder?'

Apart from the jangling of the keys...

Jules automatically felt for them in his trouser pockets and said, 'Listen, I know this doesn't sound to you like an emergency. But I spent a long time on the other end of the phone, working for 112 in Spandau.'

'Oh, really?' The policewoman sounded sceptical.

'Yes. And so I know you're not going to send out a special unit for me right away, but I'd be most grateful if you would put me on T7.'

'I see,' she said, now almost sounding convinced.

By mentioning the abbreviation he'd signalled that (a) he really was an ex-colleague who knew the procedures and (b) he wanted to be logged in the system as a 'case' so that if the situation escalated dramatically, he wouldn't have to go through all the details again when he called back.

'Will do, Herr Tannberg. One more question. How big is your apartment?'

At that moment he felt a breath of cold air on his cheeks and the door to the child's room slammed shut.

Oh, my God...

If he'd been holding a glass he would have dropped it again, this time in horror. Somewhere a window or door must have opened, producing the draught.

'Around one hundred and forty square metres. It's a period flat,' Jules replied, standing up from the stool. 'Six rooms.'

'And have you searched them all?'

'Yes,' he said, telling a half-truth.

Right before their telephone conversation he'd opened every door but he hadn't checked inside each cupboard or behind the sofas. Something which he had to do now. Just as soon as he'd found out why the door to the nursery had shut.

Still in his socks, he wandered down the corridor, holding his mobile.

'What was taken?'

'A kitchen knife.'

'Is it valuable.'

'It's from IKEA.'

'I see,' the policewoman said again; it was becoming a cliché. 'Is there a threat at present?' she now said, tapping away at her keyboard once more. 'I mean, have you had an argument or trouble, or can you think of any other reason why someone might be in your flat unlawfully?'

Jules stood outside his daughter's room and gently pushed the handle. He wondered how the operator would react if he said the following:

'*Well, how should I best put it? A woman who's trying to kill herself before the Calendar Killer does has predicted that Germany's most-wanted criminal is also going to show up at my place to kill me.*'

If anything was going to plunge his case to the bottom of the waiting list it was these words, so Jules replied, 'No, I'm not being threatened and nor can I think of who might try to play tricks on me.'

He opened the door, expecting to go insane when he saw the open window. And the chair beside it. And the curtain billowing in the howling, snowy wind, as if it were waving him over: '*Come closer. Come and look at how Fabienne jumped out.*'

But when he entered the nursery his daughter was lying there exactly as before. Breathing deeply and sleeping even more deeply. The slamming of the door hadn't woken her; the window was shut. What had caused the draught?

'You haven't got any enemies then?'

'This is what makes it so weird,' Jules whispered as he checked the window in the bedroom. 'Believe me, I'm not usually the anxious type.'

As if punishing himself for the lie, he flinched when he suddenly heard the melody.

Behind him. Melancholic, deeply sad minor chords. And they faded as abruptly as they'd sounded.

What the...?

'Then I'm afraid there's not much I can do for you except log your details,' the woman said, but he only heard her voice as if from far away, as now he was straining to work out whether that really was Chopin he'd just heard.

'Please call again if you've got more reason for concern.'

'Hmm.'

This was too much for Jules. For the sake of politeness he should at least thank the operator before hanging up, but not only was he wondering if the classical piano music had actually come from the hallway, but his father was phoning too.

Without saying goodbye, he ended the call to the police, shut Fabienne's door behind him and took his father's call in the hallway.

'What have you found out?'

'Never ring me again, my boy.'

Jules froze, but not because of the draught that had disappeared along with the music. His father sounded like he used to at home before things turned violent: aggressive, filled with hate, even though he was whispering. Jules could barely make out what he was saying. The fact that a dog was howling in the background only made the conversation more bizarre.

'What's wrong?' Jules asked.

'Have you lost it?' His father coughed, then whispered more forcefully, 'I'm going to delete your number. I don't ever want to have anything to do with you anymore.'

39

The tinnitus in Jules's ear was drowned out by the hissing and static that flooded the line whenever his father stopped talking. The howling of the dog had stopped soon after Jules heard a heavy door shut with a dull thud.

'Have you been drinking again?'

'No, but it's the first thing I'm going to do when I get home.' His father was talking louder now, although still in a hushed voice.

'Tell me what's up. Did you go to the twentieth floor?'

'I didn't even step into the lift.'

'So what happened?'

'Cindy told me it's members only.'

'Cindy?'

'The bird from reception, but what the fuck does that matter now? She was at the end of her shift and I caught her as she was leaving Le Zen to go to the underground.'

Jules heard his father's leather soles crunch. Judging by the sound he was walking in a very tall room with hard tiles.

'Cindy said there was a sort of club on the twentieth floor and I needed an invitation from Lousanne or someone.'

'That's right,' Jules said. 'Klara told me about her too.'

'Oh, really? And did she mention what goes off up there?'

Jules heard another crunch, but this time it wasn't the soles of shoes. It sounded more like the bottom of a door scraping against a concrete floor. Then he heard the dog howl again.

Or were there several of them?

'Anyway, I know what *goes off* there!' he told his father. 'Sadist parties. Every last Saturday in the month. It's where Klara was seriously abused. That's why she's trying to escape from her husband.'

To death!

'Nonsense,' his father hissed, lowering his tone again. Jules knew exactly what he looked like right now. Lower jaw jutting out defiantly, one hand gesticulating nervously while an angry vein throbbed on his brow. 'She's telling you nothing but lies.'

'Le Zen, lift, twentieth floor, Lousanne, Violence Play,' Jules said, repeating what Klara had told him.

'Okay, maybe she was telling the truth about those.'

'What was she lying about then?'

'Don't be like that.'

Jules stopped by a small chest of drawers at the end of the hall. Above it hung a mirror with a golden sunray frame.

'I swear I've got no idea what you're talking about. For fuck's sake I don't even know where you are!'

'On the stairs of the carpark of horror.'

'You're driving?'

In the dim glow of the nightlight Jules could see that his nose was still encrusted with blood. But before cleaning himself up in the bathroom he wanted to search all the rooms in the apartment one by one. Even though he didn't know how and why anyone would have crept in there, he began with the one he'd omitted before: a tiny storeroom to his right.

'No, I came out here by taxi. But you owe me far more than the twenty-five euros that cost, my boy. Thanks to you and your psycho friend I need to see a shrink now too. I'm never going to get these images out of my head. I fear they've burned themselves onto my retina.'

As Jules was pressing the handle, down the line he heard another door scrape the floor. And again Jules heard howling, only this time it sounded even more agonised. For the first time he also thought he heard human voices. Murmuring, laughter. *And moaning?*

In his mind's eye he saw his father pulling open the heavy fire door to the carpark level and watching a group of people torture a dog. To Jules's horror the howling suddenly had a different timbre. Not like any animal howl he'd ever heard; it sounded human.

'What's going on there?'

The door to the storeroom was jammed.

'Cindy said there was a rumour that the Saturday evening event in Le Zen was a children's birthday party in comparison to the afterparty that supposedly takes place in a disused carpark one block away. You know damn well what they do to the women here, but still you sent me.'

You sanctimonious arsehole! You used to get turned on by Mum's screaming and now you're playing the moralist, Jules wanted to shout, but his father would have hung up and blocked his number. Maybe for just a day or two, but he would no longer have been of any help tonight. However much Jules loathed him for what he'd done, he needed him right now.

'Where the hell are you?'

He shook the door more forcefully, but it appeared to be locked.

Or is someone holding it shut from the inside...?

It occurred to Jules that in the worst-case scenario he didn't have anything to defend himself with. In a hopeless gesture he grabbed the bunch of keys in his pocket for possible use as an emergency knuckleduster.

'I slipped in behind a vehicle just before the rolling shutter came down again. The carpark is slated for demolition, behind the Europa-Center, a stone's throw from the entrance to the aquarium. According to the signs it's going to be knocked down in a couple of months. Till then only level 7 is in operation.'

'What's going on there?'

'Don't play the innocent with me.'

Get to the point! Jules wanted to scream, but to avoid getting his father side-tracked he declined to react to his provocations. At the same time he wondered if he could risk opening the door with force. It was wooden, not particularly robust, but the cracking and splintering when he smashed it off its hinges would wake the whole building.

'There must be six cars here, each with a woman inside. Or, more accurately, in the open boot area. And at least half a dozen men standing around each car.'

Jules paused. A swarm of the most diverse thoughts and feelings buzzed around his head, as uncontrolled as the snow outside the windows.

'Okay, the city is full of perverts,' he murmured.

'Perhaps it isn't news to you,' his father hissed. 'But I might have found out something from that Cindy which will come as a bit of a surprise.'

'What?'

'Lousanne's full name. The one in the rental contract for the twentieth floor.'

'What is it?'

'I'll give you three guesses.'

Jules closed his eyes, his fingers still holding the handle that seemed to be getting ever hotter, like a branding iron trying to burn itself into his hand.

'What name?'

He didn't want to hear it, but of course his father wouldn't spare him the answer:

'Klara Lousanne Vernet.'

40

KLARA

The drive from the railway arch was barely five minutes. That was all it took from purgatory to the hell behind Breitscheidplatz.

'Head down!' Martin ordered. But rather than give her time to obey his command he shoved her head forwards so it hit the plastic panel with some force. The handcuff which it seemed she'd be shackled to all night dug painfully into her wrist again.

That'll be another abrasion, she thought, her head on the dashboard. *If you'd been brave enough to leap from the climbing wall you would have been spared this injury and all the others that are going to follow tonight.*

Would he force her to pull out a tooth too?

Klara felt herself being thrown outwards by centrifugal force as Martin shot up a winding ramp at breakneck speed. The car's engine whined like the motor of a cheap sewing machine. Her eyes blurred with tears, she tried to form a picture of her new location.

'Where are we?'

'What does it look like?'

A cliché.

It looked exactly like the place women are terrified they'll be raped in. And that was the very reason Martin had chosen it.

The car stood diagonally on the deserted level of an above-ground carpark, jammed between two concrete pillars braced against the low ceilings.

Apart from a dusty VW Beetle with no tyres, five bays along, there was not another car in this space that must span four tennis courts. Most of the markings were barely visible, due to the dirt and pigeon shit. The grey concrete walls were daubed with graffiti and the overhead lighting didn't work; the power had probably been cut off long ago. The place would have been in total darkness if it hadn't been for two construction lights. One stood to her right near the emergency exit, the other to her left in front of a huge, grey-green tarpaulin, blocking a view of the street. Passers-by gazing up from below must think that works were going on at night, suspecting nothing of the true horror playing out here.

'The actual party is on level 7,' Martin told her, unclipping his seat belt. 'But we have our very own stable.'

'Stable?'

'Where do you think mares in heat are taken for disciplining?'

To a condemned carpark?

'Normally eight to ten men are allowed to tame you at the same time,' he said factually, as if explaining the rules of a parlour game. 'And it's a good idea to come in an SUV or estate car as it gives the studs more room. But when you're improvising you can't be too picky.' Martin patted the steering wheel.

'Please,' Klara said, attempting the impossible and debasing herself by begging her husband: 'Let me go. You can keep

Amelie, I know you're good to her. I'm nothing but trouble for you. If you let me go now I promise you'll never set eyes on me again.'

'You don't understand. You've never understood me.'

He looked at her sadly, appearing to believe the nonsense he was spouting. 'I love you. Even when you make mistakes. Even when you bring me rye bread in bed though you know I only like loaves made with wheat. Even when you put the cutlery in the dishwasher with the handles facing up, though I must have told you a hundred times that they don't clean so well. Even after I'd punished you for this and hate myself because you've made me do it again. Even then, I love you.'

'No husband who loves his wife will do this to her.'

'Wrong. Only weak men let their wives go to seed. It's like children: they need rules. It's no sign of love if you let them get away with everything. On the contrary, when parents fail to pay attention to manners it's pure laziness and weakness. You could even call it a crime, for the children of anti-authoritarian parents will grow up unfit for life and become bad parents themselves, in turn producing idle children unfit for life.'

'You're not my father.'

'And yet I'm ironing out the mistakes he made when bringing you up.'

'No, Martin. You're sick. A dickless arsehole consumed by inferiority complexes who lets other men beat his wife. You let them humiliate her to break her wings. Because you couldn't bear it if your beautiful, smart and confident wife were to fly away. You think you've got me under control like this. But it's merely committing suicide for fear of death.'

Paradoxically Klara couldn't help grin as she told her husband the unvarnished truth for the first time in their toxic marriage. Unconsciously she used words she'd just heard from Jules over the phone.

'Thank you,' Martin said, patting her hand. 'Thank you for making it easier for me. Because, believe me, I'm not going to enjoy what's about to happen either. I won't watch. It would break my heart. But, who knows, we might analyse the video together later on.'

Klara looked around, but she couldn't see a camera.

'It's on its way,' Martin said, reading her thoughts. 'The stable rules are quite simple. The man who pays the most has the most rights. He gets a GoPro in case he wants to watch it all again afterwards.'

'Eight men?'

'On level 7. I booked the feral stable with Lousanne. It's for the most insubordinate mares. Those who need more than just punishment. From a single man who can mete it out with the utmost severity.'

Martin didn't need to say anymore. In his furious eyes Klara could read what remained unspoken: *Women aren't just broken here. They're destroyed.*

'You'll be visited by the highest bidder,' he told her, seemingly revelling in the fear in her eyes. *He's selling me off. This insane, disturbed fucker has put me up for auction.*

Membership of Lousanne's 'gentlemen's club' gave you an account with an international money transfer service, through which you could pay your 'club dues' in real time. This was how Martin had explained it on their way back from that night at Le Zen, as if she might find the information interesting given the state she was in. It was typical of Martin. The moment her husband was no longer sexually aroused he began regretting his excesses, which made him talkative.

Almost as if he thought the abuse was less heinous if its details were discussed quite openly in the victim's presence.

'I hope this special treatment will be a lesson to you,' Martin said, getting out. Clearly excited, as Klara could see and hear.

'You fucking bastard!' she screamed after him without fear of making things worse, for she knew that what was coming couldn't get any worse. It was precisely why she'd planned her suicide.

'You sick, perverted cunt!' she screamed even louder, but Martin was so far away that he couldn't hear her anymore.

She screamed, kicked, wept, cut her skin again on the handcuff and almost dislocated her shoulder because she was hanging from the handle with all her weight. And yet she couldn't do anything to improve her hopeless situation. Exhausted and out of breath from her pointless exertions, she hung her head. Thought of the handcuff keys out of reach beside her seat. Wondered whether she might be able to grab hold of them if she put her shoulder out of joint, then shook her head because she'd never be able to withstand the pain. And as she shook her head, at the moment when she heard a heavy door shut to her right, she noticed something.

She looked to her left, to the driver's side.

Was this possible?

Footsteps came closer. At half the speed of her heartbeat, which grew ever stronger.

That can't be right... can it?

Klara bit her lower lip to prevent herself from crying out in excitement.

If she were right, then Martin had just made a serious mistake.

41

JULES

Jules went crashing into the wall at the moment his father began running.

He'd wrenched so hard on the door to the storeroom that the handle had come off and he'd gone flying backwards with it in his hand. He jarred his shoulder and the pain made him drop the bunch of keys he'd repurposed as a knuckleduster. The mobile was still in his hand, but he was on the verge of losing the connection to his father. Rustling, crackling, scraping. Footsteps smacking on a hard surface.

From the sounds in his ear, Jules surmised that Hans-Christian Tannberg had put the mobile in his pocket and was racing up the carpark stairs.

'Dad?'

All he heard was 'Shit!' followed by several other curses, muffled and obscured by the noise his clothes made rubbing against his body as he ran.

Although his father was hard to understand, Jules was in no doubt that he was in serious trouble. He'd probably peeked through the door to the carpark once too often. Somebody was after him, intent on apprehending the uninvited witness to the 'party'.

'What's going on?'

'I'm... on... the stairs...' his father panted. Then: 'Oh, no... locked...'

When Jules thought he heard a metallic rattling like someone shaking a chain link fence, the connection was cut.

'Hello?'

Jules rubbed his painful shoulder and checked the display of his mobile.

CALL FAILED, it said, as if the conversation with his father had never happened. Not for the first time Jules wondered about this when a telephone call was dropped because a phone was out of coverage.

He pressed redial and let it ring. Once, ten times. Twenty times. His father didn't have voicemail, and so after thirty rings the mobile operator automatically switched to *engaged* and Jules had to try again.

At the same time he opened the door to Fabienne's room for what must be the fifth time that night. Here everything was still peaceful and quiet.

No intruder, no empty bed, no change.

'My little one,' Jules whispered as he sat on the bed. Her breathing was heavy but regular. There seemed to be a pause in her dreaming from earlier on. He pulled the duvet up further and a thought stole its way into his mind that made him freeze.

What if it's not just a harmless cold?

He felt her slightly damp forehead and thought of the pills in the orange juice.

Jules grabbed the Hello Kitty water bottle from beside the bed and took it out of the bedroom to examine its contents for residues in the bright light of the kitchen, even though this was daft. He hadn't seen anyone in the flat, hadn't heard footsteps and the door to his daughter's room hadn't moved a millimetre.

And yet Jules felt certain that he'd missed something.

But what?

As soon as he was back in the hall his mobile vibrated, indicating another call, just as the sound of a rattlesnake's tail signals danger.

'Dad?'

'As I live and breathe. Christ, that was close.'

'Where are you?'

'Back in a taxi. I just want to get out of here. They almost had me at the rolling shutter, but it was so rickety that I could push it to the side and squeeze myself out.'

His father laughed euphorically, clearly on a high from having escaped danger by a whisker.

'They were going to beat me to a pulp, that's for sure.'

'Who are *they*?'

Jules moved away from the child's room whose door he would rather have locked. But apart from the bathroom and front door, none of the other doors in the apartment had keys. Which made it even more bizarre that Jules couldn't open the storeroom.

'The perverts from the carpark party, who do you think? No idea who they are. Three blokes, all wearing balaclavas.'

'Any distinguishing features?'

'Yes. I can describe one of them in detail. But you won't like it.'

Out of sheer nervousness Jules almost took a sip from the Hello Kitty bottle.

'What do you mean?'

He heard his father complain about the route the taxi driver was taking ('I don't care if the city motorway is faster, it's more expensive, you scoundrel!'), then he said, 'He had light-blond, longish hair. Like a hippy. It stuck out from beneath the balaclava. Slim, sporty, about your age. Ring a bell?'

'No.'

'He was holding a tonfa in his right hand.'

'And?' Annoyed, Jules was now in the kitchen where he put the bottle beside the sink.

Any old fool could go online and order truncheons like the ones the police used. Having to worm every bit of information out of his father was increasingly getting on Jules's nerves.

'I don't know what you're trying to say.' He held the transparent bottle up to the ceiling light, but couldn't see anything. No impurities, no bits and certainly no pills. But when his father went on talking he felt as if the bottle were filled with poison and that he'd just taken a big swig from it. For Hans-Christian Tannberg said:

'Would you know who I'm talking about if I told you that the guy had a paragraph sign tattooed on his middle finger?'

42

Jules, who was about to put the bottle back down beside the sink, stopped mid-movement, just like Fabienne and Valentin used to do when playing musical statues at children's birthday parties.

'That's impossible.'

'Why?'

'Because Caesar's in a wheelchair.'

'Since when, my boy? Were you there when the doctors discharged him after the accident? Have you read his patient file?'

'No, but—'

Jules's tinnitus, his buzzing stress companion, was back.

'No you haven't,' his father interrupted him. 'He wouldn't be the first person to feign being confined to a wheelchair. You've no idea how many insurance fraudsters I've convicted for that scam.'

'Caesar's on a date. He told me about it. She's in a wheelchair too.'

'So he says.' His old man sighed. 'Give him a call if you don't believe me.'

'What would that prove?' As he spoke, Jules prowled around the kitchen island. 'If he doesn't pick up, he's busy with Ksenia.'

'You're afraid of the truth,' his father said in that strange sing-song tone that had driven him nuts even as a child. Grinning narcissistically as if he had a monopoly on wisdom.

'Don't hang up!' Jules barked, putting his father on hold, and from his favourites list called his best friend's number. It took a while to make the connection. Then there was a brief surge of white noise, like when making a long-distance call years ago.

This is so ridiculous...

Of course Jules knew that his father must be mistaken. There was no way Caesar was in that carpark, certainly not without his wheelchair.

But then, when the number finally rang, Jules had what was almost an out-of-body experience. Because the ringing in his ear wasn't the only thing he could hear; the music that had given him a fright only a few minutes earlier started up again.

Classical music.

Sad, melancholic minor tones.

Chopin?

At a stroke Jules felt as if he'd been transported back to that terrible moment on the day of the tragedy in Prinzregentenstrasse when he'd tried to run past the police officers into his own flat. Driven on by the certainty that he was about to make a horrific discovery. Jules now had a similar feeling when he realised that the source of the piano melody was just a few metres away.

Jules blinked, rubbed his eyes and felt like keeping them shut for a long while. The name of the piece came back to him: Prelude No. 4.

The piece that Caesar loved so much he'd made it his ringtone.

43

Jules looked at his screen, checked again that he'd dialled the right number and there it was in big letters: CAESAR (Magnus Kaiser). This time there could be no doubt where the ringtone was coming from.

Back down the hall, a few paces in the direction of Fabienne's room. He walked slowly, taking each step deliberately, as if trying to avoid slipping on an icy surface.

That's impossible. It can't be happening.

The melody grew louder the closer Jules came to the front door. Once there, he paused for a moment, then put the key in the lock and opened the door. This movement would normally activate the sensors in the stairwell, but even when Jules crossed the threshold the bulbous ceiling light, which usually bathed the staircase in a sulphur-yellow glow, remained off.

The darkness intensified the terrifying effect the sight of the screen had on Jules.

The photograph had been taken two years earlier in the Olympic Stadium when Hertha were playing RB Leipzig. Jules was provocatively wearing an FC Union Berlin scarf and, like Caesar, he was holding a beer and shouting something at the team or the referee. It almost broke his heart that Caesar had chosen this background picture to accompany calls from his best friend, for Jules recalled that the picture had been taken by Dajana.

But is that what we really are? Best friends?

Jules cut the call and at once the mobile phone on the doormat outside his apartment stopped ringing. Chopin faded out, the screen went black and the image of the two friends at the football match disappeared. Along with the hope that there might be a harmless explanation for all this, which with a bit of effort Jules would find.

'Caesar?' he called out into the stairwell. Finding the mobile was almost less of a surprise than the fact he hadn't heard the old lift, given that its sliding brass-plated door cracked through the building like a whip when anyone opened it.

'He wouldn't be the first person to feign being confined to a wheelchair. You've no idea how many insurance fraudsters I've convicted for that scam.'

The thought of his father's outrageous accusation reminded Jules that he'd left him on hold.

'Are you still there?' he asked when he returned to the call as he went back into the apartment, holding Caesar's phone in his other hand. He tried to unlock it to see when it had last been used, but it was secured with facial recognition.

'Let me guess, he didn't answer,' his father said.

'Worse than that,' Jules replied.

By which he didn't mean that he'd found his best friend's mobile outside the door to his flat. Nor even the question of how and, more importantly, why he'd put it there silently. His answer related to the door to the storeroom, the handle of which he'd yanked off because it was stuck.

Or locked?

Now the door was open.

44

KLARA

'No *means yes.*'

Probably the most deceitful thing men said when asked why they'd gone on when their partners had asked them to stop.

'*Please, you're hurting me.*'

'*Stop!*'

'*I don't want to!*'

Klara knew that in a few seconds, just as soon as the 'highest bidder' was here, these phrases would be meaningless. Martin's slave auction had lasted what felt like less than ten minutes, and now a tall man was walking slowly from the emergency exit towards the car. Just a few more seconds, then the broad-shouldered man with the gait of a tipsy seaman would 'use' her and only hear what he wanted to hear.

Yes.

Go on!

Harder!

Once during a lunch break, a female work colleague of hers had joked about 'money-grubbing cows' who waited years until reporting a rape, usually when there was money at stake because the 'alleged monster' had made his fame and fortune.

Klara felt so sick that she had to throw up her homemade sandwich in the loo. She couldn't bring herself to explain to this colleague how you felt like refuse when the sperm ran from your torn vagina into your bloody panties. How you'd rather cook your skin under a boiling-hot shower for a year than have your rape documented by a stranger immediately after the event. How it was mostly men who recorded the circumstances of the crime, but nor could you bear women's hands touching your defiled body to secure evidence. For a trial in which it would be your word against another's, in which the other side would try to present you as a slut *(there are even videos of her being flogged by other men)*, and in the end, if it went really well, the man would leave court with a suspended sentence while you yourself would carry the shame around your whole life long.

Klara shook her head and cried.

No, she wouldn't say anything today either. Even if the guy, who despite the night-time cold was only wearing a white, long-sleeved T-shirt and black jeans, broke every bone in her body.

For the umpteenth time Klara pressed the button to lock the doors from the inside, even though she knew her efforts were pointless because with immense foresight her husband had left the lid of the boot open to guarantee the highest bidder easy entry into the vehicle.

The 'player' (as the participants in these perverted evenings were called) had kept his side of the bargain. The payment had to be already requested from his online account – those were the rules. He'd transferred the slave fee to Martin, which meant he could do with her as he pleased; she would have to put up with it all. In all likelihood this scum thought the same as Martin: women wanted it anyway. And he'd paid for it, so it was his right.

No means yes.

Especially when it came to a married woman who was obliged to obey her husband. What was it that a high-ranking politician had once said in the Bundestag to justify why rape within a marriage should remain unpunished? 'Overcoming one's partner's lack of desire is part and parcel of married life. The husband is not trying to commit a crime – some men are simply rougher.'

Oh, yes, they are.

I bet Martin's found me a particularly 'rough' specimen, Klara thought, instinctively holding her breath when the man stopped about five metres away from the car and eyed her like a predator sizing up its prey. She was on the verge of screaming. Even the thought of what was about to afflict her as she was helplessly shackled to the handle caused her physical pain.

I've got one more chance, she thought. *One very last chance.* Klara leaned to the side, extending her fixed arm as far as she could, and with her left hand tried to reach the driver's door, or more accurately the side pocket where Martin had put Hendrik's pistol – *and forgotten it!* 'You stupid idiot,' she said out loud, drawing strength with every curse she uttered with her husband in mind. The stupid cunt had actually got out of the car without taking the gun!

Compared to the handcuff keys, the pistol was substantially bigger and not stuck, which made it easier for Klara to grasp. Her heart pounded against her ribcage like the hoof of an angry horse. The euphoria at getting her hands on the barrel was so great she couldn't feel the pain in her wrist anymore.

Almost.

Bingo! Klara thought, although at that moment the weapon escaped from her grasp again. Not because it had slipped from her sweaty fingers, but because the distance between them and the side pocket had increased. The 'player' had beaten her to it and opened the driver's door.

As the courtesy light came on, Klara's last iota of resistance dissipated. What was about to occur heralded her end. Only now it wouldn't be Klara making the decision. And it would involve pain inflicted on her by a stranger.

The huge man who was far too large for the tiny car (and far too large for a petite woman's body) fell onto the seat; this alone set the car rocking.

'Hello, love,' the man said, closing the door. Then he turned to face Klara. 'So, we meet again.'

45

'I'm sorry?'

In an instinctively defensive movement Klara put her free arm in front of her chest.

She'd never seen this man's face before, and yet he felt oddly familiar. Everything about him was powerful, but not coarse. The angular head, which matched the rest of his muscular body, made to look even bigger by the dark locks of hair that stuck out. The large, veiny hands that gripped the steering wheel like others might hold a toothpick. The chest muscles that threatened to pop the buttons from the shirt. Everything was unfamiliar – and yet it wasn't.

Maybe – the thought made her shudder – Martin had 'paraded' her to him one time; perhaps he was even the masked man with the dog lead at that sadistic Le Zen evening.

The 'player' put the GoPro camera on the dashboard, but set it so the lens was pointing to the side rather than capturing anything inside the car. Presumably he was too excited. Presumably it was his first time at the 'stables'.

'Come on, hurry up,' he whispered, and Klara wasn't sure what he was getting at.

Did he want her to get undressed?

Start undressing him? Unzip his trousers?

The man felt in the side pocket, took out the gun, but seemed totally uninterested in it and kept searching, including the tray by the gearstick and the drinks holder in front of that.

'Where's the key?' he asked without looking at her.

'On the floor by my seat,' Klara said. What point was there in prolonging the inevitable? He would want to untie her at some point when she was no longer in a position to offer resistance.

'Not that one,' the man said, his eyes fixed on the seat cushion.

Strange.

She thought she'd heard his voice before too.

'Where's my car key?'

My?

Klara gasped for air.

How was that possible?

'Hendrik?'

'No, I'm Father Christmas,' he joked, opening the glovebox. 'Have you still got it?'

'What?' She was so perplexed that she'd already forgotten what the man had asked her. The man who was evidently Hendrik without his Santa costume.

'My car key!' He pressed the start button but the engine didn't switch on. 'I hoped I'd left it in here. Do you know where it is?'

She shook her head. Partly as an answer to his question, but mainly because she couldn't make head or tail of this new situation.

'What are you doing here?' she croaked. With this question

her fear returned, and with the fear the hoof started kicking at her chest again.

Was this some obscene game that had been prearranged? Had Hendrik been controlled by Martin from the beginning?

'I'm trying to get my car back. And, as it seems, getting you out of the shit too.'

She couldn't fail to hear how animated he was. But – and for the first time this gave Klara a spark of hope – not in a sexual way. To her it seemed as if he'd rather be anywhere else in the world apart from here.

'We've got to hurry. The guy who's been auctioning you one level below said he's going to come and check in five minutes. Probably sooner when he sees the GoPro's not working.'

Klara couldn't help shaking her head.

'But... I... I don't understand... How did you find me?'

'You saw me in my Santa costume. How do you imagine I earn a living?'

'From Christmas parties?'

He laughed. 'In the middle of the night? Look, love, I'm a stripper. I get my kit off at hen parties or other women's piss-ups. Like at the Forsthaus.'

In spite of her miserable situation Klara couldn't help but give a faint smile.

'That'll explain the handcuffs and pistol then.'

'Props.'

He pulled the pistol from the side pocket and pointed the barrel at the manacle around Klara's right wrist. 'No bullets. It's a fake, like the children's toy around your wrist. But the handcuffs have held up remarkably well – much better than I'd expected.'

He reached between the upholstery and the hard plastic

panel beside the seat; his fat fingers managed to gather up the keys with impressive speed.

Hendrik leaned over to her, presumably to free her from the shackles, but Klara instinctively recoiled. 'No, leave me alone!'

'No?'

'This is a trap. I'm not going to be fucked over here.'

He tapped his head. 'Are you out of your mind? I've come to set you free. I chucked my costume in the bin so I could get a taxi driver to take me. I've been freezing my balls off in jeans and a T-shirt just for your sake because you tried to nick my car. The moment we're out of here, I swear I'm going to get some answers out of you.'

'Not before you give me a plausible explanation of how you found me.'

Henrik rolled his eyes. 'And you reckon this is the time for that?'

'If your explanation lasts longer than ten seconds it's a lie and I'm screwed anyway.'

'Okay.' He sighed. 'That arsehole who abducted you and brought you here in my car – I heard him yell he was taking you to the stables.'

An icy shudder ran down Klara's spine, not only because the inside of the car was getting colder the longer they stayed here in the carpark.

'Oh, and of course you knew at once what he meant by that?'

'I'll tell you again: I'm a stripper. I know all the perverted sex events in the city, even the illegal ones.'

'That's bullshit. Only members know when and where this thing happens.'

Hendrik muttered that he couldn't be bothered with this now. Without asking another question or waiting for Klara to come back at him, he grabbed her arm and freed her from the handcuff in a jiffy.

He must be well practised at this.

'Right, let's get our arses out of here pronto!' he urged. 'It won't be long before the bloke who abducted you notices that there's bugger all in his account.'

'You didn't transfer the money?'

'Of course not, love. Like I said, I'm not a member here. I tapped around on my phone like I was doing a transfer. I told him it might take ten minutes because there was quite a lot of activity on my account, but I'd get going straightaway. I mean, he knows where he can find me.'

Klara nodded; that made sense. Because in theory only members knew about this party, all those present would automatically assume that they had transfer accounts. But how then had Hendrik got in here in the first place?

'This is a trap!' the voice of reason screamed into the left side of her brain.

'So what? You were going to throw it all away tonight anyhow,' the resigned, exhausted voice of her heart countered.

Henrik stared at her with steel-blue eyes, which despite their colour looked astonishingly sad, and took her hand. 'Come on. It can only be a matter of minutes before that perv comes back because he realises he'll never see a penny of my money.'

'More like seconds,' Klara whispered, turning her head to the side, back to the emergency exit through which her husband came storming towards them. With two men in tow who seemed to be armed.

46

There were three of them. And those were weapons in their hands. The nastiest your opponents could be equipped with if you were weaker like Klara, or only armed with a toy pistol like Hendrik. Martin and his two balaclava-clad companions were each wielding a long knife in their right hand. Ready to slice, stab and shred.

'Who are you?' Martin shouted from a distance.

Klara winced, even though his roaring was considerably muffled by the windscreen. She'd seen her husband furious on countless occasions, often to the point of incandescence. But never before had she seen the murderous intent flare so intensely in his eyes.

'None of your fucking business, you wanker!' Hendrik yelled back.

Martin, now only a few metres away, threatened him with the knife. 'Get out, you big baby, and I'll kill you.'

Hendrik scoffed at him. 'Moron! You're only strong when you're up against someone else without a pair!'

Martin turned angrily to the men flanking him. 'I ought to have known. I've never seen his ugly mug before. And no one's ever offered so much for my slut of a wife.'

The sidekicks nodded in silence.

'No one's ever messed you up like I'm going to when I get my hands on you,' Hendrik threatened.

'Get out of the bloody car, then!' Martin barked. Klara's eyes switched between Hendrik and her husband, while the two of them stared each other down, each willing the other to blink first.

'If he comes close enough the trick you attempted might just work,' she heard Hendrik mutter, barely moving his lips, like a ventriloquist.

Even though Martin was still an arm's length too far from the car, Hendrik pressed the Hyundai's start button – in vain, of course.

If only Martin would come closer...

'Come and get us, then!' she yelled at her husband through the window and showed him her middle finger. 'You stupid bastard! Want to know who this is beside me?'

She gave Martin a smile oozing with revulsion. 'This is Hendrik. My fling. Did you think you could control me? Like fuck you could. I've been shagging Hendrik for months.'

Turning to Hendrik, she pulled his head towards her, gazed into his steel-blue eyes, pressed her lips to his and gave him a French kiss.

As expected, they didn't have to wait long for Martin's violent reaction. Her husband stomped forwards and brought his fist down on the bonnet. At that moment Hendrik pressed the button and the engine started.

Not.

Martin laughed and brandished the knife.

'So, which of us is the idiot now?' he asked. 'Did you think I'd have the key on me? Fool!'

Pushing aside the short, overweight guy to his right, who also had a suit to go with his knife, Martin went to the passenger door.

'Open!' he ordered. The man on the right took out the radio key and pressed it to release the central locking.

Martin put the knife between his teeth to take off his coat, which he flung on the floor like a gauntlet. Then he rushed at the car.

One of the chief criticisms Martin had levelled at Klara time and again over the course of their marriage was: *'You just don't think!'* A mantra that preceded almost every beating. Very often he was wrong. Mostly Klara thought too much, tried to juggle too many things in her head *(he likes his beer to be ready in front of the telly for kick-off, but it has to be cold, so when's the right time to take it from the fridge without him feeling he's got to remind me?)* and that was her own downfall. But this time Martin was right.

Klara didn't think, didn't weigh up the possible consequences of bending over Hendrik's seat – and thus his torso – to take the toy pistol from the driver's door just after Martin opened the passenger door. Just before he grabbed her by the hair and the pain shot to her sinuses as he dragged her out of the car and onto the concrete floor.

'Let her go!' she heard Hendrik shout, and judging by the noise he'd leaped from the car. Klara had so many tears in her eyes that she couldn't see a thing, on all fours on the filthy floor of the carpark. She just felt that familiar mixture of sensations – pain, fear and despair – fuelled by a large dose of anger that enabled her to rear up against Martin in every sense of the word.

With a scream that sounded as if she were in labour, she

sacrificed the bunch of hair that was still in his grasp and wrenched her head to the side. Turning ninety degrees on her knees, she stood up, pointed the gun at Martin and yelled something unintelligible. A mixture of: *'Now you're screwed'*, *'Still feel so strong?'* and *'I'm going to stick this gun up your arse and hope the bullet comes out your gob'*.

She wanted to scream all of this at the same time, but she was far too worked up and terrified to articulate her words properly, for she knew the pistol was merely a bluff. But her act was so convincing that Martin's sidekicks put their hands up, the fat one even dropping his knife.

'Nice and calm, now, Klara,' she heard Hendrik call out as he hurried behind the car to her.

Which unsettled her.

She'd learned that fear often had positive side effects. If, like soldiers in action, you'd experienced it often enough, it sharpened the senses. You paid attention to nuance and tiny details that remained hidden in everyday life. Such as a man addressing you by your first name even though you hadn't yet introduced yourself to him.

How does Hendrik know my name?

Distracted by this thought for a split second she lowered the gun by a centimetre. Martin must have noticed this briefest moment of carelessness and he exploited it. Cruelly and effectively, by kicking her between her legs, just as he used to enjoy doing when she'd come home late from work and left him alone with Amelie for too long.

The tide turned. From 'hopeless' to 'total disaster'. Martin grabbed Klara's arm, which wriggled in resistance, and shoved his own weapon in her face. Which was a mistake. For the blood that now gushed from Klara's nose like a fountain also sprayed the hand still clutching the toy pistol. It was about to slip from her grasp, and as Martin's fingers were soaked with blood too he couldn't get a grip on the gun. At that moment Hendrik leaped from behind, but he was too late.

In a desperate attempt to keep hold of the fake gun, Klara had been clutching the handle so firmly that now she pulled the trigger.

By mistake, she thought when she saw Martin fall back, behind Hendrik who in the melee must have muscled in beside her.

Klara dropped the pistol but didn't hear it clatter on the floor. Her ears were numb from the deafening bang, its echo still raging in her head.

'What happened?' she asked, but didn't hear this either. It was as if someone had plugged her ears with cotton wool.

'Klara…' Hendrik's lips mouthed.

Again he called her by her name, but now he was looking at her as if no longer certain she were really there. Astonished, helpless. Injured.

That's what a husband must look like who loves his wife more than anything else and witnesses her betraying him, Klara thought, mystified that Martin hadn't taken advantage of the situation and overpowered her. He actually had fallen back. Dropped the knife and copied his masked assistants by turning around and running back to the stairs, speeding up with every step.

Still completely in shock, Klara almost called out why he was doing that, even though it was precisely what she wanted: Martin was leaving her alone. Hopefully forever.

Where are you going?

Why are you letting me go?

What happened?

She turned to Hendrik and found the answers to the questions dancing around her head: she saw the stain.

At first it reminded her of a butterfly, then the map of an island, spreading from the chest of Hendrik's white T-shirt to his kidneys.

'What...?' she asked, still deaf and incapable of articulating a complete sentence.

Her breath formed a cloud, just as the pistol had done when the bullet left the barrel. With a bang.

That's impossible. He told me...

Hendrik staggered. Klara took a step closer and was about to grab his arm, but she wasn't quick enough. Hendrik pressed his hand over the gunshot wound and fell forwards. First to his knees, then to the side, then he lay on the cold, grey concrete floor in the foetal position, right beside the pistol which evidently wasn't a toy after all.

'I thought it was a prop!' Klara groaned. 'You told me it didn't work.'

She too got to her knees and stuck out a trembling hand, but didn't dare touch him. Her gaze fell on the coat that Martin had discarded. She picked it up to lay it over Hendrik's body. The first aid poster in her practice said it was important to keep injured people warm. Was this true for bullet wounds too?

Bloody hell, you've shot someone!

The coat felt heavy, which couldn't be down to the bunch of keys because the fat bastard had taken that with him. Klara felt the inside pocket and discovered a mobile phone. *My mobile!*

Shaking more severely, Klara was too nervous and her

fingers too sticky with blood and sweat to unlock the screen and call for help.

Hendrik meanwhile was moving his lips. Gradually her hearing returned and now she could make out traffic noise drifting up from outside. But Hendrik's whispers were so feeble she couldn't understand what he wanted from her. Eight storeys below them a vehicle accelerated with the whine of a racing car.

Klara's mind, by contrast, was working at the speed of a caterpillar.

Fetch help.

I. Must. Fetch. Help.

She remembered that you just had to hold down the home button to be connected to the emergency services.

'*Help, you've got to come to a carpark,*' she would tell them without knowing where it was. But surely they'd be able to pinpoint her mobile. '*There's a man here who's been shot,*' she'd tell the operator.

I don't know who he is.

Nor how he knows my name.

She saw Hendrik move. Saw the gun next to him.

Just before he could get hold of it, Klara kicked the pistol over to the abandoned VW Beetle. Then she headed in the same direction, as quickly as her painful ankle would allow, the phone to her ear, trying to call for an ambulance.

Towards the exit.

However much she hated herself for this, she had to put her own interests first. She had to leave Hendrik on his own.

Before she fell for another of his lies, which would mean her losing either her mind or her life.

Possibly both.

47

JULES

In the first few weeks after Dajana's suicide Jules would regularly wake up feeling he was dying of a heart attack brought on by grief. These symptoms, which usually came on around midnight, had eased off recently, but now he felt the fatal signs again as he switched on the light in the storeroom: the metal ring constricting his chest. The sweating that first burned his forehead, but would soon cool down and give him the shivers.

And of course the heart that felt far too big, as if it had gorged on its own blood and could no longer pump the contents of its chambers back into the arteries.

Jules clutched his chest, unable to turn his gaze from the storeroom door, which earlier had remained obstinately shut, but now stood wide open.

'Are you there?' his father asked, still in his ear.

'Yes.'

He felt another twinge around his heart, so painful that he had to hold his breath. It reassured him to feel Dajana's suicide note in his breast pocket. Even though its contents were more horrific than anything he'd ever read, it lent him some security to carry around part of that person he'd been most intimate with in life. Besides, the end of the note also contained sentences in which she spelled out her love for him. Such as:

Do you remember our first kiss at school?

The wonderful years that followed.

How I loved all those letters you always surprised me with. Beneath the pillow, in the fridge, among my sports things. In the glovebox [...] Basically I wanted to believe we really had made a pact even though we never got married.

How he cursed himself for never having taken this step. Never having proposed to her, never having given notice at the registry office. Now there weren't any photos of them pledging their vows at the altar, nor a video of a first dance, which would have been to 'Somebody' by Depeche Mode as the lyrics were so apt and you could dance it like a waltz even though it was in four-four time.

In fact there was hardly any documentary evidence at all of their extraordinary relationship. Not even a photo album because Dajana believed you stored the important images in your head rather than on your mobile. And so their treasure chest of concrete, tangible memories was as sparse as the wooden shelves of the storeroom, which contained just a few detergents, a box of clothes pegs, spare parts for the hoover and a pack of lightbulbs. There was enough free space between the shelves to store more things too.

Enough space for a person to hide.

'I need to comb the apartment again,' he told his father.

Jules picked up the cardboard pack of lightbulbs.

'What? How come? And why *again*?'

'I don't know what's going on here.' Jules slipped into a pair of Crocs beside the front door. 'I've got the feeling that someone's hiding here.'

'In your flat?'

'Yes.' He told him about the locked storeroom which was now miraculously open.

'And when I called Caesar just now his phone rang on the mat outside my front door.'

'Do you think *he* was in the storeroom?'

Jules took two bulbs from the pack of six and a pile of old tea towels, then shut the door from the outside again. 'No, no way. Why would his mobile be outside the door then? Besides, he's in a wheelchair.'

'Which, as I already said, could be a disguise.'

'But that's nonsense. Why would he do that?'

Merely feigning such a disability – and for months on end – would require tremendous, almost fanatical motivation. If only to sneak secretly into other people's flats.

And slip pills in my juice…

'Didn't you tell me that Caesar was in love with Dajana too when he was younger?'

'That was back in eleventh class.' Jules unfolded a tea towel on the floor and laid a bulb on it.

'Unrequited love leaves deep psychological scars. Maybe he never got over the fact that she chose you over him. Maybe he holds you responsible for her death because you didn't prevent her suicide.'

'And so he's taking revenge?'

'It's perfectly possible. And this Klara woman might be

helping him. It seems quite obvious that there's a connection between them. He wouldn't have been in the carpark otherwise. Maybe the two of them are trying to intimidate you psychologically.'

Jules tapped his head. 'You've just demolished your own theory. If you saw Caesar in the carpark he couldn't have been here, could he?' With his foot Jules gently lowered his weight onto the lightbulb he'd wrapped in the tea towel on the floor. As hoped, it broke quietly into shards. Even his father seemed to have heard nothing; he didn't ask about it at any rate.

'Okay, I'll give you that one. Caesar can't be in two places at the same time. I've just got back home, by the way.' Jules heard his father call the taxi driver a rip-off merchant and demand a receipt, doubtlessly to claim compensation first thing in the morning.

Jules used this break in the conversation to scatter the lightbulb shards using the tea towel outside the door to the nursery. Then he crunched another bulb and put more bits of glass by the front door and storeroom.

If anyone went through these doors he'd hear it.

Hopefully.

Now that he'd secured the entrances and exits to those places he'd failed to find anyone, he began his thorough search of the other rooms, beginning with the spare room.

'Something else has crossed my mind,' his father piped up again, slightly out of breath; he must have taken the stairs up to his flat rather than the lift.

Jules flicked the switch, but the bulb above the double bed that was a generous size for a guest bedroom, didn't come on.

Dajana loved having guests, Jules thought, well aware that he'd never invite friends for the night again.

'Might there be a third party involved?'

'I don't think so,' Jules replied, even though at that moment he had good reason to agree with his father.

At any rate he saw the reflection as soon as he kneeled to shine the torch of Caesar's mobile beneath the bed, where there was barely enough space for a grown person to lie. And yet there it was: something white. Bloodshot.

An eye?

Then Caesar's mobile rang.

48

KLARA

Please! Answer!

Klara stamped her foot nervously on the floor of the taxi she'd got into right outside the Palace Hotel. On her instructions the driver had headed for Wilmersdorf first, even though she didn't want to go there at all.

But I had to give the guy some destination, didn't I?

Or was it a woman?

Klara was in such a state that she hadn't paid any attention to who was behind the wheel. But whether the driver was male or female, the best thing would be for her to get to the nearest hospital.

Or straight to the cemetery.

She felt as if her body were on the verge of shedding its skin. Everything about her seemed alien, beginning with the head – she got the impression that Martin's blow had made it swell to double its size. Her nose might be broken and the pain beneath her skull was throbbing, particularly behind her eyes, which now felt too small for their sockets. She'd howled tears and snot on her convoluted way out of the carpark, from which lots of vehicles suddenly left without taking any notice of her, as if the gunshot from Hendrik's pistol had been the starting signal for some crazy race. At least it ensured the main exit was open, allowing her to escape outside.

But not to her freedom.

As the pain raged inside her head, she knew for certain that it wasn't over. Not even for tonight.

Right now they were cruising up Tauentzienstrasse towards the Gedächtniskirche.

The driver (*a man!* as she could see in the rear-view mirror, with white hair and a dark moustache) looked blankly as he handed her a packet of wet wipes.

'For your face,' he told her.

Klara nodded gratefully and cleaned her nose. She must look dreadful, although apparently not so dreadful that Erdjan Y. (as it said on the brass plate by the air vent) had been put off taking her as a fare.

Klara suspected that he'd seen his fair share of battered women coming out of hotels. He must take her for a mistreated prostitute, and that's basically what she felt like. Used and empty, even though there hadn't been any sexual activity.

'Your friend okay?' Erdjan asked.

'What?' It took Klara a moment to realise that as she was getting into the cab he must have heard her talking to the emergency services and giving them Hendrik's location.

'Yes, I hope so.'

She had no experience of gunshot wounds and she wondered whether it might even be a good thing that he was lying on a cold concrete floor on level 8, because that could possibly reduce the flow of blood.

'But he's not answering?'

Erdjan nodded to her in the rear-view mirror and with

his thumb and little finger gestured an imaginary telephone which he held to his ear.

'No,' she said, although she ought to have explained that she hadn't tried to contact Hendrik. But the 'no' was also true of the call she was actually trying to make. After letting it ring at least twenty times she hung up.

Shit!

Where are you when I need you?

The taxi stopped at some lights beside the Europa-Center with a view of the Gedächtniskirche. Years ago newspaper vendors here used to thrust the latest headlines in people's faces around this time of night. Today, in the internet age, where every printed headline was virtually yesterday's news, it was no longer worth their while. And certainly not in this shitty weather.

These days no sensible person would be here of their own accord unless coming home from their shift or having to go off to a poorly paid menial job. The young people out partying, who wouldn't be deterred by the mush and the ice, congregated in the hip areas in the east of the city, which was why you could count the passers-by here on the fingers of one hand. And so Klara found it all the more astonishing that from inside the taxi she thought she recognised one of them.

'Oh, no!' she cried. Erdjan asked her if she needed more wipes, but the horror she'd seen in the entrance to a building couldn't be removed cosmetically.

The man was standing at least fifty metres away in the muted light of a large glass door, which seemed oddly familiar to Klara, but she couldn't focus on it now, nor did she want to. She needed her last ounce of concentration to work out if she'd fallen victim to her own imagination.

'What's wrong?' Erdjan asked, glancing over his shoulder.

'Nothing,' she protested, although this nothing felt as if she were losing her mind.

And seeing ghosts at every turn.

But this ghost is real!

It had to appear some time.

I'd just forgotten it.

If only for a few seconds.

Klara had never thought it possible she'd be able to forget him, but for a while she had forgotten. She'd pushed him out of her mind, and on the very day he'd selected for her death.

Tall, his sporty body in a long, dark coat with the collar turned up, emphasising his slim neck.

Was it really him? Or was she seeing things?

Just as in the bloody wet wipes in her hands she suddenly saw organs oozing from her body, and in Erdjan's moustache the bushy tail of a rat that was sitting around his neck, ready to leap into her face at any moment.

Klara glanced at her mobile.

Of course it's him. He knows where I am. He's tracking my phone.

And the ultimatum has expired.

As soon as the taxi pulled away she started to doubt herself again. Had she really seen him? Was her mobile actually bugged?

Or have I finally gone mad?

She was terrified that if she turned around now she'd glimpse Yannick waving at her. Making the same gesture with his thumb and little finger to imitate a phone.

It took a superhuman effort not to turn around. Instead she desperately pressed redial on her mobile.

49

JULES

No. That wasn't an eye under the guest bed shining eerily in the light from Caesar's phone.

It was two eyes!

And they were staring at him. Accusingly. Wide open and screaming. As if dead – but they moved. Blinked.

At the moment when the *ghost?* (Jules couldn't think rationally right now) moved beneath the bed, he dropped both phones in shock, both his and Caesar's, which had suddenly started ringing and was now silent again.

He must be naked, Jules thought, and a repulsive image in his mind intensified the real horror. He imagined a wiry, muscular sex offender, his body smeared with butter – *how else would he be able to crawl his way under there?* Into the farthest, darkest corner beneath the double bed.

'Come out!' Jules shouted, surprised at how composed and calm he sounded, given that he just wanted to run away. One heartbeat later he was no longer able to suppress this reflex.

The stranger's slim hand shot out from under the bed and grabbed one of the mobiles from the oak parquet floor. Like a spider seizing its prey, the hand hauled it back into the darkness beneath the bed.

To make sure he didn't lose his own mobile to the intruder, Jules quickly seized it and weighed up his options as he withdrew to the door. The blue-grey duvet was rumpled and a pillow lay on the floor as if the intruder had made themselves comfortable in the bed and perhaps had even dozed off.

'Who are you?' Jules called out. 'And what do you want?'

He could, of course, have lifted up the mattress to reveal the stranger's identity, but even though Jules appeared to be physically superior, all he had for a weapon was a tea towel with a smashed lightbulb, whereas the stranger might be armed with a knife.

No, not might be. *Definitely was!*

Playing it safe, therefore, Jules left the room, shut the door and was about to call the police when he noticed that the screen of his mobile was black. The battery was finally spent.

50

Jules raced through the living room and into the study, where he opened the rucksack he'd left under the desk. His portable charger must be in there somewhere. He couldn't find it at first, but as he rummaged deeper the lead attached to it got wrapped around his finger.

He immediately connected his mobile to the power pack and heard a crashing. A sound like furniture being shifted made its way down the corridor of his flat.

Not watching where he was going in his Crocs, on the way back Jules tripped over a curled-up rug. Again the mobile slipped from his grasp, and although the phone stayed connected to the portable charger, this time it smashed on the floor and the screen cracked like armoured glass hit by a bullet.

Please, God, no.

Although he could still see the charging battery symbol, it didn't guarantee he'd be able to make a call with his broken screen.

Jules grabbed the dining table, pulled himself to his feet and kept running, now without the rubber shoes, back to the nursery, the room with the most important living thing that needed protecting in this apartment.

Right now he would have given his right arm for a landline, but all he had was his mobile, which as a result of his stupidity might not work anymore.

In the hall he stepped on the glass shards that dug through his socks. He felt no pain because he was so on edge from the appearance of the 'ghost', who of course wasn't a supernatural being but a flesh-and-blood human.

Armed.

And maybe no longer cowering under the guest bed, *but already in Fabienne's room...*

The ghost must be a master of camouflage, having crept its way through the flat undetected by Jules. Even though he had searched, but not thoroughly because he couldn't imagine what motive the invisible intruder might have. Unless they were simply crazy and wanted to see blood.

A child's blood!

Jules jerked open the door, far too loudly and rashly.

'Daddy?'

'Sorry,' he whispered to reassure her. 'I'm sorry, little one. Are you okay?'

'Yes,' the wonderful, innocent being answered with that sleepy, distant voice unique to small children who are so tired they fall asleep again immediately, despite having been woken by a loud noise.

Or ill people...

'That's it, sleep tight, sweetheart,' Jules said to her and left the room, although not before checking under the bed again.

Nobody there.

No eyes. No hands. Just dust and a box of paints and... *wood?*

There was no doubt – Jules had heard a clatter. The sound

was coming from the next-door room, as he realised when he was back in the hall.

Wood on wood. The typical sound of a window being slammed open and closed by the wind.

He took a large step over the shards of lightbulb, but had to grit his teeth when he stepped on another piece of glass he hadn't noticed.

Jules returned to the spare room and of course found himself in the dark again – the overhead light hadn't miraculously started working. This time he couldn't use the phone torch, because his mobile wasn't sufficiently charged to start up.

In any case there was no point in checking under the bed because it had been overturned. The ghost (as Jules was still calling the intruder) must have got up beneath the slatted frame and pushed it over along with the mattress.

And then gone to the window…?

Which was open!

The right-hand window in the double casement moved backwards and forwards in the draught, as if it were waving Jules over. But he stayed where he was, making sure no one was lurking behind the mattress now standing on its side. He also slowly opened the farmhouse wardrobe, just in case someone was hidden inside who might surprise him from behind. For the hundredth time he glanced at his mobile; he finally saw the logo and heard the salvation of the guitar melody that signalled sufficient battery to start up. Three seconds later he saw to his relief that the mobile was still working. The first messages pinged in. Two texts, one WhatsApp.

And a call!

'I can't talk now,' Jules barked into the phone and was about to cut him off.

'Stop, wait!' his father cried. 'You're in danger. I've found something out about Klara!'

'Not now.'

'Yes, my boy, it's important. Do you know where she is?'

'No, but if she gets back in touch I'll try to guide her here.'

'Good God, no. Don't get too close to her. Whatever you do, wait till I'm there!' was the last thing he heard his father say before he took a second call, which had been waiting all this time. A powerful gust threw the window fully open and made the glass rattle in the frame. So loudly that Jules couldn't make out who was on the line to begin with.

Only that the person was crying.

And begging him for help.

51

'I'm losing my fucking mind.'

'Klara?'

She looked at her forearm. Her tears had already smudged the number she'd scribbled on it with Hendrik's pen.

'I thought you'd given me the wrong number. Why didn't you pick up? I tried again and again.'

Klara had asked Erdjan Y. to stop at the next possible parking spot until she worked out where she could flee to.

'Trouble at home?' her driver had asked and then driven past ten parking bays until he stopped outside Kurfürstendamm 195, to combine his enforced stop with a curry sausage.

Yes, let's call it 'trouble at home', Klara thought, eyeing the fast-food outlet that was known for staying open twenty-four hours a day and serving food on china only. Which went hand in hand with the luxury boutiques and celebs' hairdressers that flanked the restaurant set back from the street.

What should I do? Where should I go?

She felt drawn to her daughter, but surely Martin would be waiting for her at home.

Klara was so desperate for Jules's advice that she must have rung him twenty times, but he hadn't answered till now.

'You switched off your mobile!' she reproached him.

'It ran out of battery.' Jules sounded like she did. Not as tearful, but anxious. He was whispering too.

'Really?'

'Don't you trust me?'

Her eyes filled with tears. 'I don't trust myself. That fucking experiment. It made a complete mess of my head. Do you remember what you asked me earlier?' She was babbling, but she couldn't help it. Klara was worried that if she stopped talking she'd have a crying fit.

'When I told you what the supposed Dr Kiefer revealed to me in the clinic park: that I was clinically dead during the experiment?'

'I'm sorry, I've got a problem here at the moment...'

'You asked if he'd been telling the truth. Yes, he had. I really was on the verge of death, and this was right after I was injected with the drug that brought on the hallucinations. Nothing that happened after that was real.'

'You mean your conversation with the Spanish doctor, the strange translation...' Jules still sounded hassled, but also as if an important riddle had just been solved.

'... everything up to Kernik leaping to his death,' Klara said. 'None of it ever happened.'

'What are you saying?'

'The artificially induced hallucinations affected me far more intensely than the other guinea pigs. I had to spend three further weeks in Berger Hof until I was able to distinguish between madness and reality, but only just.'

'And now you're not sure if you're still suffering from the side effects of this experiment?'

Klara groaned in agreement. 'Christ, I'm not even sure if

you're real, Jules. Maybe I'm just imagining all of this, my entire life – maybe it's the result of the brainwashing. I—' Klara abruptly changed the subject in the vain hope of finding a way out of the gloomy carousel of her thoughts. 'What did you mean, you've got a problem?'

'I'm no longer alone. We have an intruder.'

This unexpected piece of news came as such a shock to Klara that she thought her nose had started bleeding again, but when she checked with her finger all she felt was an encrusted scab beneath her nostrils.

'An intruder?' she asked with a lump in her throat.

'Yes.'

'Yannick!' Klara blurted out, although she corrected herself immediately.

No. It couldn't be him. She'd just seen him standing in the street near Breitscheidplatz.

Assuming that was him.

For if she allowed her imagination free rein, from a distance she could even see similarities between Erdjan at the sausage outlet and her tormentor.

I'm going insane.

'Sorry, I see him everywhere,' she said, probably throwing up more questions for Jules than explanations.

Astonishingly his next remark was cryptic too: 'Like a ghost.'

'A ghost?'

'Describe Yannick for me again,' he asked.

'Mid-fifties, beard, blue eyes, longish black hair, washboard stomach…'

'Hmm. That doesn't sound like the guy under my bed…'

Under your bed?

'More the complete opposite, but—'

'What do you mean *but*?'

The sensation that her nose was bleeding grew stronger again, but this time Klara didn't touch her face. She watched Erdjan return with a bottle of cola, his entire face a cloud of breath. He must have gobbled the sausage and chips inside, apart from a few last morsels he was chewing with visible enjoyment.

'There's someone I know who partly fits your description,' Jules said. 'Apart from the age. But everyone says the beard makes him look older.'

'What's his name?'

'Magnus Kaiser. Known as Caesar.'

52

Klara's tension had reached a new level. Although she hadn't eaten anything proper in days, her stomach was rumbling like after a feast. 'He works for the telephone companion service too. I'm doing his shift for him,' Jules said.

This information seemed to have given her the piece of the puzzle that completed a terrible picture: 'Are you saying that I ought to have been talking to this Caesar guy tonight rather than you?'

'Or with another volunteer. It's all random.'

'Nothing tonight is random,' Klara said, thinking out loud. Then, just as Erdjan was opening the car door, she came to a decision. 'Where does Caesar live?'

'Why do you want to know?'

'Didn't you say you have to face up to the danger?'

'You don't sound as if you're in a state to do that tonight.'

'Tonight's all I've got left.'

According to the ultimatum that the Calendar Killer had given her, Klara was already living on borrowed time.

'If, by 30 November, you haven't managed to end your marriage to your husband I will kill you the moment day breaks.'

Erdjan had got back into the car together with an odorous fug of frying oil and ketchup. Klara felt hungry, another new sensation for her besides the sudden thirst for action.

'Do you know what, Jules? In all the madness that must have taken hold of Yannick, there's one thing he's completely right about,' she whispered, although Erdjan could barely hear her. The taxi driver had switched on the radio and turned up an electropop song in which someone who sounded like Dave Gahan sang about pain he'd got used to. *Of all the topics!*

Erdjan hummed along. He appeared to be enjoying this bizarre tour, which was hardly a surprise as the meter was already standing at thirty-three euros and there was still no destination in sight.

'I have to stop playing the role of the victim.'

'My words exactly,' Jules agreed with her.

Klara nodded, euphoric at the thought that everything which had happened tonight marked a turning point. She was still weak, still lacking any energy. And she was definitely more frightened than ever before. But she had been prepared to die. She'd braced herself for excruciating pain until her death, first on the climbing wall, then in the garage and later in the carpark. And each time she'd evaded death.

'Until this evening I thought that ending my own life would mean I still had a modicum of autonomy. But in truth I was just scared about further pain.' It didn't terrify her anymore. Perhaps because the fact that she was still alive after all she'd been through today seemed to be a sign. Perhaps the limit of cruelty a woman can sustain had already been reached. This is what war reporters must feel like, who spend so long standing in a blaze of gunfire that they no longer worry about their own mortality when heading for their next mission. Not because they don't fear dying, but because they accept death as part and parcel of their job.

'I've come across people who've committed suicide for reasons that are far less comprehensible,' Jules said with his nice, soothing voice. She wondered for the first time what her companion looked like.

The song (it was in fact 'A Pain That I'm Used To') finished and Klara heard a crunching sound on the other end of the line, as if Jules were opening an old wooden window, which went with the wind noises that ensued. Then he uttered a bewildered: 'Oh, fuck!'

'What's wrong?' Klara asked, agitated.

'Pestalozzistrasse 44, third floor,' she heard Jules say. 'Caesar's address. But call the police if you really intend going there. I fear I can't help you anymore.'

'Why, what's happened?' Klara asked, giving Erdjan a sign that they could set off again.

She now had an address; that was something.

'Talk to me, Jules!'

'No time for that,' her companion gasped. Now he sounded like someone climbing steep steps. 'It looks like I've got to save someone else's life first.'

53

JULES

The 'ghost' might be a magician, Jules thought, when he saw the telephone on the windowsill.

A master of deception. Like an illusionist who uses every means of distraction, such as putting substantial pressure on the right wrist of the clueless audience member, so as to pilfer the watch from the left wrist.

Because the human brain can't focus on multiple intense sensations at the same time!

Viewed from this perspective the mobile phone on the windowsill could also be a distraction from the real danger, for obviously it was the first thing that caught Jules's eye when he opened the window.

The sleet had let up – it was merely drizzling now – which allowed him a good view over the ledge that ran the length of the entire building here on the third floor, interrupted by eagles' heads carved decoratively into the stone every five metres. There was enough room for somebody to stand here, maybe even to move slowly on the ledge, albeit not in winter when the weather turned it into a wet slide.

And yet, the 'ghost' must have escaped this way with astonishing rapidity and lowered himself down the bent gutter pipe for, try as he might, Jules couldn't see him anywhere. Not in the front garden, not on the pavement, not on the path to the shore of the lake.

Only the mobile on the windowsill.

When Jules picked it up he saw that it was Caesar's. The movement had activated the lock screen and Jules was able to read the first line of a text message:

PLEASE ANSWER. I KNOW YOU'VE FOUND MY MOB…

With Klara's voice squeaking in his ear, Jules leaned over the sill. 'Oh, fuck!' he exclaimed, then he just had enough time to reel off the address as he extended his hand to the fingers.

But he didn't have a firm grip; he was just touching the top two digits clamped around the cold stone of the ledge. Whether he liked it or not, he would have to climb out.

'Why, what's happened? Talk to me, Jules!' he heard Klara say.

'No time for that. It looks like I've got to save someone else's life first,' Jules groaned, tossing his mobile back into the room.

Climbing out onto the ledge, he kneeled to brace against the storm and looked down with one hand firmly gripping the window frame to stop him from falling. And to give him an anchor when he grabbed the arm of the person hanging on for dear life. One hand on the stone ledge, the other on an electrical wire he'd pulled out of the render.

Jesus Christ…

The intruder looked up desperately at him but said nothing, his energies probably vanishing.

So many vessels in his eyes had ruptured from the exertion that they were no longer merely bloodshot, but one big sea of fire. Jules reached for the hand holding the electrical cable.

The cable had wrapped around his wrist like a loop – fortunately so, for without this additional support the guy would have already plummeted onto the roof of the entrance. It also made it easier for Jules to pull him up. As did the fact that he was a flyweight.

'Stop kicking,' he yelled at him. The stranger's vitality must have been awakened and he now looked as if he were trying to salsa.

When Jules heard the window frame crack he feared that it would break free from its bracket at any moment and go sailing – along with him and the intruder – twenty metres downwards. But it held firm, supporting Jules as he pulled up his arm and hauled the stranger over the icy stone.

'Who the hell are you?' Jules asked, now in a puffing and gasping competition with the intruder. He didn't let go of the man until he'd pulled him over the windowsill and into the room, the electrical cable still around his arm like a tourniquet. The blue of his face, frozen by the winter wind, was so intense that the boy – Jules couldn't describe him any other way – looked as if he'd been made up as an alien for a science-fiction film.

The next thing that caught Jules's attention was the scar on his left cheek. Then he realised that it wasn't a scar, but a sleep line, as if the intruder had recently been lying on a pillow.

Then Jules wondered about his age.

So young?

'What the hell do you want from us?'

The stranger, still silent, couldn't be older than eighteen.

Probably younger, if the pimples beneath the fluff on his upper lip were anything to go by.

'What are you doing here?'

The answer he got smelled of salt. Slightly rusty and viscous.

Jules hadn't seen it coming. The blade of the breadknife, wedged in one of the intruder's sneakers and concealed by his jeans, was now stuck beneath his ribcage.

Jules collapsed forwards, almost cracking his knees when he fell onto them. He saw the blood drip and collect in a rivulet on the parquet.

He wanted to shout something else to the ghost – which had never been a ghost, only a mortal danger – but he couldn't remember what and for what purpose.

The killer with the boy's face unwound the cable from his wrist.

Jules's last thought before he toppled to the side was: *I saved the life of the man that murdered me.* Then he heard the absurdly young offender leave the room. Open the neighbouring door to the child's room. Heard it close and furniture being shifted about, no doubt to block the door.

Fabienne! He yelled the name of his daughter, but only in his thoughts. Jules was tormented by the realisation that he'd failed again. Then he blacked out.

54

KLARA

'You could have walked this,' Erdjan groused, disappointed that the lucrative tour had now come to an abrupt end. Kurfürstendamm to Pestalozzistrasse wasn't even a post-prandial stroll.

Klara paid the forty euros with her mobile and would have given much more if the taxi driver had forbidden her from getting out of his car.

Or if he'd insisted on driving her to a hospital rather than abandoning her outside this warmly lit, late-nineteenth-century apartment block.

The annual rents in this magnificent building must be equivalent to the price of a mid-range car. If the apartments were owned, those who lived there had either made it or staked everything on their million-euro loan.

Klara got out and looked around. She tried, among the cream stucco and Ionic columns, to find some indication that she'd been here before. Wondered if the organic shop on the other side of the street or the vegan café looked familiar. Or the Russian sign in the window of the antique lamp shop.

But even the names on the brass plates by the door meant

nothing to her. Nor could she see a Magnus Kaiser, although there was an empty nameplate on the third floor.

Was this the building where Johannes mutated into Yannick?

Where I had both the most wonderful and horrific experience of this year?

Klara recalled that on that evening, the entrance to the building hadn't been locked. She hadn't paid much attention to it, although she did think it strange that in such a smart area nobody seemed to worry about unauthorised entry. No doubt the doors to the individual apartments were secured several times over, but residents in this part of town were usually sent paranoid even by the idea that the homeless might bed down for the night in the marble stairwell when it was cold outside.

Klara couldn't help thinking of the 'professor' from Savignyplatz, who was probably only a stone's throw from here with a very sore mouth, waiting for the dawn of the next day. She felt sad.

Her breathing was heavy as she pressed the curved handle of the wrought-iron door, and she was panting when she discovered that this building was unlocked too.

Her heart in her mouth, Klara entered a vaulted corridor, passing chrome-plated designer mailboxes on her way to the stairs. On that fateful evening he'd waited until they were in the apartment before removing her blindfold, which was why the red carpet on the wooden stairs didn't stir any memories.

Was it the third floor?

Taking out her mobile, she tapped the number for the police and left her finger hovering above the call button.

Jules said she ought to notify them.

But didn't he also say that the police aren't any help when it comes to domestic violence?

Perhaps that didn't count in the case of a killer who tried to make someone end their marriage by issuing the threat of horrendous and ultimately lethal torture. But what if she were mistaken? What if the Caesar guy who lived here had nothing to do with her suffering?

Klara was already on the police radar after one far-fetched statement. If she now called them out on a wild goose chase, her future credibility would be shot.

If I have a future.

When she arrived at the heavy oak door with a white stain on the third floor, Klara had to laugh at her naivety. She was totally unprepared.

So what are you going to do now, you silly cow?

Ring the doorbell?

Or look for a spare key under the mat? Run through number combinations in her mind like in a Hollywood film and switch off the alarm system – which the apartment would inevitably be equipped with – with a lucky guess at the last moment?

Such crap. Maybe I should just…

Klara took a really deep breath as if she were about to undertake a lengthy dive, and for a second her powers of reason abandoned her. No matter how she looked at it, none of what she was going through here could be a coincidence.

Nothing tonight is a coincidence!

For the most unlikely of all the scenarios had actually happened. The door to the apartment on the third floor of Pestalozzistrasse 44 was unlocked and it opened inwards with a gentle push.

55

JULES

Unconsciousness had lasted two days. Perhaps it was only two seconds; Jules had lost all sense of time. It had vanished with the blood that had formed a puddle beneath his body in the spare room. When he came to, feeling colder than he ever had in his life, a cold that penetrated every fibre of his body, he wasted a few important moments staring at the trickle of his blood on the oak parquet. It took him a while to realise that it ran precisely to the mobile phone he'd tossed back into the room before his rescue operation.

Why didn't that young knife attacker take it?

Perhaps because he thought Jules was beyond help.

Jules himself didn't understand how he could still breathe with a stab wound like that in his side, but it must have missed all the vital organs.

Picking up a small pillow that had fallen from the mattress, he ripped off the cover and pressed it onto the wound. Then he got to his feet.

Jules swayed as he felt his way along the wardrobe to the door, then staggered down the hallway to the front door. Fingers shaking feverishly, he slipped several times trying to put the key into the lock until he finally managed to open the door.

If they needed to escape or if he managed to put the knife attacker to flight, the door should be open.

He called the police, but only heard the same message as earlier:

'Please hold! This is the Berlin police emergency number. All our lines are currently busy. Please do not hang up…'

He hung up again impatiently and pressed the handle of his daughter's room.

Gripped by a shivering fit, he began to hallucinate.

He saw Valentin on the autopsy table. And Fabienne right beside him. Dead at the hands of a madman who'd slit her throat with a knife.

'Fabienne!' he screamed through the door, which, as expected, was blocked.

In normal circumstances he would have launched himself against it for as long as it took to shift the wardrobe, bed or other furniture out of the way, even if it cost him a dislocated shoulder. But with his stab wound, this was impossible.

'Don't worry, my little one,' he called out, even though he was panicking himself. He thought of the time he'd first let Fabienne go to school on her own. How he'd followed her the whole way without her catching sight of him. Because he'd sworn to protect her from all the wrongs of this world.

How he had failed.

'If you touch a hair on her head, I'll kill you!' he screamed through the door. 'Tell me what you want and you'll get it. But leave the girl alone!'

The pillowcase was already soaked and fresh blood was dripping from it, forming another red trickle that ran back down the hall on the wooden floor.

Jules looked at his socks and nodded.

The trickle showed him the way.

He took a decision and hurried back to the spare room, where he took off his socks that were also bloody because bulb shards were still in the balls of his feet and heels.

It was lucky he didn't feel this pain because he would have slipped otherwise. The freezing stone of the ledge was probably numbing any wound. Jules had manoeuvred himself over the windowsill a second time, and for a second time was holding the electrical cable that was more of a hindrance than a help as he snuck his way along the wall.

His mobile, which he'd put in his shirt pocket beneath his jumper, was ringing. But that was irrelevant right now. First he had to avoid plummeting to his death as he stepped over the stone eagle.

Although this was different to what he'd seen in films, Jules was standing with his back to the street. He preferred to be staring at the textured render rather than a precipice.

His hands flat on the wall, he edged his feet sideways, centimetre by centimetre.

Like a waltz on black ice.

Anyone gazing up at him from below must think he was either an intruder or a suicide victim. The wind tore at his clothes, but he continued to make slow progress.

When he finally got to the child's room, Jules realised that the danger of slipping wasn't his biggest problem.

Because what was he going to do now?

Of course the window was closed. And Jules couldn't take a run-up to storm into the room.

Pressing both hands on the windowpane he peered in.

A small chest of drawers was wedged under the door handle at an angle, preventing access from the hall.

At that moment the boy's face appeared at the window, which almost made Jules lose his balance.

My God!

Jules hammered his fist against the windowpane which, although only single-glazed, was too thick to break without a sharp object.

'Leave her alone!' he yelled, striking the glass again. And again to no avail. Jules thought that in the young killer's eyes he could see him weighing up the pros and cons. Should he open the window and push Jules to his death? Or was the risk of letting him into the room this way too big?

The stranger turned away and Jules saw an unsettling movement: the guy bending down to the bed with the knife in his hand. The rain started up again. Heavier than ever.

The images blurred before Jules's eyes. All he could see was a large body that seemed to be lifting a small, motionless one from the bed.

'Fabienne!' he cried, then his mobile rang again and this gave him the solution.

Jules hurriedly thrust his hand beneath his jumper and fished it out of his shirt pocket. He stumbled because he almost pulled out Dajana's suicide letter as well, which even in this extreme situation he was not going to risk losing. It cost him a couple of valuable seconds and in the knowledge that this may have destroyed another life he struck the window with the edge of his phone. Once, twice, three times until he'd made a sufficient crack in the thick glass for him to have a go with his shoulder. With the entire weight of his body, Jules came crashing through the windowpane into the bedroom.

56

The struggle lasted barely ten seconds.

When Jules flew through the window he smothered the intruder with his bodyweight. They rolled around on a sea of glass confetti, which made it impossible for Jules to tell if he'd been stabbed for a second time or if he was being injured by the shards on the floor.

'Fabienne!' he yelled, but only in his head, beside himself with fury when he saw the madman holding the knife make for his daughter's bed.

'Leave her alone!' the stranger now barked with a voice that was astonishingly deep for his small body. 'Don't touch her!'

In the semi-darkness, broken only by the light from the street lamps, Jules couldn't see if she was hurt. But in any case, she was his priority.

I have to protect her. With my life. I have to protect her, I...

Jules threw himself onto the bed in the certainty of being slashed by the kitchen knife again, this time with fatal consequences, but all he felt was a draught. The wind hurtled into his daughter's bedroom like a hurricane, because the window was no longer there to offer resistance. The killer had toppled over the chest of drawers and run out of the room.

To fetch more weapons?

Or reinforcements?

Or... – Jules scarcely dared think this because such wishes never came true – *or to get the hell out of here?*

The heavy footsteps on the stairs suggested as much, while the door slamming shut below was another clue.

Or was it just deception?

'Daddy?'

Jules raised his head. 'Shhh, sweetie, shhh. Everything's okay, everything's okay.'

He patted her head and hoped he wasn't making any false promises that would end in her death.

When the guy comes back.

If he came back.

'Did you send him home, Daddy?' asked the most wonderful creature in the world, whose face was hidden beneath the duvet. Crying, sobbing.

'Yes, sweetie,' he whispered, for fear that a loud voice might lure the killer back. But also because he was finding it hard to talk at volume.

Jules tried to organise his thoughts, which seemed to be seeping from his head like the blood from his stab wound.

For God's sake, who was that? And what did he want?

His mobile rang again and this time he took the call.

'Finally, my boy. I'm on my way to yours,' his father said. 'What on earth's going on?'

There were thousands of answers to this question, but at the moment Jules didn't feel capable of giving any one of them, so he just groaned tersely, 'I'll tell you when you're here.'

'Okay, open the door for me.'

Jules drew the curtains in front of the smashed window to at least provide some barrier to the cold air. Then he turned the thermostat right up and sank to the floor.

With his back against the radiator he looked out into the hall and felt his energies dwindling, but he was still conscious and determined to remain so until he could be sure he hadn't failed today.

Just for once.

'The door's open,' he said, already hearing footsteps downstairs. In the hope that these weren't the killer's, he asked his father to stay on the phone for a while.

57

KLARA

'The truth isn't to be found in wine, but in violence.'

Klara remembered these words as if her father had said them to her yesterday rather than decades ago in place of a bedtime story.

She could still smell his woody aftershave, feel the tingling on her cheek when he kissed her and hear his faintly alcohol-slurred voice, the breath of which reeked of tobacco and wine, a combination that still made her feel sick today.

'Imagine your best friend is attacked on the underground by two boys. They punch her so her nose bleeds. What do you do?'

'I intervene,' she replied, full of conviction at the time, and he punished her with a look of reproach.

'You say that so casually. Any idiot can talk big and ramble on about moral courage.' A term that meant nothing to her at the time. It only became clear years later, as did the full meaning of what he was trying to tell her. 'But it's only when you face violence that your true self is revealed. Violence,' he repeated, raising his index finger, 'violence rips the mask from your face. It forces you to act. Bam!' He clapped his hands and she flinched in bed. 'There you go! If you're so scared you can't think or weigh up your options. Now the decision is made in fractions of a second: do you help your friend or run away?'

'*Violence*,' the voice from the past echoed in Klara's ears, years later. '*What do you do when you come up against it?*'

Today she could have given her father a definite answer: she didn't run away. She stayed put. She faced up to the danger, perhaps for the first time in her life, but at any rate at a time when she was closer to death than ever before. Here on the third floor, in this grand period apartment with what must be at least five bedrooms, which triggered a nauseating feeling of déjà vu.

It was as if the furniture were speaking to her as she made her way down the hall to the kitchen–living room. The pictures on the walls whispered – interchangeable black-and-white photographs of the sort you could buy in a DIY store, far too cheap for this luxury renovated apartment. The grey rug at her feet spoke softly, whereas the dining table in the kitchen almost shouted at her: 'Welcome back!'

'But I've never been here before,' she protested, as if the furnishings in this apartment had a soul she had to explain herself to.

And in fact there was nothing that leaped out at her.

Which surely the old Coca-Cola fridge or the grey sofa would have done. Who, after all, had a sofa in their kitchen?

Klara went through a sliding door into a dining room with a table that had been fashioned from a slab of walnut wood. She ran her hand across the furrows of the table edge, then felt the polished surface, but here too there was nothing that explicitly reminded her of the night when her suicide became a done deal.

In an open cabinet stood a photo frame with a picture showing a young, bearded man in a wheelchair. Behind him stood a slim guy with sad eyes – maybe his carer.

Neither bore the slightest resemblance to Yannick. And yet, the bookcase with its collection of crime novels sorted alphabetically by author name screamed at her, *'You'll see, Klara. You'll see.'*

And she did.

Not in the sitting room, not in the small study that contained just a computer and rubber plant. Nor in the bathroom. But one door further on.

She recognised the artwork on the wall.

The samurai dagger!

Her eyes wandered over to the bedside table. Or, more precisely, to the strip of switches embedded in it, one of which was on.

Which was why the water in the bed was shimmering red.

'I assume I'm right in thinking this is the first time you've fucked on top of a corpse?'

The moment that the furniture stopped yelling *'Welcome!'* at her, when the realisation burrowed into her like a tick does its victim, Yannick started talking to her again.

She heard his voice, his breath, felt his presence. Sure in the knowledge that she'd made a fatal error by going into the bedroom, she slowly turned to the door.

58

JULES

'I see your crappy lift is broken again. I'm going to need a life-support machine when I get up there,' grumbled his father, who'd complied with his request and stayed on the line.

Jules heard the heavy footsteps on the stairs and ended the call. Soon afterwards the floorboards outside his door creaked.

'Hello?' the voice resounded from the entrance. In this period apartment the echo went from room to room, seemingly getting louder rather than quieter, but that didn't matter anymore as the little one was awake anyway.

'I'm in the nursery,' Jules called out. 'With Fabienne.' He stroked her back affectionately; her head was still buried beneath the duvet.

'With Fabienne? What the hell…?'

Hans-Christian Tannberg usually wore trainers, but now leather soles were crunching the lightbulb shards on the floor.

'What's going on here?' said the voice that had now acquired a face, and it wasn't the face of Jules's father.

'Daddy?' the girl said, surprised.

'Don't worry,' Jules said, trying to prevent her from pulling back the duvet and seeing the man who had appeared in the doorway.

'Who are you?' said the tall man in a suit soaked by the rain. He had a nice-looking face.

A man many a woman would fall for, Jules thought.

'Daddy!' the girl said. She'd freed her head from the duvet.

But she wasn't looking at Jules, which was hurtful. Even though he understood her behaviour, of course, and objectively there was no reason for him to be jealous. Not after such a short time. She'd been asleep all the while, caught up in her feverish dreams.

We don't have a connection yet. She doesn't know the extent of what I've done for her tonight.

'Daddy!' she cried again, trying to wrestle free of Jules so she could get to the man in the doorway.

Her biological father.

59

The little girl wasn't Fabienne, of course. She didn't even look like her, as Jules was well aware. But his attempt tonight to save her life, at the expense of his own if necessary, had helped him imagine it was his own daughter he was protecting. And in all the commotion she had actually appeared to him as a vision from time to time.

My little girl.

The seven-year-old tried to sit up. The feverish exhaustion that had kept her in a trancelike state for the past few hours had given way to a dreadful realisation, which Jules could see in her terrified eyes: the man who'd come to check on her over the past few hours, stroking her, looking after her, even giving her medicine, was a complete stranger.

'Who are you?' the man in the door asked. Like his daughter, he was as white as a sheet and his bottom lip was trembling. 'What do you want from us?'

'Stay in bed,' Jules ordered the girl as he clutched the knife which the baby-faced killer had dropped when fleeing from the room.

'But I want to go to Daddy!'

'No, sweetie,' Jules said, showing her the blade. 'You don't.'

Her eyes grew even bigger. Soon, after a brief delay, the tears would start to flow.

'Don't worry, Amelie, don't worry...' the man called out from the door, but he was too cowardly to step into the room.

Jules shook his head and smiled sadly. 'Such words to a member of the fairer sex coming from your mouth. Who would have thought it?'

With the knife he gestured to the man to take a step back.

'Come on, Martin, let's go into the bathroom, the two of us.'

The only room that could be locked, if he wasn't mistaken.

After all, this was his first time here and he didn't really know his way around Klara's apartment.

60

KLARA

'Deep into that darkness peering, long I stood there,' Klara whispered as she turned around, 'wondering, fearing, doubting, dreaming dreams no mortal ever dared to dream before.'

Edgar Allan Poe's poem comforted her.

It drove Yannick's voice from her head. And right now she would give anything for the situation this verse described: an old man opening his front door at midnight and seeing nothing, even though he's just heard a knock at the door.

Darkness, and nothing else.

She'd love to be staring at nothing too. Seeing nobody standing in the door to the bedroom. No Yannick. No Martin. No man intent on hurting her. Even though she'd heard the heavy footsteps coming.

Which was why, of course, he was there. Smiling confidently, albeit slightly taken aback, as if surprised to find her here so late.

'Yannick,' she spluttered when she saw the familiar face she loathed.

'Well, I never,' he said, and laughed.

As if in a trance Klara pressed the phone symbol on her

mobile and called the police. Then she wondered whether she'd be able to grab the dagger from the wall before Yannick got to her, ultimately deciding against taking the risk. She ran into the en-suite bathroom, past the waterbed in which she saw a hip bone floating in the transparent mattress that was now glowing green. She felt like throwing up, but pulled herself together, shut the door to the bathroom and had a stroke of luck: she got through to an operator immediately rather than being held in a queue. 'Come as quick as you can, Pestalozzistrasse 44, third floor.'

She tried to bolt the door, but Yannick was quicker and he kicked it open.

'He's going to kill me.'

Klara jumped back onto the tiles.

Yannick remained in the doorway, just like that time he'd come out of the bathroom, only now he was looking in at her cowering in the shower. As expected, the dagger was in his hand; he'd already removed the scabbard.

This time he's not going to just cut my nostrils.

Yannick gazed down at her. Watched her like someone in a cinema who's interested in how the story continues, but not how it ends.

'What is the reason for your call?' the policeman asked.

'I'm being threatened,' she said, the mobile pressed close to her ear. Yannick frowned in amusement.

'Who by, darling?' he asked in a whisper. Soft enough that his voice wouldn't be picked up by the police's recording device. That was why he was keeping his distance.

For now.

'I'm not going to touch you,' he lied. 'This isn't even my flat. I'm going to be out of here before the cops set off.'

'He's got a weapon,' Klara said into the phone. 'He's going to kill me.'

Yannick, who was standing calmly in the door, now grinned even more broadly. 'You really haven't understood a thing, you stupid trollop. *I* was never the real threat. You were only ever a pleasant way to pass the time. I'd never have killed you, but now I no longer have a choice!'

'Can you get yourself to safety?' the man on the other end of the line asked, a touch too unprofessionally. He sounded nervous.

'No. Maybe. I don't know,' Klara stammered, fully expecting that Yannick – or Caesar, or Jo, or whatever the psychopath was really called – would snatch the phone from her hand.

But for the moment he was keeping quiet. And so Klara continued to make use of the opportunity and screamed, even though there was actually no reason to do so, for her murderous tormentor still hadn't moved.

All the same she cried, 'Oh, God, he's coming. He's found me, he…'

As she spoke, Klara reached behind her, pulled out Hendrik's gun which she'd stuck into the back of her trousers, and aimed it at Yannick.

Then she fired three shots into his chest.

61

'Hello? Are you still there? Are you okay?' Having heard the shots, the policeman on the emergency line now sounded understandably more flustered.

Klara tried to give him an answer. She opened her mouth, moved her tongue, but the words she spoke sounded as if she were under a bell jar.

'Yes, yes, I'm still here. But nothing's okay. Oh, God, nothing's ever going to be okay again.'

She took a step forwards and stood over Yannick, who looked up at her in astonishment. He'd collapsed to the floor, leaning against the heated towel rail. His right arm was shaking. A mobile phone had slipped from his hand and lay upside down on the bathroom tiles, which would soon be stained red.

Klara gasped for air in panic. Once, twice, ever faster. The detonations of the pistol had caused a sinusoidal beeping in her ears, which stopped as soon as her lungs were full.

'Hello? Please stay calm. We're on our way to you.'

'Thanks!' she said, and began to cry uncontrollably.

'It was self-defence,' she said, believing this lie that wasn't a lie, for if she hadn't pulled the trigger she'd be lying here in Yannick's place. 'I didn't have a choice.'

Klara broke down. It wasn't a charade or an act. The negative feelings that had been bottled up for years now came flooding out. She couldn't help thinking of Martin, the Le Zen video, all the broken bones, bruises, humiliation, and of how she'd been 'auctioned' tonight. The burden of the past weighed down like lead on her shoulders that were too slender for the load. She could barely climb over the dying man at her feet, the man who'd slept with her, only to daub the date of her death in blood on the wall. When she was back in the bedroom and saw the mortal remains of the Calendar Killer's victims swimming in the waterbed, all the dams burst.

Klara staggered, stumbled, shouted, wept, hissed like a wild cat and gurgled as if she were drowning. Nothing of what she was saying made any sense.

'We'll be with you very soon,' the policeman tried to reassure her when she paused to catch her breath, but it wasn't his voice that made her stop.

It was the knocking sound on her mobile that she'd initially mistaken for her own racing heartbeat.

Wiping away the tears with her forearm, Klara looked at her screen.

A bucket of ice-cold water couldn't have been more sobering.

If a call were coming from that number at this late hour, so long after midnight, Klara knew that something even worse than what she'd just been through must have happened.

62

'Hello? Frau Vernet?'

'Yes.'

Klara was already running. Out of the apartment, onto the landing. Unable to hear any sirens yet, she might have a chance to escape.

From one crime scene to another.

'What happened?'

Klara hurried down the flights of stairs. Past a woman in a nightdress who must have been woken by the shots and who, as white as a sheet, retreated back into her flat when Klara came flying down.

'Elisabeth Hartmuth, I'm Vigo's mother,' the woman said unnecessarily. Klara had saved her number under 'BABYSITTER'. Vigo lived with his mother in the building behind.

'What's happened to Amelie?' Klara asked insistently. Frau Hartmuth was a very sweet woman but terribly slow. Everything she did happened at an almost insufferably glacial pace. She spoke slowly, walked slowly, and Martin had often grumbled how Vigo even overtook her when it came to thinking.

'Well, that's one of the reasons why I'm ringing. I'm not sure but I think I have to call the police.'

'Why? What's happened?'

Klara was back on Pestalozzistrasse. Still no sirens. No blue lights. Just a gentle drizzle that froze as it hit the pavement and made every movement slippery.

'Vigo's totally beside himself. He came back barefoot, blood all over his hands and clothes. Vigo, what... no, stop that please...'

The sixteen-year-old must have ignored his mother and grabbed the phone from her hand. His message to Klara was far quicker and clearer than his mother's: 'You've got to come home right now, Frau Vernet.'

Klara hurried around the corner, slipped over on the ungritted pavement, got to her feet again and carried on. A couple giggled in a tight embrace, trying not to stumble on the black ice, and both of them fell silent when they saw Klara. Weeping, hobbling, still holding the pistol as she only now realised when catching her reflection in an advertising display. Klara had to force herself not to scream into the phone. 'What's happened to Amelie?' she said again, asking the only question that counted for her.

And from Vigo she heard one of the most dreadful answers a mother could get: 'I don't know.'

Klara stopped and stared at the brightly lit display window of a Kashmir boutique, in which there wasn't a single coat that would ever be able to make her feel warm again if her worst fears came true.

'She went to bed around eight,' Vigo said. 'I went to lie down in the spare room – must have been around ten – and was woken up by a crashing. First I thought that Amelie had reached up for a glass and it had fallen. So I got up and was about to go into the kitchen when I saw a strange man on the phone.'

'Who?'

'I don't know. An intruder, I think. To begin with I thought it was your husband or a friend, but then he said, *"Everyone in this place is condemned to death."* Fortunately he didn't spot me.'

Klara wanted to scream, but she was suffocated by the primeval fear that can only be felt by a mother on the verge of losing the most precious thing in her life.

'I don't have a mobile and you weren't on a landline, Frau Vernet.'

It was Martin who'd kept complaining that the boy didn't have a mobile, but Klara had been reassured by the fact that he just had to cross the courtyard to his mother if anything was up with Amelie.

'I was about to go back to Mum and get help.' The boy's voice was cracking. 'But the bloke heard the key rattle in the door. So I hid from him, I went from room to room, wherever he wasn't. I took some sleeping tablets from the bathroom and stirred them in his juice. I even armed myself with a knife, but then Amelie started shouting and the bloke went into her room with a weapon. Oh, God, I wish I could have protected Amelie.'

Klara closed her eyes. She heard a delivery van drive past, and in addition to the drizzle on her face felt fat drops of water drip down the back of her neck from a canopy above her head. She was paralysed. Unable to take even one more step.

'You've got to believe me, I didn't want to leave Amelie on her own. Especially not tonight as I think she wasn't feeling so well. But what could I do? He was going to kill me, for God's sake. I hid under the bed, but he found me. Then I tried to get downstairs out the window. I'm so sorry, you've really got to get home as soon as you can!'

This was the second time he'd said it, and she didn't need to hear any more. It was her cue.

Home.

Klara hung up and went skidding on towards Kantstrasse. They'd passed a taxi rank on the way here, hadn't they?

Just to be sure she checked the outgoing calls on her mobile, because only yesterday she'd phoned for a cab to their apartment in Lietzensee. All she had to do was press redial, which was quicker than googling the number.

Okay, here it is!

Again she skidded, but this time she kept her balance.

Berlin Taxis. The second outgoing number. After the twenty or so attempts she'd made to get through to Jules's mobile earlier.

Oh, Jules…

It stung her to acknowledge that once again she was facing a task she couldn't deal with on her own.

Klara sobbed and thought of her companion who she now needed more urgently than ever.

On my way home.

The most dangerous journey in the world if you were a woman. Having reached Kantstrasse, Klara looked around for taxis and saw a rank where two were waiting.

She only had to cross at the lights, a few more metres, and yet she stopped. Froze, like one of those tourist attractions who stays perfectly still until people throw money into their hat.

The call register, she thought.

Something about it was wrong.

How can yesterday's taxi be the second-last number I dialled?

Klara stood on the central reservation of the junction. Held up her mobile phone again. Wiped away the sleet that splashed on the screen.

She couldn't find it.

The call to the telephone companion service!

At this, Klara felt something shatter inside her. 'It's no coincidence,' she croaked as the first taxi on the rank drove off without her being able to summon the strength even to raise her arm.

Nothing of what had happened over the past few hours was a coincidence.

Not Martin's car being broken into, which had allowed someone to get their hands on the keys to their apartment in Lietzensee. And certainly not the fact that it was Jules she'd spoken to on the companion service tonight.

Klara pressed redial and felt as if she were in a dream from which there would never be the possibility of awakening.

This is my purgatory.

Trapped for all eternity in a conversation with a companion who told her the terrible truth over and over again, but which her mind would forever refuse to accept.

No matter how well Jules described her nightmare.

63

JULES

He sat on the kitchen floor in the dark. All the lights in Klara's and Martin's apartment were off and the curtains closed. He was better able to concentrate this way. Better able to ease the pain from the stabbing with his breathing.

He knew he didn't have much time left after now pressing the third cloth onto the wound; the flow of the blood wasn't letting up.

Jules was fine with the fact that everything was now coming to an end. And that Klara was trying to get to him as quickly as possible.

'What's happened to Amelie?' she said as soon as he took the call, asking logically the only question that could be of interest to a mother in her situation.

As a former father, Jules was reluctant to keep her on tenterhooks, but they might not get another chance to talk and he simply had to know: 'How did you find out?'

'I want to know what—'

'I'll tell you in a minute. You'll get all the answers you're looking for, Klara. I swear. But only if you tell me how you know.'

She was outside. In the background he could hear cars

rushing past. With people behind the wheels who he bet would barely afford the howling woman at the side of the road a glance.

What a shame!

If New York was the city that never slept, then Berlin was the place Jules never wanted to wake up in again.

'My call wasn't an accident.'

'No?'

'No. My phone didn't unlock when I was scrambling up the climbing wall. I didn't call the telephone companion service at random.'

'What, then?'

'It was you. You rang *me*, you arsehole! And now I want to know why. What's happened to Amelie?'

Jules nodded in acknowledgement. 'Bravo. But I did think you'd work it out earlier.'

'WHAT'S HAPPENED TO MY DAUGHTER?'

Now Klara was yelling and Jules punished her by doing the worst thing possible.

He hung up.

Three seconds later the phone in his hand was vibrating again.

'Can we now talk calmly?'

'No, yes, I'm not—'

'You're upset. I understand that.'

Maybe the only reason I'm so calm is that I've already lost a litre of blood.

'Listen to me, because what I'm about to say is very important. You're right, you didn't ring me. I called your number.'

'Why?'

'Because I wanted to talk to you. If you hadn't made it so easy for me by thinking it was an accident, I would have pretended that we at the companion service sometimes called particularly vulnerable people whose numbers were on file.'

'You nasty shit. What sort of sick game are you playing and why?'

Jules opened his mouth but had to pause before giving an answer because the stinging pain in his side momentarily left him breathless.

'This isn't a game,' he said. 'I'm being deadly serious. Did you meet Yannick?'

Klara was already fragile enough, but Jules could hear how distressed she was by this question.

'Yannick, what... I...'

'Come on, Klara, I want the truth now. Stop gabbling and pull yourself together. Did you meet him?'

'Yes.'

'And was there a struggle?'

'Sort of.'

'Is he still alive?'

'I, well...' she spluttered, 'no, I...'

Jules gave a satisfied grin. The first good news he'd had in ages. 'Congratulations! You did it.'

Now Klara yelled again. 'There's no reason to be happy – it's the worst thing I've ever had to do in my life!'

'No,' Jules contradicted her, 'it's the best thing. Believe me, Klara, my father deserved to die.'

64

KLARA

'Your father?'

Did Jules really just say that?

'Yannick is...'

Klara was still standing on the central reservation in Kantstrasse, just a few steps away from what was now the only taxi left.

Which she knew she'd never get into, as she saw the patrol car approaching. No blue light, no siren, but its objective was clear.

'That's right, my father. A nasty, sick bastard. I hold him responsible for my wife's death.'

'I don't understand any of this.'

The police car double-parked outside a pharmacy and two officers got out. Weapons at the ready, they shouted something at her.

'You can't understand, Klara. But you will, very soon.'

'You wanted me to meet him?'

And kill him...?

'Drop the weapon, drop it right now,' the policemen ordered. Now she heard sirens too. They were still in the distance, but reinforcements were on their way. Had the giggling lovebirds notified them? Or had the woman on the stairs in her nightie given a description?

What did it matter?

'So right from the start you planned everything that's occurred tonight?'

Nothing happens by chance.

Jules gave a choked laugh. 'No, I just prepared the groundwork. It's like what I was told by the wedding planner I was going to hire for our wedding, which sadly never happened: *"You can only set the parameters, it's always the guests who make the party."'*

'DROP THE WEAPON!'

Now the policemen were just a few metres away. She could see the nervousness in their eyes and the wedding ring of the officer standing closer, who aimed his pistol at her.

Klara turned away from them.

'Is Amelie still alive?'

'Yes, of course. She's fine.'

Good God. She put her head back, sobbing.

'Please don't hurt my little girl,' she said, dropping the gun.

'I would never have done,' was the last thing she heard Jules say, for then she was wrestled to the ground by the officers.

65

JULES

Ten minutes. A quarter of an hour, perhaps, if he were lucky. Even though it sounded as if she'd just been arrested, Klara would move heaven and hell to get home. If necessary in the patrol car that was taking her to the station. There was no greater elemental force than a parent whose child was in danger.

Jules knew, therefore, that he didn't have much time. Besides, it was better to keep moving if he didn't want to die here.

On the kitchen floor.

Putting his weight on one knee, he pulled himself up with the help of the kitchen island until he was fully upright. Teetering, he groped his way back to the nursery and opened the door.

He could see his own breath.

The curtains he'd closed in front of the shattered window were billowing in the wind. The room was chilling with the same rapidity as his body.

'Sorry, sweetie. I guess it all got a bit out of hand tonight.'

He switched on the nightlight, a pink Elsa figure with a warm glow. Amelie inched her way further to the wall and hid her head under the duvet again.

She was freezing, but of course she didn't want to look at him anymore either. No surprise; he couldn't hold it against her.

When Jules stepped over to her bed, she curled up even tighter. He tried to get through to her with words at least.

'Like you, I had a bad father, Amelie. And my mum was weak, like yours. But today your mum has shown courage and strength.'

As he stroked the girl's head through the duvet, he felt her body tense.

'I'm sorry.'

He turned away from the bed and staggered to the door. Exhausted by tonight. By the fight with the stranger. And by life.

At the same time he felt something quite unfamiliar. The satisfying feeling of long-awaited success – finally.

In the hall he stopped again, took a step back and looked Amelie in the eyes for the first time. She had pulled the duvet back down over her head and watched him leave the room, probably to make sure he really was going.

Those eyes were so large and innocent, and contained a deep sadness they would never altogether be free of.

'I'm really sorry,' he told her again. 'I know you don't understand everything right now. And I can't promise you with any certainty that you'll thank me one day, because you won't know of the horror I've saved you from. Unless your mother explains it all.'

He paused briefly then left with perhaps the most important warning he could give her: 'Whatever happens, Amelie, please don't go into the bathroom.'

With these words he headed there himself.

He opened the door, checked for Martin's pulse again, and when Jules was sure he was no longer alive he dipped his hand in the pool of blood on the tiled floor. He'd stabbed Martin twice with the breadknife, thrusting significantly deeper than the young intruder whose presence and intentions he'd perhaps never be able to understand.

Jules checked the time.

It was 02:34. 30 November.

He wrote this date on the bathroom wall with Martin's blood on his hands. In his unmistakeable handwriting. A squiggle at the top of the number 1. With a little imagination the figure, which he'd written on the wall at the scene of the first murder too, looked a bit like a seahorse...

66

KLARA

THREE WEEKS LATER

Waterworks.

There couldn't be a café with a more fitting name than this one in Knesebeckstrasse.

As Klara gazed at Amelie, busy drawing in a little corner the waitress had made specially for her today, she could have wept yet again.

For love.

And with relief that she hadn't lost her, even though there were many reasons she might never have seen her daughter again. Her own plans being at the top of that list. She'd come within a whisker of killing herself before Martin or Yannick got there first.

'Are you still listening to me?'

'What?'

She looked from her daughter back to the man sitting opposite her at the table.

He was in a wheelchair and indeed did look older with his beard, but Magnus Kaiser didn't resemble Yannick at all. Not in the slightest.

321

Caesar must be twenty years younger, with longer, much lighter hair, and looked more agile despite his physical disability. Before the accident he must have been a real sports freak.

'Yes, please excuse me. Until a few days ago my daughter was in a really bad way. Since her father's death she's barely eaten anything, drunk very little and been plagued by nightmares every night. For me it's a miracle to see her in such good shape today.'

'I can understand.' Caesar stirred his white coffee.

There had to be something on his mind or he wouldn't have been so persistent in asking her for a meeting. But over the last few days Klara had been so busy with lawyers and statements and their move that she hadn't managed to arrange a time. Now that it was clear she wouldn't have to be in custody before the trial (and according to her lawyer Robert Stern it was pretty unlikely she'd ever be locked up if she stuck with her plea of self-defence), she'd finally found the inner peace to be able to tackle the reasons why Jules had done what he did. And so she agreed to a meeting.

'Where were we?' she asked Caesar.

'I was just telling you about my hunch. Like I said, I was friends with Dajana. There was a time when we almost got together, but she went for Jules, which wasn't really a problem. At least not after some time had passed. We stayed good friends.'

'Really?'

'*Very* good friends. We trusted each other implicitly. We talked about everything, even her problems with Jules.'

'What sort of problems?'

'She told me about this feeling she had. She was worried that he was involved in something illegal.' He nervously rubbed the tip of his index finger on a torn part of the cuticle of his thumb.

'Anything concrete?'

Caesar frowned. 'She didn't want to say. And that's precisely what aroused my suspicions. Normally we told each other everything. But she just kept beating about the bush. It was something to do with his father, she said. And other women.'

He'd stopped fiddling with his thumb, but now his hands had found a napkin on the table, which they could scrunch up.

'I couldn't make head nor tail of it. But Dajana touched a nerve. Jules had changed. He'd always been different from other people. Quiet, very melancholic. Working for the emergency services took a lot out of him. He could never let his cases rest, he took work home with him. Once I had to drive him to an address where a woman had been beaten black and blue by her husband, because he wanted to see whether she was alright. Whether she'd left her husband.'

'Had she?'

'No. And he completely flipped out. We just saw the two of them through the kitchen window, husband and wife. Jules wanted to ring the doorbell and give the guy a sound thrashing. I only just managed to stop him doing so.' He smiled sadly. 'I wasn't in this thing at the time.'

Klara took too large a sip of her chai latte, which was still very hot.

'I don't mean to be impolite, but why are you telling me

all this? I read about most of it in the papers. I mean, you did give a statement to the police.'

He nodded and looked sheepishly at the table, as if the answer lay on the plate with the cake he hadn't touched.

'I'm here to apologise,' he said softly.

'For what?'

'I don't think anything would have got this far if I'd said something earlier.' He looked up again.

Is he crying?

'I wish I'd warned you, Frau Vernet.'

Klara cocked her head, swept a strand of hair from her brow and asked, 'You could have warned me?'

'It's a long story.'

Caesar was clearly struggling to get the words out. Finally he said, 'After Dajana committed suicide I did some research. Like I said, we had a real bond of trust. I knew her computer password and so could access her inbox from my laptop. Dajana had saved a draft of her suicide letter, which she later wrote out by hand.'

'And?'

'Your name is in it.'

My name?

The conversation was so unusual and so compelling that she'd completely forgotten to check on Amelie every minute, but now she did.

At that moment her daughter looked over at Klara and flashed her a toothy smile.

'Please don't despise me for what I did,' she heard Caesar say. She turned back to him.

'Jules is... he was my best friend. Even though he changed over the years and got increasingly bitter. He experienced bad things in his childhood: his father beat and tormented his mother until she left him and his sister alone with the madman.'

Caesar picked up the fork for the first time and stuck it into his cake, but made no moves to take a mouthful.

'This is how he explained his saviour complex and why he worked for 112. But it must have also forged his hatred of women who let such things happen to them without offering any resistance.'

'Women he killed!' Klara whispered with a glance at Amelie, who luckily wasn't picking up any of their conversation.

On 8/3, 1/7 and 30/11. All key dates for feminists, as journalists had highlighted when reviewing the crimes: International Women's Day on 8 March; the change in German legislation on 1 July 1997, making rape in marriage a prosecutable offence; and the introduction of women's suffrage in Germany on 30 November 1918.

'What's in the letter?' she asked Caesar.

'Promise you won't hate me?'

'Why should I?'

Caesar sighed. 'I should have gone to the police. But I thought it might just be the fantasies of a disturbed woman. I mean, shortly before her death Dajana was in a psychiatric clinic because of paranoia. How seriously was I to take it?'

Caesar had unwittingly stirred a memory in Klara's mind.

She herself had used similar words when she asked her lawyer if she really had to testify in court.

'How seriously are they going to take my testimony? Everyone knows I took part in an experiment in a psychiatric clinic.'

As Caesar continued to poke at his cake he continued his

confession: 'I tried to find out if there really was anything in it. I asked Jules if he could take over my shift at the telephone companion service.'

'How did you know he would call me?'

'I didn't. But I showed him how to find numbers of those women who'd rung several times before. And the file that contains information on anxieties, fears and other background material to make it easier for volunteers to keep the conversation going.'

'You *hoped* he'd ring me?'

I was Caesar's bait?

'I hoped he *wouldn't*. But around ten o'clock I ran a check to locate my laptop. I've got software installed in case it's nicked. And bingo, Jules wasn't at home. I got a taxi to take me to Lietzensee, where the GPS signal was coming from. When I saw your surname by the bell – Vernet – I was stunned. Now I knew something was wrong.'

A pause.

Klara didn't dare move, from the irrational fear that she might do something to unsettle the highly nervous man opposite her and he'd stop talking.

'Well, I took the lift to your floor. I was going to confront him, ask what he thought he was doing in someone else's flat.'

'But you took fright?'

'Yes,' he said, looking visibly ashamed. 'It might sound childish, but the light on the stairs wasn't working. All of a sudden I felt really helpless.'

'So you turned around and left?'

'Yes. My taxi had waited. Once home, I realised I'd mislaid my mobile. But I wasn't sure if I'd dropped it outside the door to your flat or elsewhere. I called my number a few times from my landline, now hoping that it had been pinched and Jules hadn't got hold of it. I even sent a text from my second mobile to the thief demanding they return my phone.'

'But you didn't call the police?'

'No. And I can't forgive myself for that.' He cleared his throat in embarrassment. 'It was cowardly of me, I know. I behaved like a little boy who hopes that if he looks away the bad thing will disappear.'

'You refused to accept that your friend was capable of the murders.'

He nodded. 'It's too monstrous. Unbelievable. Maybe you'll understand me when you've read it yourself.'

Caesar pushed himself away from the table and reached for his wallet. Klara was about to insist that she pay the bill, when she saw him place an envelope by her cup.

'Please don't hate me,' he said again.

He turned on the spot and wheeled himself to the exit.

Klara watched him wait for another customer to open the door, then disappear in his wheelchair from her field of view and into Knesebeckstrasse.

She checked that Amelie was still busy drawing. With a racing heart and sweaty palms, she felt the sheets of paper in the envelope.

Then she took a last gulp of the water she'd ordered in addition to her chai latte.

Finally she opened the envelope and read Dajana's suicide letter.

67

My darling Jules,

I wish everything had happened differently.

I wish I'd never found out. I wish my hunch had been wrong. But I recognised your handwriting, the playful curve you finish your 2 with. The squiggle on the 1 that makes it look like a seahorse. You are the Calendar Killer. You leave the date on the walls of your victims.

Do you remember our first kiss at school? The wonderful years that followed. How I loved all those letters you always surprised me with. Beneath the pillow, in the fridge, among my sports things. In the glovebox. It always amused me that you signed them off with the date, like a contract. Basically I wanted to believe we really had made a pact even though we never got married. Even though you never gave up the flat where you were born. You said you couldn't live there anymore because of the bad memories from your childhood, but I knew throughout all those years you lived with me you took the occasional bit of time out there and didn't leave it empty. Because you needed your freedom. Now I know what you used it for and my mind simply can't comprehend it.

To begin with I was sick with worry that you were meeting other women in Pestalozzistrasse. I knew how helpful and kind you were. You told me yourself how sometimes after work you'd get into the car and drive to where the callers lived to see whether everything was alright. Because you couldn't bear the emptiness you felt after your shift or the uncertainty over how the call-out went.

If only you had just cheated on me. How much easier it would have been to cope with jealousy than what your father confirmed to me. Despite the dreadfulness, despite everything, I still doubt myself and wonder if I'm not to blame too. After all, my jealousy made me stalk you. And that's how I found them, the bloodstained clothes you thought you could clean secretly in the laundry room. The tiny red drops on the enamel, which found their way onto the sink from your hands because you didn't scrub them thoroughly enough before coming to bed after your 'night shift'.

Then I saw the photo in the newspaper, the blood on the walls, the death date the Calendar Killer left behind for his victims, and I recognised your handwriting. I admit, I almost managed to close my eyes to the truth with my therapy at Berger Hof. You noticed the change in me, believed my lie that I had burnout because of the children and the stress that your job also inflicted on me. How simple I found it to convince you I needed psychiatric treatment. Did you use the time to commit your atrocities? I told the therapists at Berger Hof that I was suffering from paranoia. Because it's easier to believe in a lie than to live with the certainty that you love a murderer.

But your father put an abrupt end to my self-delusion

when he came to visit me in the clinic. I'd hoped he was going to bring some proof of your innocence because, yes, I confess, I put him onto you, Jules. I couldn't have known that he didn't need to do any research. I thought the photos of your bed he brought me would have shocked him too. How wrong I was! Did the two of you laugh at my naivety? Or was he acting completely on his own when he told me the whole truth? The latter, I hope, because I can't get out of my head the treacherous smile that was carved on his face when he told me I had to be very brave.

The two of you were a team, he said, and you carried out the killings together. I know he relished my pain and impotence. I can still feel how utterly numb I was when he held my hand and took me to the window in the clinic, sure in the knowledge that nobody would believe this story if it came from me, the psychologically fragile patient. But maybe he really thought that I'd understand you. That you had good reason to punish women for willingly returning to their tormentors. Your father smugly showed me a young woman, another patient, who was sitting in the park, lost in thought. Her name was Klara Vernet...

'Flowers?'

Klara gave such a start that her knees crashed against the underside of the table.

'What?' she snapped at the street vendor, who couldn't have chosen a less appropriate moment to shove a bunch of roses under her nose.

'No!' Klara couldn't bring herself to be polite. Otherwise she would have felt sympathy with the poor devils who had to pass on their meagre earnings to some mafia-like family head.

She first made sure that the man in a hoodie, who reeked of smoke, wasn't going to bother Amelie, then waited until he'd shuffled outside empty-handed in his laceless trainers before embarking on the final section of the nightmarish revelations that Dajana had written in the last, desperate hours of her life.

Your father smugly showed me a young woman, another patient, who was sitting in the park, lost in thought. Her name was Klara Vernet, he said, and he'd chosen her as his next victim. She suffered sexual and mental abuse from her husband, but she wouldn't leave him. Even though, irony of fate, she was so scared she'd had the number of the telephone companion service saved on her mobile for years. The two of you had decided she was going to die on 30 November, your father said. Like your first joint victim.

Since I came back from the clinic I've been all over the place, but you haven't noticed a thing. You don't think about me anymore because you're struggling with your demons. As far as Valentin and Fabienne are concerned you're still the caring father, but for me you're just a shell without a soul these days, although that's something we have in common.

You and your father chose a date for Klara Vernet and I settled on a date for myself. Which is today.

I know you'd never have done anything to me. That, and the knowledge that in spite of everything I still love you, makes it unbearable for me to go on living. Maybe I'd have managed with you on your own. I might have been able to tame your dark demons – who knows? But with your father as the evil mentor at your side? No chance.

That's too much for my head to deal with, beyond my strength and my will to live.

Farewell, my darling Jules. Now I'm going to slit my wrists. Maybe I'll manage to call you one last time on 112 before my energies fade. Hear your voice, which used to give me support, confidence and hope. Maybe I'll be able to hold onto it and you can accompany me on my final journey.

I don't suppose anyone but you will ever read this letter. But if they do, then I bet they're thinking: 'How can a mother leave her children with a murderer?'

I'm sure even you would say this too if I'd told you of my intentions. And maybe one look into your eyes would weaken me, and I'd lose the resolve to carry out my plan.

But I know I've got to do it. You were always closer to the children than to me. And they've distanced themselves further ever since I've become an emotional wreck. I'm utterly exhausted, but at the same time so furious with you. My death will punish you, I know it will. Because I know how much you love me. And how much my suicide will make you suffer. Perhaps, and this is my hope, the shock will put you back on the right track, which has been blocked for me forever. And then I know you'll be a good father to the children, just as you were always a good husband to me.

I love you so much, despite everything,
Dajana

68

For a while she'd been staring into space above the letter when the spoon started to rattle in the saucer. Klara, mentally still trapped in the morbid world that Dajana's words had drawn for her, took some time to realise that it was her mobile causing the vibrations on the table.

'Hello?'

'How are you, Klara?'

At these first few words from the caller the temperature inside the café sank to what it was outside in the street. Instinctively Klara reached for her scarf she'd laid over the chair beside her. At the same time she checked that her daughter was safe.

'Jules?' The name she'd once found so beautiful that she could imagine giving it to another child of hers, was now so loathsome that she felt sick when she uttered it.

'Don't worry, I won't keep you long. And I won't ring you again either. This will be our last call, ever.'

In addition to her scarf Klara also picked up her puffer jacket and stepped outside the café, all the while keeping an eye on Amelie through the floor-to-ceiling window.

'I'm calling the police.' Her words were enveloped by

condensation like the vapour from an e-cigarette. It was just below freezing, but the emotional chill she felt was far stronger.

'They never come quickly when you need them.'

'Oh, yes, I forgot. I mean you *are* the 112 Killer.'

When the press found out who was responsible for the murders they renamed Jules.

'I'm speaking from experience because I tried calling for help myself that night. I thought your daughter was in danger. I'd rather hand myself in than put a child's life at risk.'

Through the recently cleaned shop-like window Klara waved at Amelie, who'd been looking for her mother, but now seemed reassured to see Mummy on the phone outside.

'Oh, how honourable of you. But you were the only danger to Amelie. You fought the babysitter!'

'I read the papers, Klara. I know what happened. And I'm really sorry about Vigo. I'd taken the key from your husband's glovebox, knowing that on the last Saturday of the month he always comes home very late.'

After partying at Le Zen. Or at the 'Stables', Klara thought, wondering how many therapy sessions she'd need until she'd be able to talk to someone else openly about all of this.

'I didn't know anything about a babysitter. When I arrived he must have already been asleep in the spare room.'

Klara snorted contemptuously. 'Did you think I'd leave my child on her own?'

'Have you already forgotten? You were going to leave her alone forever,' Jules retorted. The recollection of her failed suicide attempts had a sobering effect on Klara. In truth Jules's suspicions had been spot on when they spoke on the phone that night: all her suicide attempts had been half-hearted cries for help. The abortive leap from the climbing wall, the inept attempt to poison herself with car fumes.

A pregnant woman pushed a pram across the road and stopped outside a shop selling maternity clothes.

Statistically, one in four women experience domestic violence. For most of these it gets worse during pregnancy because the man feels even more worthless. These were the thoughts that shot through Klara's mind as she watched the woman.

I wonder if she's afraid of going home?

She looked back at Amelie, who was sitting with one leg bent beneath her and whose only problem at the moment was which colour she was going to use for the trunk of the palm tree.

'What do you want?' she asked Jules.

'To put something right.'

'You don't have to. I've read Dajana's suicide letter.'

'Caesar must have given you a copy. That's what I was worried about.'

Klara shook her head and lowered her voice, even though a group of teenagers was approaching from the station, hollering loudly.

'You're sicker than I thought.' Nauseated, Klara now forced her words out through gritted teeth. 'Team killing? Together with your own father?'

'No, not at all. I had virtually nothing in common with my biological progenitor. He loved torturing people, I didn't. He wanted to scare women, I wanted to help them.'

'By killing them?'

The teenagers had chosen the playground right next to

the café as the place to rehearse their football songs. The playground was actually for children up to the age of ten, but the yobbos didn't seem to care.

'By showing them they have to act. I showed the victims that there is a way out of the trap. Yes, you have to put the pressure on. That's why I set an ultimatum. I'm happy that my motivation is now public knowledge. Otherwise you women will never understand.'

'What is there to understand about not being allowed to kill people.'

'But that's exactly what women like you do, Klara. What do you think your daughter would have become if you hadn't freed yourself? She would have learned a pattern. That it's perfectly normal for Daddy to hit Mummy, torture her, humiliate her. That the only way out is suicide. You would have made Amelie the next victim.'

Klara paused, furious that in outlining his twisted view of the world Jules had highlighted a sad truth. Amelie too would have learned from her parents how to be a victim. How would Klara have turned out if her mother had summoned the strength to stand firm against her husband?

'You must have heard of my sister, Rebecca.'

'She doesn't give interviews,' Klara replied.

'If she did, she'd tell reporters how much she suffered from my mother's feebleness. My mum never did anything to defy my father. She put up with everything he threw at her. And so Becci learned, consciously or unconsciously, that a woman's natural role is to accept the dominance of her husband, silently and submissively. If my mum hadn't left when she did, my sister would now be just as much of a victim as you are, Klara.' Jules corrected himself at once: 'As you *were!* You don't know how great an achievement it was to get Yannick out of the way.'

'Your father!' Klara hissed, nodding lovingly at Amelie and relieved to see her daughter go back to her drawing. 'Your killing assistant!'

'Wrong, my father just piggybacked on my efforts.'

Klara faltered. 'Wait. Are you saying he never killed anyone?'

She heard Jules click his tongue disparagingly. 'He was far too cowardly for that.'

'But I don't understand! How did he find out you were the Calendar Killer if you didn't tell him?'

Jules gave a deep sigh, then said, 'One day there was some water damage in the apartment below me. I was at work and uncontactable. Thinking it was my bed, the neighbour called the caretaker in a panic. The caretaker rang my father as he knew he used to live there and was still registered as the co-owner. My nosy old man organised a locksmith and took advantage of the situation to have a nose around the flat.'

'And he discovered the waterbed?'

Along with its horrific contents.

'He didn't say anything; he acted as if everything was normal, but I'm certain he took the opportunity to go through the entire apartment and found the folder with all the documentation under the bed.'

'You photographed your victims?' Klara felt like throwing up.

'Only the dates on the walls.'

'Only!' she groaned.

'You ought to understand, Klara. I've seen hundreds of cases like yours. Time and again women would call me for help, but when I sent them help they stuck by their men and let themselves be beaten, tortured, raped, killed. I wanted to set an example, purge those affected, make them shed their roles as victims. And in your case I actually seem to have had some success.'

'You're seriously deranged.'

'Hmm, maybe you're right, but I'm convinced I'm far less insane than my father ever was. All his life he got a kick out of tormenting women. He loved wrecking my mother both physically and psychologically. Her fear was like a drug for him and he was addicted to it even after she died. He got a thrill from seeing happiness die in a woman's eyes. Seeing his words and deeds destroy all the joie de vivre inside her.'

Like with me, Klara thought. *When he slept with me only to reveal that I'd been to bed with a monster.*

'He lied to you to poison your soul, Klara. Just like he lied to Dajana and drove her to her death.'

Klara scoffed. 'I see, are you saying your girlfriend would have been able to cope better if she'd known the truth? If she'd known that you alone were to blame for the calendar murders?'

'Yes. That's what Dajana said explicitly in her suicide note. If you read it carefully, you must have realised that deep down it was never her intention to take her own life. Just like you, Klara.'

'How do you know?'

'She tried calling me beforehand! Because she knew that my voice would stop her.'

Klara nodded automatically. How had Jules put it? *She was in despair, but in the end her death wish wasn't as strong as her motherly love.*

She didn't know it at the time, but these words described her too that night.

'Whatever, Dajana would still be alive even if I'm wrong about this,' Jules continued. 'My father's solely to blame. If he hadn't dished up those lies to Dajana, it wouldn't have got that far. My wife wouldn't have slit her wrists. My children wouldn't have died.'

'But you would still be a murderer.'

Jules gave another deep sigh, but agreed with her. 'You're right, I am a murderer. But that night I saved you, Klara.'

'By getting me to face your father?'

Jules had made her dance like a marionette on invisible strings. Made her think she was on her way to Caesar's, whereas he'd lured her to his apartment.

Jesus Christ, he even left the doors open for me.

'I stopped you taking your own life, Klara.'

'So that your deranged father could do it instead? The fucker was going to stab me,' she hissed.

'I'm not sure he'd have really been capable of that. Once again: my father didn't kill any of those women. Although I admit I completely brought him out of his shell that night. I played the innocent. Pretended I didn't know he'd tried to share the credit and told you he was Yannick. By guiding him to Le Zen I almost got my father to investigate himself.'

'To torture him?'

'Yes,' Jules said. 'And to get him to make a mistake.'

'You put him onto me!'

'Yes, but I didn't leave you completely defenceless.'

Klara nodded. 'You hoped I'd use the dagger on the wall!'

'And just for once in your life go that extra mile, exactly.'

The waterbed. The Japanese dagger. Tannberg's trench coat, shredded with bullets. His body, first doubling up, then collapsing like a detonated chimney.

The memories of her last few minutes in Jules's apartment flashed in her mind like photographs cast onto the wall by a slide projector. As it had then, her pulse started racing, while fear pressed down on her chest like a lead weight. 'But what if I hadn't killed him? If I'd just come home to say goodbye to Amelie one more time...' Klara whispered.

Jules continued her train of thought: 'I'd have killed you.'

She groaned. With those words he'd confirmed the nightmarish hunch which had haunted her every night since. He'd lain in wait for her in her own apartment!

'It's not something I would have done with any pleasure. But it would have been the only way to break the chain. I couldn't allow Amelie to become a victim too.'

Klara glanced into the café again and saw Amelie waving to her to come back in and look at the half-finished picture.

'One day, when your daughter's old enough, she'll realise that her mum's a heroine who doesn't let men push her around, but takes control herself. Even though of course I'd have preferred it if you'd got rid of your own husband. But I took care of that for you.'

Back in the café, Klara took off her scarf and puffer jacket, her face burning from the sudden change in temperature. The waitress raised her eyebrows, but Klara smiled and gestured that she didn't want anything else for the time being. Apart, perhaps, from a call trace on the man known as the Calendar Killer.

'See it as a gift from me,' Jules said. 'You know that Martin deserved to die.'

'Nobody does,' Klara protested half-heartedly. 'You'll pay for it.'

'I already have. When Dajana died, my life lost its meaning.'

In her ire, Klara almost spat the next words: 'You're mentally ill and you know it, don't you? You're trying to tout your perverted actions as assistance, but you used me. I was your tool.'

'Wrong. All I did was accompany you to a door. You took the decision yourself to go through it.'

'You're a monster!'

'Oh, come on!' Jules was actually giggling. 'Of all the men in your life, I've been the most harmless recently.'

Klara laughed hysterically, earning her nervous glances from two women at the neighbouring table, whose conversation had been interrupted.

'Harmless?' she said, feeling like running outside again so she could shout at the top of her voice. 'What about the body parts you'd collected that were floating in your bed?'

'Not as a trophy, but a reminder. My mother was to be a permanent reminder of my goal.'

'Your mother?' Klara closed her eyes and once again saw limbs swimming in the blood-filled memory bank of her consciousness. Once again she was lying on the waterbed, alone with the thoughts of what she'd done there with Yannick, feeling really queasy, though for the first time she realised whose bones had been beneath her.

'I thought your mother…'

No, she corrected herself in her mind. Of course his mother hadn't just upped and left. She was Jules's first victim. Because she hadn't faced up to his father.

'For years her remains lay buried in our garden. Later

I looked for a better place for them,' Jules said. 'Do you understand now what a bastard my father was?'

'The apple doesn't fall far from the tree.'

'Wrong,' Jules contradicted her forcefully. 'I'm not a liar like he was. All his life he went from one lie to the next. Until his death. He was worried you might tell me something on the phone that would put me onto him. It was almost funny how frantically he kept trying to make me break off the conversation with you. He wouldn't stop telling me to hang up. He said you were a liar and a madwoman, and I shouldn't believe a word you said.'

Klara nodded silently. That couldn't have been particularly difficult for Hans-Christian Tannberg. After all, she had just been in a psychiatric clinic.

'In the end the best he could come up with was to try to frame Caesar.'

'To divert attention from himself,' she said.

'Yes, it's ludicrous. I've no idea how he thought this would get him off the hook. Maybe he didn't really, either. He was making it up as he went along, but at some point he ran out of ideas and there was only one option left.'

'He had to catch me,' Klara inferred.

'Exactly,' Jules said. 'That's why he went straight to my apartment when I told him that's where you were going.'

Klara shook her head. She had to give Jules one thing: he'd orchestrated this cat-and-mouse game to perfection, and with two players who didn't know at any point who was the cat and who was the mouse. Reluctantly she had to acknowledge the perverse ingenuity behind this plan. Jules had put them in a situation from which only one winner could emerge: Jules himself. If she hadn't managed to kill Hans-Christian

Tannberg before he'd killed her, Jules would have made sure that his father was banged up for the other murders too. Klara was convinced that Jules hadn't notified the police that night to come to her rescue in Pestalozzistrasse, but so that Hans-Christian Tannberg was caught in flagrante as the Calendar Killer.

'Now you know the whole truth, Klara.'

As if this were a cue, she opened her eyes again. Nothing around her had changed. The waitress was still behind the counter, the women were chatting, her daughter drawing.

'Adieu,' Jules said, using the old-fashioned phrase.

Something inside Klara was screaming at her to end the call right now and throw the mobile – now contaminated by this conversation – into the bin. But another inner voice forced her to threaten Jules openly: 'You know I'm going to do all I can to make sure they find and punish you.'

'Of course I do. If you've learned one thing from that night, it's that you have to stand up to men.' He laughed, sounding oddly proud.

'Are you going to keep killing?' Klara asked.

'Does the chai latte still taste good, or has it gone cold?'

Klara went as white as a sheet. She stared at the glass, which she hadn't touched for so long that the foam had dissipated.

'Where are you?' she said, looking around.

Apart from Amelie and the two women, there were only another couple of customers in the café, who were sitting away from her, near the loos. A short man with a high-pitched voice was talking to a friend when Jules said, 'Look on the chair next to you.'

Klara glanced to her right. When she saw a rose there her heart missed a beat.

'That's my parting gift to you. From now on I'll remain your invisible companion.'

At that moment the bell on the door rang and a tall, broad-shouldered man entered the café.

'Well, that's it for today,' Jules said before hanging up. 'Your boyfriend's here.'

69

'You look like death warmed up,' the man laughed, planting a kiss on Klara's forehead. When he was with her he tried to tone down his Berlin dialect, but didn't always succeed.

'Hendrik!' Amelie exclaimed with delight, and leaped to her feet to jump onto this mountain of a man as if he were a bouncy castle.

In Hendrik's arms and in front of his voluminous chest the seven-year-old looked like a fragile porcelain doll, *which is what she basically is*, Klara thought, straining a smile as she dropped the rose beneath the table.

Klara told her giggling daughter not to be so boisterous, but once more Hendrik acted as if the bullet had passed straight through his body decades ago rather than just a few weeks ago, and as if he hadn't undergone an emergency operation. Although his recovery was incredibly rapid, Klara knew that he was still taking painkillers every day.

'Did you bring me something?' Amelie asked and, as ever when he came to visit, he took a little present from his pocket. Today it was a bag of sherbet powder that would very soon be all over Amelie's dress and the floor of the café. Beaming, the girl hurried to the counter to get a glass of water before returning to her drawing table.

'She's so like you, Klara.' Hendrik smiled as he watched Amelie. Klara felt a slight twinge, as she always did when he called her by her name. That fateful night they first met she'd wondered in the carpark how he knew it. Of course he'd heard it from Martin. The bastard had 'auctioned' her under her real name.

'Who were you just on the blower to?' Hendrik asked, dropping onto a chair with a crunch.

'Stop being so nosy.'

Klara felt comfortable in the presence of this unusual man who did actually earn his living by undressing in front of strangers.

'But only down to my crackers,' as he stressed.

'It was my lawyer,' Klara lied. Later she'd tell Hendrik about her conversation with Jules, when Amelie was asleep and she herself was unable to doze off – again. There was no better stimulant than a nightmarish past.

'Right then, what are we three lovelies going to do today?' Hendrik asked. As Klara had discovered over the last few weeks, he found pauses in conversation and moments of silence unnecessary. On the other hand – and she had to grant him this – she'd never have gone on a date with him if he hadn't badgered her so much.

It began on her very first visit to his hospital bed. Klara wanted to apologise for what she'd done; full of beans, Hendrik had started gushing like a waterfall. It still felt like a bad dream that the bullet had been fired from the pistol in her hand and hit him.

'*Why was the gun loaded?*' she asked him when they saw each other again. He put on a sweet, mischievous, almost pathetic face and answered: '*Jealous geezers. You know I'm a stripper, right? Well, I can't tell you the number of times I've been attacked by blokes wanting to know if their women were a bit too fruity on the hen night. So I got myself a piece as a bit of insurance.*'

For his own 'safety' he always kept his costume on after the performance too. '*Till I'm home. So no one sees my face and ambushes me in the carpark.*'

He knew full well that there was more than just a little paranoia involved here and he was overexaggerating wildly. Basically Hendrik was a rather shy man who compensated for his insecurities through weight training, erotic posing and a live weapon that he'd never intended to use. Because of a prior conviction (for three years he'd 'forgotten' to itemise VAT in his accounts) his firearms licence had been revoked. He'd have to answer in court again for the unlawful possession and inappropriate custody of the pistol. He'd told Klara all this over their 'make-up' coffee in the hospital cafeteria.

'*Yes, I lied. The gun was real. But I thought you were a madwoman, skipping through the woods and hell-bent on nicking my car. I didn't want you fiddling around with it so I told you it was useless.*'

Klara leaned forwards and stroked his paw-like hand, which she hadn't touched intimately before, simply because it was far too early for that – assuming it might ever happen at all – and asked, 'Did you find it?'

Hendrik nodded and pulled out the envelope. The second

man who'd placed an envelope on this table for her today, only Hendrik's one was much fatter.

'How much is it?' he asked.

'A lot.'

She'd asked him to fetch the money from the safe. From the apartment in Lietzensee she'd never step foot into again.

'I think around ten thousand euros.'

This was the 'gaming money' Martin kept at home.

Hendrik whistled through his teeth. 'Wow, and what do you need the moola for so urgently today?'

Klara peered out of the window at the railway arches on Savignyplatz, which she could just about make out from there.

'I'll be right back,' Klara muttered, getting up.

She asked the bewildered Hendrik to look after Amelie for a bit and went to the door.

'Where are you going?' he called after her. She smiled at him as she turned back.

'I'm trying to do the impossible.'

Put something right.

'Perhaps I'll succeed.'

Stepping outside into the cold winter air, Klara was struck by the idea that 'perhaps' was both the most dreadful and the most hopeful word on earth.

She cautiously approached the homeless man's sodden mattress. He peered out at her from beneath a plastic tarpaulin with apprehension in his eyes. A look which made her realise that once you'd inflicted pain and fear on someone, you could never take it back.

But sometimes it's possible to make the memory more bearable.

Perhaps, Klara thought, reaching for the envelope to give

it to the professor, in whose sad eyes she could make out something akin to hope.

If she weren't mistaken.

Perhaps.

ABOUT THIS NOVEL

Berlin, 1 April 2020

I'm afraid this is no April fool; I'm writing these lines at a time when together with millions of other people I find myself in a real thriller by the name of 'Corona'.

My head is bursting with the flood of information I've been pumping into it for weeks. Yesterday my mobile notified me that my average daily screen time over the past few weeks has been eight hours and twenty minutes! (A full three minutes longer than usual!)

Right now live news updates are informing me that Italy has extended the ban on foreign travel until 13 April, Lufthansa is putting 87,000 people on reduced working hours, in Panama men and women are only allowed out on alternate days, and the number of people in the US who've died of the Covid-19 virus has risen to 4,000. Germany has reported 69,346 cases of infection and 774 deaths. It's 1 April. And nobody knows where this is going to end.

But there is hope. And if you're reading these lines then my hope has been fulfilled. For at the moment, at 10:37 Berlin time, I've no idea if *Walk Me Home* will appear on time in autumn. Of course there are far more pressing problems at the moment than the publication date of a psychological thriller. But if you're now holding a physical copy of the book, it means that printers are still functioning, the supply chains haven't completely broken down and that the book trade still exists in some form. (If you're reading an e-book, then at least the internet is still working – that's something too.)

I've just done a DPA interview in which I was asked whether the scenario we all find ourselves in is the basis for a thriller. I gave an unequivocal answer: 'No!'

I've often been criticised in the past because the events in my books aren't realistic. Because many of the crimes are improbable and merely a product of my imagination. Today I say, 'Thank goodness!'

I write for entertainment. For this reason I don't want to exploit the real suffering in the world in all its detail. I've never understood why so-called critics think I ought to aim for the outcome where someone – a surviving husband, for example – reads my book and thinks, 'Well researched, Herr Fitzek. The serial killer executed my wife in exactly the same gruesome way!'

The next thing I was asked was why we read such horrifying stories in the first place. Wouldn't it be better, given the current catastrophe, to enjoy something more 'lightweight'? (Whatever that means.)

My answer to this was 'No' as well, and I took the opportunity to clear up a major misunderstanding. You see, people who don't like thrillers are often completely at a loss as to how people can enjoy engaging with death. The mistake in this question is: good thrillers engage first and foremost with life!

Even before Corona, many readers of my books had suffered tragedy in their lives, something I know from all the messages sent to me at fitzek@sebastianfitzek.de. (Sorry I can't answer them all.)

If narrowly surviving a road accident, getting over a serious illness or the premature death of a close relative allows a chink of light, it's the realisation that each stroke of fate makes us think about how precious life is.

All those things I took for granted before Corona: going to the cinema, shopping with friends, dinner at the Italian restaurant, summer holidays in Greece, playing tennis...

The catastrophe – and this is the only good thing about it – has reordered my priorities. For example, it's shown me how great an online community can be, but how much more important real contact with my fellow human beings is.

A good thriller confronts us with a fictitious danger and trains our empathy. Ultimately it also allows us to think about ourselves. How would we react faced with an extreme situation?

As I see it, violence, which features prominently in this book, tears the mask from our face. And believe you me, each of us wears one. Even our clothes and hairstyles disguise us. (I, for example, hide my love handles with baggy shirts, while my haircut prevents my receding hairline from looking like a runway. Or at least I hope it does; please don't spoil the illusion.) In the face of a catastrophe, however, we're 'naked'. We no longer have time for big words and long-term plans. We have to act – and immediately. Which is why it's said that a crisis brings out the best and worst in people. Let me be more specific: a crisis exposes people. It shows us who we really are. For this reason I'm happy to keep throwing my protagonists in at the deep end and get a diabolical pleasure from watching them struggle. But for me this pleasure vanishes when the waters of fiction wash over into reality. As far as I'm concerned, it then stops being fertile ground for entertainment.

In the time of Corona, how often the old writers' saying has proven true: reality is stranger, more horrific and more outlandish than fiction. We authors often have to modify the real truth to make our fictitious lie credible.

Talking of the truth:

A telephone service to accompany people on their way home really does exist! Just visit www.heimwegtelefon.net. As I mentioned above, however, everything in my thriller relating to the 'telephone companion service' is solely the product of my imagination. I've also allowed myself a little creative licence when it comes to the technology and how the service works. The real *Heimwegtelefon* is for everybody, whereas 'my' telephone companion specialises in calls from women.

ACKNOWLEDGEMENTS

To prevent my imagination from silting up somewhere between my laptop and Nirvana, I've had to rely on the support of a large number of people, all of whom I want to thank. (And must! You wouldn't believe how huffy some people get just because I forget to mention them by name here. In 2007 this happened to a good friend of mine, and even now he still finds it hard to prostrate himself before me by way of a greeting!)

I'm fully aware that for someone who can't bear acknowledgements in other people's books, mine end up being absurdly long. At the end of a book I find it silly to come across a barrage of names that mean nothing to me as a reader. But to make it clear how many people are involved in the production of a book, while not merely bombarding you with names of strangers, once again I'm taking a (rather lengthy) middle way. This time I'm going to give those involved a short introduction so you get to know a little about the person behind the name.

And so, from the bottom of my heart, I'd like to offer my thanks to the following people:

Carolin Graehl & Regine Weisbrod

Photographers have a standard phrase they use during shoots: 'Super, great, perfect... We'll just do that once more.' I get similar-sounding comments from my two wonderful editors, Carolin and Regine, when they've read the first draft of my manuscript: 'Really exciting first draft. We've just got two hundred and fifty questions.' And yet again each one of these has made the book a far better work.

Doris Janhsen

My publisher is always silently and secretly furious that she has to wait months before getting anything to read, because of course I've got to go through those two hundred and fifty questions first. At least that's what Doris says. But maybe she's quite happy about the period of grace, as it allows her to keep Droemer Knaur going so well. There couldn't be a better publishing home for an author like me.

Josef Röckl

Anyone who thinks that finance people always have to be dry and sober is wrong when it comes to Josef. And right at the same time. In the official PR photos he personifies the seriousness I'd expect from the CFO of a business, someone who devours balance sheets like others binge on TV series. But when after work he takes his jacket off for a publishing dinner his joie de vivre is as infectious as... (hmm, maybe I'd better stop talking about infection given the current situation; you know what I mean!).

Sibylle Dietzel, Ellen Heidenreich & Daniela Meyer

They must have muscle ache from throwing their hands up in horror, for whenever I tell my publishers, 'I think I've got an idea of how the book might look,' this means a huge amount of extra work for the poor production department. I remember *Pupsi & Stinki*, where I asked for each copy of this children's book to have a whoopee cushion, as a result of which the entire publishing house had to test dozens of fart cushions for 'quality' (none passed the test). Whether it's numbering the pages backwards, sticking Post-its between the pages or outer packaging for a book – they make it possible!

Bettina Halstrick

Although she's gone independent with Giraffenladen, her marketing agency for books and authors, Bettina hasn't managed to get rid of me. Well, her work was so good it thwarted her plans in this regard.

Hanna Pfaffenwimmer

If it were up to her, I'd do a reading in every bookshop in Germany, Austria and Switzerland. And if there were five hundred and fifty days in a year, the Droemer head of events would happily organise it all for me. But I'm afraid I write books too... (Sorry, Hanna, it's an annoying habit; I've no idea when I picked it up.)

Steffen Haselbach

On his business card it says publishing director for fiction. On my mobile he's listed as 'Mr Magic' because he never fails to come up with the most brilliant book titles. Anybody who thinks, 'It can't be *that* difficult and the titles aren't *that* unusual,' has never spent hours racking their brain over which title isn't too hackneyed, but not too bizarre either, and most importantly not already the title of another book. (Parents trying to come up with baby names know what I'm talking about.)

Helmut Henkensiefken

His agency is called ZERO, but he and his team are anything but nothings. They design Germany's best book covers, and not just for my novels. But for me Helmut has been a hero ever since he was the first person to take a photograph of me that even I was happy with. (I think I'm about as photogenic as a deep-sea monster.)

Katharina Ilgen

I've never seen the head of Marketing & Communication not laugh. (Maybe I should stop stuffing my jacket into my trousers in meetings.) It's more than a pleasure to be looked after by her so professionally but also so sympathetically.

Monika Neudeck

You'll spot her at the Frankfurt Book Fair because she's the one clearing a path through the crowds to take me to my next appointment with the force of a nightclub bouncer. She's so sporty that one glance at her reminds me of my unused tickets for the gym. Like Katharina, she's always in a good mood too, no matter how hectic the public excitement they both deliberately whip up.

Antje Buhl

Another bundle of dynamite in the publishing house, although her explosive power is more like enriched uranium. (I realise it's hard to put a positive gloss on this association.) What I really want to say is that the high levels of sales she manages to achieve year after year is incredible. To use a Chuck Norris joke: when she coughs, even Corona gets out of the way.

Barbara Herrmann & Achim Behrendt

I love the sense of humour of our authorities, especially our ministry of finance, which right in the middle of the Corona madness (i.e. exactly when nobody was going to work unnecessarily and all companies were facing a very uncertain future) announced it was going to run a tax audit on the firm that manages me: Raschke Entertainment. If I hadn't used all my powers of persuasion on Barbara, she's so dutiful that she actually would have abandoned her quarantine and searched with Achim for the requested documents.

Micha & Ela Jahn

I suspect they both hate Father Christmas as much as a

mother friend of mine who told me she was so angry at this – and I quote – 'fraudster!' Her reason? While she runs herself ragged getting the nicest possible presents for her children, 'he takes all the credit without lifting a finger'. Similarly, I think that very few people who order a present from fitzekshop.de know that the packet is wrapped and hauled off to the post office by Micha and Ela personally.

Sabrina Rabow

Her PR work is as outstanding as her dog is sweet. And if you were to see a picture of Ole, you'd realise that there is no greater praise. I can only recommend to everybody her perfect, smart, sensitive and strategic consultancy work. (Unless you're looking to become famous by writing psychological thrillers. In that case, hands off – no way...)

Manuela Raschke

Best friend, sparring partner (not in the gym – that's her husband Karl-Heinz, although I'd be more inclined to describe him as 'sparring victim'), manager... she warrants so many descriptions. But the most important thing for me is that I can always trust her in any situation. Apropos, Manu, seeing as I can't get you on the phone anymore: why have my accounts been blocked and are now in your name? And why have you changed your address to the Cayman Islands?

Sally Raschke & Jörn Stollmann

If you ever read one of my social media posts, it'll have gone via Sally's desk first. Don't worry, I write them all myself, but I'm about as good at technology as a fish is at chopping wood. Although thanks to all the live videos during quarantine I now understand Instagram much better. But nowhere near as well as Sally, who with Stolli is responsible for all my online activity, organising the text, layout and images.

Of course that's not her only job, besides looking after my website and a host of other things. Similarly, Stolli does far more than sticking funny pictures beneath my Facebook entries. For example, he waters the plants, takes out the rubbish and dusts the books. Sometimes, if his crazy schedule allows, he designs covers, games and comes up with ideas for children's books.

Franz Xavier Riebel

Your typical Berliner. In other words, he lives in Prenzlauer Berg and wasn't born here, but in Bavaria. Nonetheless he's managed to acquire German as a foreign language and this allows him to scrutinise my texts with his eagle eyes.

Angie Schmidt

There's no event without Angie. I don't mean you'll meet her at every party in Berlin, although I can't exclude the possibility. (As someone who's stuck to his desk and rarely to be found dancing bare-chested in techno clubs at the weekend, I can't say much about the partying of other Berliners.) We're talking about my readings here!

Christian Meyer

What the secret service is to presidents, Christian Meyer is to me. Not that authors need bodyguards. I mean, we're not influencers luring thousands of teenagers to signing sessions in supermarkets. (While we're on the subject, my dry shampoo 'Writers' Delight' is now twenty per cent cheaper with the discount code 'Fitzi'!) But I've enjoyed having him by my side for ages now. Without Christian I'd never manage those long distances between readings!

Roman Hocke

A musician recently told me that his contracts with record labels included rights not only for Germany and the world but for the universe too! No joke. Perhaps just in case someone puts a radio station on Mars. When he heard this, the best literary agent in the world (in the universe, I mean) went all dewy-eyed and considered renegotiating the contracts of all his authors. (But please, Roman, don't forget to leave the exoplanet '51 Pegasi b' out of mine. I want to go there some day when I get fifty light years of holiday.)

Pegasi might also be a good idea for a work outing with your wonderful team, thanks to whom the AVA International literary agency is such an important player: Claudia von Hornstein, Susanne Wahl, Markus Michalek and Cornelia Petersen-Laux.

Sabine & Clemens Fitzek

'Fitzek, Fitzek... I know that name from somewhere,' the nurse said who was giving me a vitamin D injection in January. (My doctor said my vitamin deficiency was comparable to victims of abduction who are held prisoner for three years in a coal shaft. He's got some strange patients.)

On a scale of embarrassment from one to ten I felt I was at two hundred, as I'd put on my most ugly pair of pants that day. I'd never been told to take my jeans off before for a routine discussion of my thyroid levels. And by one of my readers!

But as I was trying to convince the nurse that any similarity with my name was pure coincidence, she asked me, 'Are you related to Sabine Fitzek, the famous neurologist?'

My relieved answer was, 'Yes, I'm her husband, the neuroradiologist. My wife and I help my brother with the research for his books.' (Sorry, Clemens, now the nurse thinks you're the one in our family with the ancient pants full of holes.)

Linda Christmann

Talking of family. To describe how she'd managed to enrich my life so much in such a short period of time would even go beyond the scope of a Jojo Moyes trilogy. It's remarkable enough that she's not put off by the grim look on my face when she drills me with intelligent questions about my first draft, to which I don't have an immediate answer. Such as: 'Do adults commit domestic violence because of specific things that happened in their childhood?' or 'Are there courses where you can learn how to act as Father Christmas in public?' or 'Darling, why are your hands always covered in blood when you come up from the cellar...?'

Regina Ziegler

Nothing's impossible. If there's anyone who lives by this motto, it's Germany's first and most successful female film producer, who I have far more to thank for than just the film versions of *Cut Off* and *Passenger 23*. For example, the best Königsberg meatballs in the world, which I hope will be on the menu again the next time you give me your intelligent suggestions as first reader about the rough draft.

Well, the production department just called, said I shouldn't waste so much paper again and just briefly mention by name those people who aren't so important to me. Marcus Meier and Thomas Zorbach from vm-people: please feel ignored.

One of the jobs these two had to do – they're also partly responsible for Fitzek marketing – was to crouch in the middle of the night behind a Portaloo brought by forklift truck to some eerie wasteland belonging to German railways, surrounded by industrial and construction refuse, just to get the perfect setting for a Fitzek psycho book trailer. (I really must get to the end now. The longer I keep going with these acknowledgements, the more amazed I am that all these people are still working with me.)

As ever, I'd like to conclude by thanking all the wonderful booksellers, librarians and organisers of festivals and events. Right now almost all your wheels are at a standstill, even though to my mind you're as important as any other industry in the world. People ought to be stockpiling culture rather than loo paper and pasta. I really hope that our shops which offer mental nourishment will open again soon!

Please keep in good health!
Goodbye

Sebastian Fitzek
Berlin, 7 April 2020, 13:44.

(Yes, I really did spend six days writing these acknowledgements. Now you can see just how much work it is. I haven't managed to finish all the series of *Game of Thrones* in between...)